Sh
Hop- ♡
Helen

ISBN-13: 978-1544282121

ISBN-10: 1544282125

EDUCATED IN MURDER

Copyright @ 2017 by Helen Gray

All rights reserved. Except for use in any reviews, the reproduction or utilization of this work in whole or in any form by any electronic, mechanical or other means, now known or hereafter invented, including xerography, photocopying and recording, or in any information storage or retrieval system, is forbidden without the written permission of the author.

This is a work of fiction. Names, characters, places and incidents are either the product of the author's imagination or are used fictitiously, and any resemblance to actual persons, living or dead, business establishments, events or locales is entirely coincidental. Any references to historical figures, places, or events, whether fictional or actual, is a fictional representation.

Cover by Cynthia Hickey

HELEN GRAY

Educated in Murder

AUTHOR NOTE

If you've read any of my previously published novels and novellas, I hope you enjoyed those romances.

Educated in Murder is a departure from that genre. Authors have typically been expected to write in only one genre. Personally, I enjoy reading romance. But I also enjoy a good whodunit. So I decided to break from tradition and write a mystery. I had so much fun with it that I ended up with a series.

I hope to continue writing in both genres—and that you'll give the mysteries a try. But it's okay if you prefer one over the other.

After much consideration, I've decided to write both under my own name rather than use a pen name. But the covers and titles will be designed to make it easy for you to distinguish the difference in the two genres.

If you happen to enjoy this book and want to continue the series, the next two titles are *Preyed in Murder* and *Coached in Murder*.

If a man say, I love God, and hateth his brother, he is a liar: for he that loveth not his brother whom he hath seen, how can he love God whom he hath not seen?   I John 4:20

Chapter 1

Toni Donovan shivered in the nearly zero temperature, hugging her coat tighter to her. She stood next to Jenny and John Zachary at the edge of the church parking lot, watching the living nativity scene.

Members had constructed a crude stable, and Toni's two sons, ten-year-old Gabe and eight-year-old Garrett, stood at the edge of the stable, gazing toward Mary, Joseph, and the baby Jesus. Dressed in costumes of robes and scarves over their winter coats, Gabe's left eye was partially covered by his bath towel turban, and Garrett looked peculiar in his orange turban and bright red mittens. A young girl dressed as an angel stood on a bale of hay behind them. Two men and a teenage boy portrayed wise men.

Jenny edged over near Toni, also shivering. She laughed, but it came out quivery through chattering teeth. "It's good to see the sheep back on its tether."

Toni nodded, grinning. The night before, the sheep had pulled from its tether and run away.

"A farmer called the radio station this morning and reported a sheep with a rope dangling from its neck grazing in his pasture with his cows. The youth director and I went and got it." John chuckled as he told the story.

Over six feet and almost three hundred pounds, John was a mild mannered guy with brown hair worn in a neat, short style. It amused Toni to see the gentle giant with his wife. Only four feet eleven, Jenny was a bubbly redhead who loved to cook almost as much as she loved music, which she taught at their local high school. John and Toni both taught science. Not only were they colleagues, but they attended the same church and were close friends. Classes had dismissed right after lunch, two days ago, for the Christmas break.

"When is Kyle due home?" Jenny asked.

"Later tonight," Toni answered. "He hated missing this." Her husband was a commercial pilot for Heartland Air Transport, and the Christmas season inevitably meant extra runs—like the one that had kept him working late tonight.

Jenny shivered again and glanced up at the sky. "The forecast is for more snow. I hope it holds off until this is over."

John cleared his throat. "Have you heard that Jack Rayford is calling around asking if anyone has seen Marsha?"

The mere mention of their school superintendent brought such a boil of anger in Toni that she thought her ears would pop off. She hated the woman, as did other staff members. In thirty-four years of living, Toni had never hated anyone before. She had hated situations and experiences, but never a person. She shook her head and fought to keep her voice calm. "I've been busy and haven't talked to very many people. What's the story? Do you think she may have left him?"

John shrugged. "If she has, I hope she keeps walking."

Toni's mouth tightened. It made her feel a little more justified in her feelings, knowing that others disliked the woman as much as she did. But it still frightened her to experience such a strong negative emotion.

"I know that resentment is high and morale low among the high school and junior high teachers, and I suspect it's as bad in the elementary," Jenny said in an angry tone. "The woman is a tyrant. She penalizes all teachers for the lapses of two or three, targets those she doesn't like, and caters to her favorites."

John became still, his gaze focused on his wife and Toni. "It sounds like we need to be praying for her."

Toni stared at her big colleague, surprised at his comment. "It's hard to do that when she treats us like second-class citizens," she said after several moments, not sure how she could pray for Mrs. Carter while strangling with resentment. The best she could manage right now was pray that the woman had truly left town.

"Why don't we go inside for a few minutes and get warm," Jenny suggested, wrapping her arms around herself while still shivering.

The evening concluded without incident, but Toni had trouble going to sleep that night. She didn't know what was wrong, but it was more than just unhappiness over her job. All she wanted was to help Kyle provide for their family and keep them safe—and to provide knowledge and training that would benefit her students' lives. She should check the state education website and see if there were any listings in the area yet. Maybe it was time to call neighboring districts and see if they anticipated any openings in her field. But this was Christmas Eve. She couldn't make any decisions right now. She finally fell into a troubled sleep.

*

"Mom." Softly. "Mom, wake up." Louder.

Toni struggled from the depths of sleep as a small hand tugged at her shoulder. She reached over, flipped on the bedside lamp, and blinked when the glare hit her eyes. The sight of her older son's worried expression and rumpled hair sent alarm skittering through her. She bolted upright in the bed. "What's wrong?"

Gabe clenched his fists, his brows pulled together below a fringe of ash brown hair. "Garrett's being spooky." His voice was shallow and strained.

Toni reached for her robe. "What do you mean?"

"He must be having a bad dream. He's flopping around and saying weird things. I don't know if he's awake or not."

Toni followed him down the hall to the room he shared with Garrett, tying the belt of her robe as she went. She and Kyle had suggested more than once that the boys have their own rooms, but they insisted they liked being together because they had their video games and equipment set up the way they liked and didn't want to change.

Garrett's small body trembled and thrashed on the bed, his mumbling unintelligible.

Toni sat on the side of the bed and placed a hand

on his arm, being careful not to startle or frighten him. "Garrett," she said softly. "Wake up, Son. It's me, Mom."

He shivered and mumbled some more.

Toni reached down and gently pulled him into her arms. "Ssh...wake up and talk to me, sweetheart. Tell me what's wrong." She cradled him against her chest.

Garrett opened his eyes to slits. "Harry Rabbit," he whispered through a gap in his front teeth, his eyes large and tear-filled.

What about Harry Rabbit?" Toni asked softly.

Several months earlier the boys had found an injured rabbit at the edge of the woods behind their house, his leg broken. Determined to save the animal, they had built a pen in the corner of the yard and nursed him. After some discussion about the differences in a rabbit and a hare, they had named him Harry Rabbit. Three weeks later Harry died, and the boys donated his body to science, specifically to Toni's forensics class at the Clearmount High School.

The students had placed the rabbit's body on the ground under a milk crate where they could observe and monitor him to learn about the skeletonization of a carcass. Gabe and Garrett had not viewed the rabbit during that process.

Was the animal's death just now coming back to haunt Garrett? Toni hoped not. The boys had been concerned about the rabbit, and naming him Harry had been a game rather than a symbol of long-lived attachment. When he died, their attitude had been philosophical, saying they wanted Toni to put his body to scientific use.

She smoothed the soft brown hair back off Garrett's brow. "What about Harry Rabbit?" she repeated.

"He's dead," Garrett whispered in a small hiss, his body trembling.

"I know he's dead," Toni crooned. "You did everything you could for him, but he was too weak to survive."

"I saw him," Garrett mumbled. "And something big and black."

She frowned. "Big and black? What do you mean?"

"Don't know." He burrowed his head into her chest.

"Can you describe it?" She wasn't sure how much to probe with him only half awake.

He shuddered and took a shallow breath. Then he looked up, his eyes opening a little wider. "Its eyes were big and round and black. His bones showed. There was something big and black next to him. Something that's missing. It's dead." Garrett shivered once more and went limp in Toni's arms.

"It's okay. Everything's all right. It was just a dream," she assured him. "Why don't you go back to sleep while I hold you. Can you do that now?"

He nodded drowsily, his eyes drifting shut.

Toni held him a little longer, and then gently eased him back onto the pillow. As she tucked the covers under his chin, she noticed Gabe perched quietly on the edge of his own bed. She went and sat next to him.

"Is he all right?" he asked in a small voice.

"I think so. He just had a bad dream."

Gabe's dark eyes clouded. "Sometimes he moves around in the bed and makes little noises. But not like tonight. He was talking about Harry Rabbit."

Garrett's words echoed in Toni's mind. What could have upset him? "Maybe he was worried about the sheep running away."

Garrett had been upset when the sheep ran away from their live nativity, but thrilled when he found that it had been found and returned.

"A sheep is bigger than a rabbit, and it could have been dark in his dream. If he was dreaming about animals, he could have remembered Harry Rabbit. The sheep was another animal he liked--and they both went away," Gabe reasoned in rambling fashion.

Toni didn't have any better explanations. "Maybe you're right. So do I need to tuck you back in, too?" She grinned and gave him a fake punch on the shoulder.

"No." With a quick shake of his head Gabe crawled under the covers and peered up at her. "I'm glad Garrett's okay."

"Me, too. Good night." Toni turned off the light and returned to her own bed, still troubled by Garrett's behavior. Lights arced across the window and into the driveway. Kyle was home.

She got back up and met him at the door. He dropped his bag on the foyer floor and gave her a brief kiss. Then he tousled her shoulder length tresses. "Your hair says you've been asleep. So how come you're up now?"

His deep voice made Toni's heart rate clip along faster. Way too handsome, her six foot one, sandy haired husband still made her toes curl just by touching her or looking at her in a certain way. He wasn't perfect, but he was honest, caring, and a good provider. He always put her welfare above his own and was a good father to their boys. When he was home.

She loved Kyle, but she feared that his job was becoming more important to him than his family. Toni understood how much he loved flying, but it often kept him away from home days at a time, and it was hard having him gone so much. Her time was consumed by two kids, a demanding job, and church and school activities. There was never enough time in their busy schedules for just her and Kyle, like there had been earlier in their marriage. She feared they were growing apart.

Toni eased back. "Get your shower while I fix you a snack. Then we can talk."

"It's a deal."

Ten minutes later she faced Kyle across the kitchen bar while he ate a ham and cheese sandwich. "Gabe woke me because Garrett's tossing and mumbling scared him."

Kyle paused with the sandwich at his mouth. He lowered it, frowning. "Is he sick?"

Toni shook her head. "No, he was just dreaming. He talked about Harry Rabbit, and something big and black. Something that's lost."

The crease between his brows deepened. "Garrett finds things we lose. And there have been a couple of eerie coincidences surrounding his dreams. As for Harry Rabbit, it's been months since he died."

Toni nodded at his sandwich. "Go ahead and eat.

You know how it is with his dreams. Odd things can trigger them. It might have been the sheep."

He started to take a bite, but paused again. "Sheep?"

"You *do* remember that the boys were shepherds in the church's live nativity last night and again tonight …I mean last night," she amended, glancing over at the clock on the microwave. It read two a.m.

He nodded and bit into the sandwich so hungrily that Toni guessed it had been a long time since his last meal.

"When they started to let the alternate cast take their places and go inside the church for hot soup and warmth, the sheep that was tethered to a stake in the ground next to Garrett pulled its rope loose and ran away. No one could catch it."

He swallowed. "So it's still running around town?"

Toni grinned and shook her head. "The radio carried an announcement for us. I quote, 'The people at the church across the street have lost their sheep and don't know where to find it'. But a farmer found it in his pasture, and it was rescued."

Kyle chuckled, but then sobered. "So how does this cause Garrett to dream?"

Toni shrugged. "Maybe it doesn't. But Gabe's theory is that Garrett liked Harry Rabbit, who went away. He also liked the sheep, which is bigger than a rabbit, and it also went away. Only it's not black."

Kyle's eyes narrowed in confusion.

She raised her palms. "I don't know. There's probably no connection, but I can't tell what goes through Garrett's mind. If his imagination is getting out of control, I want to help him. On the other hand, I don't want to be an alarmist."

Kyle set his half eaten sandwich down and took a big swig of milk. "He's a good natured kid who doesn't seem to have problems. I agree that we shouldn't make too big a deal of him finding things, or dreaming. But let's pay more attention. If we notice anything too abnormal in his behavior, we'll talk to the school counselor."

Toni drew a long breath, knowing she would be the one doing any talking to anyone. "Okay. I'm feeling more stress than I realized, and I tend to overreact to things when I'm tired. I feel better now that I've talked it over with you."

*

After church Christmas morning Toni, Kyle, and the boys went home with her parents for Christmas dinner. Russell and Faye Nash lived in a small subdivision about a mile outside the city limits on a secluded, tree covered hillside.

Toni's brothers, Bill and Quint, arrived as she and her mother were setting the table. Bill, two years younger than Toni, lived in Clearmount and worked for the postal service. Quint, five years younger than Bill and three inches shorter than his brother's six foot one, was in the army and stationed at Fort Leonard Wood. Because of truck problems, Bill had gone to the fort to get him.

After dinner, they moved to the living room with their coffee and Cokes.

"So what do you think happened to her, Quizzy?"

Toni rolled her eyes, as she knew Quint expected. Growing up, their parents had referred to the boys as their dynamos and Toni as their inquisitive child. The boys had dubbed her Quizzy, and still used the nickname when they wanted to irritate her.

"I have no idea."

The subject had come up during the meal, and both her brothers had shown keen interest.

Bill spoke up. "My guess is she left old Jack, but she'll turn up after she thinks she's been gone long enough to teach him whatever lesson she intended. Dear old Jack will be so grateful he won't ask questions."

Toni understood Bill's attitude. He worked with the brother of Janet Rayford, the wife Jack had cheated on and dumped for their school superintendent.

Faye topped off the guys' coffee cups. "If that's the case, I guess Jack got what he asked for. But I can't help but wonder if something really bad has happened to her. Maybe she's been in an accident."

"I have a theory," Bill said, his voice quieter.

"Let's hear it." Russell put his cup down and gave his son a trooper-like stare. Recently retired from the Highway Patrol, their dad was sixty-two and not yet quite sure how to keep himself occupied. Toni knew he would be much more content when baseball season opened in the spring and he could watch his beloved Cardinals play.

"I think she probably decided she made a mistake in hooking up with Jack, and went back to her former lover for a holiday fling."

Toni stared across the room at Bill. "There are no secrets in small towns."

"What's the dirt?" Quint glanced from face to face. Not having been around much since high school, he no longer knew the local scuttlebutt.

"She's supposed to have been having a relationship with Jimmie Huff, the director of special services at the school," Toni explained.

Quint frowned. "Another man?"

She shook her head. "Woman."

"That's not such an unusual story in itself," Bill said. "But I can see where it would cause trouble for the superintendent to be involved with another staff person, especially one below her in the pecking order."

"There's been so much talk that I didn't give it much credence," Toni said slowly. "But even if it were true, something in my gut says that's not where she is."

"Want me to track her down?" Quint asked, eyes glinting.

"No!" was the simultaneous response.

Faye gathered empty cups and glasses. Then she paused and looked from Toni, to Bill, and then to Quint. Five years younger than her husband, she was about a hundred and fifty pounds and five foot three, with salt and pepper hair. She still worked part-time as a nurse practitioner at the local clinic. A high-energy person, she doted on her husband and children, but she could be stern with them. "I don't know what I'm going to do with your dad. He lost his glasses back in the summer, and he's forever hunting his keys."

Quint grinned. "What's he lost now, his patience with you?"

Faye gave her youngest an exasperated shake of her head and started toward the kitchen. "He's lost one of his hearing aids," she said over her shoulder.

Garrett's uncanny ability to find things that were lost came to mind, but Toni hesitated to mention it. She went to peek out the door and see if the boys were still in the front yard.

*

The remainder of the holiday vacation passed quickly. Bill took Quint back to the fort Monday. Then Toni, Kyle and the boys went to Springfield and spent a couple of days with Kyle's parents. Dan and Barb Donovan had lived in Clearmount most of their lives, but had moved to Springfield to be near their two daughters and have easy access to hospitals after Dan suffered a stroke and had to take an early retirement from the Corps of Engineers.

By the time they returned home, the town was buzzing about Marsha Carter's disappearance. Friday at the beauty shop Toni learned that it had been made an official missing person case and an APB put out on Marsha's car.

Shortly after that, she met Sandy Douglas, her principal's wife, in the grocery store and learned that Marsha's car had been found parked at the airport at the west edge of town. Three industries shared the industrial park. Local business people and a few aviation enthusiasts used the small airport adjacent to it for business trips, freight, and personal jaunts.

An eerie feeling crept up Toni's spine as she envisioned an abandoned car out there. Something definitely was not right. The knots forming in her stomach destroyed her appetite, and she couldn't concentrate on business for the questions spinning through her brain.

Toni's parents spent New Year's Day at her house. After supper they settled in the living room. The subject of Marsha's disappearance came up again.

"That's an odd place for them to find it," Faye commented when Toni mentioned where the car had been found. "Could she have taken a private flight out of town?"

Russell spoke up. "Buck said they've checked every flight that's been in or out of there since last Friday." Buck Freeman was the Chief of Police and his longtime friend.

Toni rubbed a hand over the goose bumps on her forearm. "I'm not usually an alarmist, but I have a bad feeling about this."

Russell nodded. "Me, too. The police got a tip from someone saying she had been seen out at the river retreat area. They've had boats on the water and the K-9 unit searching out there, but they've found no sign of her."

Toni's emotions were jumbled. She did not like or respect their superintendent, had even wished she would leave the district. But never once had she envisioned anything happening to the woman. Guilt rose in her because she couldn't muster more grief at the possibility of Marsha being gone.

"I'd like to hear the news now," Kyle said as the movie the boys had been watching came to an end.

Gabe turned off the DVD player and found the local news channel. A newscaster was already reporting the story.

"The Clearmount police are investigating the disappearance of Mrs. Marsha Carter, superintendent of the Clearmount School District, who was reported missing Saturday the twenty-second. Yesterday her car was found abandoned at the industrial park. When the police forced the locked doors open, they found some personal items inside, but her purse and briefcase were not among them. No evidence of injury was found."

Marsha's picture appeared on the screen.

"Mrs. Carter is described as five foot four inches tall, a hundred and thirty pounds, with strawberry blonde hair and blue eyes. Anyone with information that might help locate her is asked to contact the Clearmount Police Department."

The impersonally stated facts struck Toni hard. She now believed the worst.

They played a board game until midnight, but Toni couldn't focus on it. All she could think about was her missing boss. After greeting the New Year, her parents went home.

"What's the matter? Can't you sleep?" Kyle asked an hour later as Toni tossed and turned in the bed.

"No," she mumbled. "Too many things on my mind."

"What kind of things?" He pulled her into his arms.

"Dumb things," she said, afraid he would think her silly.

"You're worried about Mrs. Carter." His hands stroked her back and shoulders.

"I guess. I can't stop thinking about it. And there

are these crazy pictures floating through my mind, mostly of animals."

"Animals?"

"Uh huh. Sheep …and rabbits with big black eyes …and Marsha's car sitting abandoned at the airport. It's all jumbled, like I should be understanding something."

"Why don't we get some sleep? You can think about those things tomorrow when they won't seem so dark. Happy New Year."

Toni woke about six o'clock and tiptoed to the boys' room. When she opened the door, she heard Garrett tossing and turning. She slipped inside and held him until he stopped mumbling about Harry Rabbit. Then she went back to bed.

The troubled thoughts that plagued her were beginning to coalesce into a dreadful possibility. Garrett's dreams about Harry Rabbit, combined with all the circumstances, were forming a picture, an idea that she couldn't shake. The first time Garrett had found something someone lost, Toni had accepted it as a simple coincidence. Then he had found Kyle's lost knife. More incidents had followed.

Other than Kyle, the only person she had ever talked to about those uncanny findings was John Zachary. Should she talk to him about this? No, he would call her crazy if he knew the path her mind was taking.

And she was going to feel downright foolish tomorrow morning when she arrived at school and discovered Marsha present.

Chapter 2

Dark thoughts plagued Toni Monday morning as she dropped the boys at the elementary building, drove on up the street, and pulled into the high school parking lot. She tried to pray, but no words would form.

Located a mile outside of town in front of a rolling hillside, the school was fronted by a large strip of concreted parking lot. The eastern portion housed the middle school, with the high school to the west. The district served about twelve hundred students, with a faculty of nearly a hundred, and about sixty support staff.

Toni's stomach knotted when she noted the vacant parking spot where Marsha Carter's silver car usually sat. She grabbed her purse and hurried inside.

In the staff workroom she checked her mailbox and found a memo amongst the usual junk mail and catalogs. When she read it, she breathed a sigh of relief. There was to be a faculty meeting right after school in the cafeteria. Marsha was on the job and running true to form. For once Toni welcomed a meeting on short notice. She hurried to her classroom without stopping to chat with anyone.

Inside the room, she donned a white lab coat over her red satin blouse and charcoal slacks, flipping the ends of her hair out so that it just brushed the collar.

Bookshelves crammed with bulky textbooks lined the front half of the right wall. The back half housed a row of computer desks. An emergency eyewash station stood at the front of the left wall, and a multicolor plastic DNA spiral occupied the rear. Student desks and worktables filled the center of the room. A centrifuge and a thermal cycler, used in genetic fingerprinting exercises, sat on the counter along the back wall. An aquarium inhabited by a turtle and a lizard stood in front of the windows. Test tubes and micropipettes graced the desks.

Toni's class schedule consisted of three sections of general biology, one of advanced biology, one of forensics, and an anatomy and physiology class that she taught from as much of a medical perspective as she could at a secondary level. The forensics class was an evolving thing, and Ken Douglas, her principal, gave her a lot of latitude with it. She added units or activities when she found challenging ideas or lesson plans at workshops and conferences, as well as implementing ideas of her own.

Within minutes of the beginning of class Toni realized that her relief had been premature. The students buzzed with speculation about Mrs. Carter's whereabouts. Toni struggled to keep them focused while the same questions ran on a parallel track in the back of her brain.

During lunch the staff talked exclusively about Marsha's disappearance. Back in class, Toni had to forcefully block everything but science from her mind. As soon as the room emptied after her last class, she hung her lab coat in the supply closet and began to put materials away. She was tidying her desk when John Zachary stepped inside her doorway.

"You ready to see who's in charge of today's meeting and hear the latest?"

Toni shoved her desk drawer closed and grabbed her purse. "Let's go."

When they entered the cafeteria, they saw that several staff members from each building had already arrived. More were filing through different doors and following their natural tendency to cluster by departments. The elementary teachers sat in a group on the east side of the room, the high school staff on the west, while the middle school gang flocked around the refreshment table.

There was a subdued buzz in the room, an overpowering atmosphere of curiosity and tension. Lingering odors of the pizza lunch served to eight hundred junior and senior high school students three hours earlier blended with the invisible vibrations.

A crack of thunder startled Toni. She stared up at the row of small windows across the top of the wall. They were cloud darkened, and rain was beginning to splash against them. With a sigh of resignation she accepted that, by the time the meeting ended, it would be too dark to carry out the idea germinating in her mind.

"Let's sit here." John indicated a vacant table on 'their' side of the room and stepped over the attached bench to sit at one end of it. Toni slid in beside him.

"I'll join you if you don't mind," someone said

from behind them.

Toni looked up as Coach Jordan Hopper scooted onto the seat to her right, sandwiching her between him and John.

"I hope this doesn't take too long," he said into her ear. About forty, Jordan was still dark haired, tall and athletic. He had three kids, and a wife who taught physical education in another district.

Toni gave him a stern look. "I should report you for skipping out on the Christmas party."

He formed his famous ear-to-ear grin, not the least bit repentant. "I had important computer work to do." A bit irreverent, he had been with the district longer than Toni and was working on his specialist degree in hopes of becoming a principal.

"Sure you did," Toni said, her tone saying exactly the opposite.

He gave her a wink. "Well, a professional development survey was a lot more important than Marsha Carter's mandatory party." His tone turned acerbic on the word mandatory.

"No argument there. But aren't you concerned about her now that she's missing?"

He shook his head, his lips forming a line that resembled a sneer. "Nah. She's like a bad penny. She'll turn up."

"Okay if I join you guys?" Lisa Baker stopped behind them. Taking her welcome for granted, she slipped onto the bench to the right of Jordan. Dressed similarly to him in black sweat pants and a bright red sweatshirt, she wore a red headband over her shoulder length ash blonde ponytail, typical attire for the physical education teacher and girls' basketball coach.

Attractive in a sporty way, Lisa was divorced with no children, an eight-year veteran of the district. She was tall and wiry, with well-toned muscles. Her voice was deep and husky, probably from the smoking habit she indulged whenever she could sneak outside the building.

Toni spoke to her across Jordan's back. "Thanks again for helping me clean up the gym after the Christmas party."

"No sweat," Lisa brushed off the gratitude. "Keeping it clean is one of my duties."

The Student Council and Science Club, the two student organizations Toni sponsored, had provided the tree for the staff party, set it up, and decorated it. Then Toni had sent the students home with the assurance that she would dismantle it afterward. Lisa Baker and Ken Douglas had noticed her working alone and stayed to help.

The principal's arrival at the front of the room claimed their attention. Ken stepped to the podium, stress lines visible in his face, his body language tense, and his dark hair rumpled.

"Good afternoon, staff." He paused to clear his throat. "This meeting was called in an effort to keep you informed. I promise to keep it brief. I know there has been a lot of talk and speculation about Mrs. Carter."

He ran a hand around the back of his collar. "As most or all of you know, our superintendent has been reported missing and did not show up for work today. The school board and administrators have met and discussed our situation. I'm afraid I don't have any solid information for you, but the board wants you to know that they have every confidence in your ability to focus on the welfare of our students and move forward. The police are looking for Mrs. Carter, and any information they give us will be shared with you as we're able. I'll do my best to keep you informed. You're dismissed."

After the abrupt dismissal, Toni was more troubled than ever, but reluctant to share her misgivings. She got to her feet with the rest of the staff.

Jordan grimaced. "Ken's in a tough situation."

Toni's sense of well-being, already at an all-time low, dropped another notch. She liked Ken Douglas and had a lot of sympathy for him. He was only thirty-two, intelligent, and in his second year as a principal. He worked hard at his job, but she knew he faced some stressful issues. "I know the board doesn't always support decisions he makes, largely due to Mrs. Carter's influence. Her disappearance has to have him uneasy about who's in charge around here."

"She tried more than once to get the board to fire him," John reminded them. "They refused to go that far, but they can't block everything she proposes. Ken has to be worried that she's going to eventually succeed."

Toni took heart at John's reference to their superintendent in the present tense.

"Ken's wife quit teaching last year to have their baby and stay home with it, and I heard recently that she's pregnant again," Lisa interjected. "That makes his job more essential to him than ever."

"Well, I hope the tyrant is gone for good," Jordan

said with open animosity. "Ken isn't the only one who would be better off." He glanced at his watch. "Gotta run."

"Me too. See you two tomorrow." Lisa followed Jordan toward the north exit.

As she watched them leave, Toni's gut wrenched.

What was happening? She didn't understand. And she was scared.

Toni walked beside John back to their classrooms, her low-heeled red pumps clicking on the concrete floor. "As much as I hate working for our superintendent, I'm worried about her," she admitted quietly.

He stopped at the little alcove where their classroom doors faced one another. "My feelings are mixed, too. I can't stand the woman, but I never wished for anything bad to happen to her."

"Maybe it hasn't," Toni said, her voice laced with doubt as they parted ways.

With the efficiency of long practice, Toni tidied her desk and prepared for the next day. On a worktable she laid out a supply of plastic bags, extra pencils, and other supplies necessary for tomorrow's DNA fingerprinting lab. She was gathering her purse and book satchel to leave when John appeared in the doorway.

"I can't find my scientific calculator. It's not all that valuable, but my parents gave it to me as a gift several years ago, and I hate to lose it. Do you, uh ... have your boys gone home yet?"

Toni read his mind. "They should be waiting for me in the front lobby by now."

"I have Popsicles in my refrigerator."

Toni rolled her eyes. "You want Garrett."

John nodded and gave her a wry grin. "Can't hurt to try, can it? I'd really like to find it."

Toni sighed in mock exasperation. "All right. Get out your bribes, and I'll be right back." She tossed her bags back onto the desk and took off down the hall.

"Hey, guys," she called as she reached the lobby where Gabe sat against the wall near the door, his backpack stuffed behind his spine and his trombone standing upright beside him. Garrett stood in front of the display case, studying the athletic trophies. "How would you like to come up to John's room for a Popsicle?"

"Sure." Gabe gathered his things while Garrett grabbed his backpack. As they darted up the hall, Toni had to hustle to keep up with them. Her boys were adventurous and kept her on her toes, but she loved them dearly. Gabe, about seventy-five pounds and four foot six, was a fifth grader with a love and aptitude for athletics. His hair tended to curl around the edges just like his dad if not kept trimmed. Garrett, a third grader, was about three inches shorter, had darker hair, and weighed about sixty pounds. He liked to fix things. If Toni had a small gadget that quit working, she would let him tinker with it. If he got it to work—which he sometimes did—that was great. If he didn't, it was no loss.

"Hi, Dr. Z," they greeted in unison as they entered John's room ahead of her.

John had attended dental school, but by the end of his second year had realized he wanted to drop out. He had finished, but never took the board exams—and was still paying off his school loans. After a series of dead-end jobs, he had gone back to school and earned his teaching certification. Friends for years, he and Toni joked about how he had twisted things around, getting his Ph.D. first, then his bachelor's, and then a master's in biology. John taught physical sciences, chemistry and physics classes, while Toni had the life science classes.

Tables were organized for group study, but everything was arranged in a mirror image of Toni's room. The one thing identical was a work counter across the rear of the room.

The boys pulled out chairs at the first table and sat in them, their backpacks tossed on top of it. Gabe leaned his trombone case against the tabletop.

"Here we go." John emerged from the supply closet at the corner of the room, a half sized can of soda in each hand. "How about a Coke?" he asked Toni.

She gave him a you-know-I-never-turn-down-a-Coke eye roll.

He placed the ones for the boys on their table and went back to the closet. This time he returned with two Cokes, plus two Popsicles that he handed to the boys.

They thanked him, and Gabe stuck his Popsicle in his mouth. But Garrett didn't immediately unwrap his. He sat quietly, his eyes sweeping the room. "Where's your computer?"

"I had problems with it, and the technology director came and got it." John's fondness for the boys was evident in the warmth of his voice. "But my scientific calculator is missing."

Garrett's small brow wrinkled. "What kind of

calculator is that?"

"It looks like this." John reached inside a desk drawer and pulled out the box in which the instrument was usually stored. He handed it to Garrett.

Garrett studied the picture. "That's neat. You lost it, huh?"

"Sure did. And I use it a lot. I've turned this room upside down hunting for it."

Grinning, Garrett looked down at the floor, and then up the ceiling. "Looks right side up to me."

"Okay, smarty pants." John gave him a fake punch in the arm.

Toni pretended to ignore them and sipped from her Coke as John perched on a lab stool near the desk. She drew a long breath. "Days like this make me wonder why I ever went into teaching."

John shook his head. "I hear you. What is it you've got in now, ten years?"

She nodded. "If I live through this one it'll be eleven."

One disadvantage for both of them could be those very years of experience. There was less earning disparity in teaching than many professions, men and women starting at the same base pay and advancing on the same salary schedule. But districts experiencing tight budgets had a tendency to hire less experienced teachers because they could get them for less money. Some set a limit on how many years of experience they would recognize, meaning that she and John might sign on at another district and have to start on the salary schedule at less than their actual experience. The idea of taking a pay cut, while adding the expense of a long commute, held no appeal.

"I'm only a couple ahead of you," John said. "My first two years were at Poplar Bluff, and then I came back here." His family owned the local Ford dealership, and he had grown up in Clearmount and attended the local schools.

"I hate the thought of making that hour drive to Poplar Bluff every day, but I'm thinking seriously about applying for a position down there for next year," Toni said, rotating the Coke can in her palms.

"Well, this is about the time for positions to start being listed. I'm wrestling with the same thought." John darted a glance over at Garrett.

Her youngest son had quietly risen from his chair, still clutching the calculator box and sucking on his Popsicle, and walked slowly around the room. He stopped near a window, paused a moment, and then moved on. When he reached the corner of the room near the supply closet he stopped again and studied the heat and air conditioning controls. Then he squatted on the floor and placed the calculator box on the floor beside him. He put his Popsicle on it.

"Don't bother him," John whispered, anticipating Toni's intent of avoiding a potential mess in the floor. "He's okay."

Garrett lay on his stomach and peered into the small space under the wall-heating unit. Then he reached under with his right hand and swept it back and forth. Suddenly he grunted and pulled the hand out. He turned and faced John, the missing calculator in his hand. "Is this what you were looking for?"

"How does he *do* that?" John muttered.

Toni shrugged. "I don't know. It's happened several times now. I don't know what it means, but I appreciate you keeping it between us."

"What about Kyle?"

"It's happened a few times at home, and we've talked about it. It's pretty amazing, and baffling, but we don't want to make a big deal of it." She considered mentioning the dreams, but decided against it.

John walked over and took the calculator Garrett held out to him. "I know what must have happened now. It was in my coat pocket yesterday. I remember dropping my coat when I took it off to hang it in the closet. This must have fallen out of my pocket and slid under there. Thanks, pal. I owe you." He shook Garrett's hand, the one without the Popsicle.

Garrett grinned and held up the Popsicle. "You paid in advance."

They both laughed.

Toni picked up her purse and satchel. "How about we all go home now."

"What time's Dad supposed to be home?" Gabe asked when they reached her red van.

Toni slid behind the wheel. "He said he should be there in time for supper."

She turned left out of the school parking lot, drove up the highway about a quarter of a mile, and turned right onto a paved road that wound back to the Country Club and golf course. About a mile back, she turned into the estates and drove to a ranch style home that sat in front of a wooded hillside. She and Kyle had bought it two years earlier. She parked in the garage.

An hour and a half later, freshly showered and padding around in her fleecy blue robe and house slippers, Toni donned potholder mitts and pulled a steaming chicken casserole from the oven.

"Smells great," Kyle announced from the kitchen doorway. He stepped inside, tossed his hat on the dryer, and crossed the floor to give Toni a quick peck on the cheek.

"Be careful," she cautioned, balancing the dish carefully. "This is hot."

"So are you," he returned, his brown eyes dancing.

"Get washed up and it'll be on the table," she ordered, sidling past him.

After the meal the boys went to their room, and Kyle helped Toni clean up the kitchen. "How was your day?" he asked as he shoved the clean casserole dish into the cabinet.

"Tiring. My classes went fine, but the faculty meeting afterward wasn't really informative. Marsha still hasn't been found, but her car has." She flexed her aching shoulder muscles.

"She'll show up." Kyle put down his dishtowel and came up behind Toni at the sink. When he began to knead her tired shoulder and neck muscles she silently purred.

"How can the board tolerate her?" he continued. "It's bad enough that she treats you teachers so badly, but to brazenly break up the board president's marriage is too much. She's probably getting tired of him and playing hide and seek."

Toni tipped her head to the side as his hands did their magic. "I don't understand how Jack could leave his wife and kids for her."

Jack Rayford and Marsha Carter's affair was

believed to have started soon after Marsha's appointment to the position of superintendent. When Jack's wife found out about it a few months later and evicted him, he had moved in with Marsha, who was already divorced. He was now in the process of a bitter divorce of his own. His son, Josh, was a college student, and his daughter, Sidney, was in Toni's forensics class. Toni hoped the girl didn't divulge her role as perpetrator of the simulated classroom crime in which Toni had asked her to participate.

"Do you really think you want to change jobs?" Kyle worked his fingers up and down her neck. "Would you like to just take a year off? You can, you know. Or we could try for a little female rug rat."

Toni gave an elongated sigh. "I know. But I don't think I would be content not teaching." She knew they both spent too much time and energy in their jobs, but they liked what they did. "I'll give your suggestions some more thought and make a decision soon. Thanks for understanding."

*

A sound woke Toni during the night. Instantly alert, she detected that it came from the boys' room. She slipped out of bed, went down the hall, and eased their door open. Peering inside, she could make out Garrett's form tossing restlessly on his bed. Again she tiptoed to his side and eased onto the mattress beside him.

"Harry Rabbit," he mumbled, followed by more sounds she couldn't decipher.

Very gently she reached over and drew him into her arms, moving her hand over his brow in a soothing caress. "It's all right, son. Everything's all right. Go back to sleep."

Toni held him that way until she was certain he was asleep. Then she eased him back down onto his pillow and crept from the room. She crawled back into bed, but lay there wide-awake, tossing and turning. She reached no conclusions about her job, but did make up her mind to talk to John Zachary first thing tomorrow. That decision made, she fell asleep.

*

Driven with purpose, Toni bypassed the workroom the next morning and went to find John. Almost certain she remembered his name on the breakfast duty roster for the week, she entered the cafeteria. He stood to one side of the room, monitoring the students.

"What's wrong?" he asked as she approached, his eyes moving over her hot pink jacket that she had hoped would camouflage the worry on her face and the loss of sleep in her eyes. It obviously hadn't helped.

"I need to talk to you. Can we eat lunch together in your room?"

"Sure," he said, grasping her need for privacy.

Toni went on to class. As soon as the lunch bell rang, she grabbed her sandwich and green grapes and made a beeline for John's room. He sat at his desk, already eating a lunch that made her sandwich look unappetizing in comparison.

A bachelor until last year when he met and married Jenny, his life had changed dramatically. Because of the short, twenty minute lunch break, he had been a "brown bagger" and brought an apple and ham sandwich every day. Since his marriage he brought sealed lunch plates of leftovers and delicious munchies that Jenny prepared for him to pop into the small microwave in his storage room.

"I have the most awful thing in my head that I need to put to rest," she began without preliminaries, sinking into a student desk. "You're the only person besides Kyle who would understand."

John placed his elbows on his desk and leaned forward. "Does this have anything to do with our missing superintendent?"

Toni nodded. "All the talk …and some other things, have caused me to wonder if…if…"

"Something has really happened to Marsha?" John prompted. "What are you thinking?"

Toni took a deep breath. "Before I run my thoughts by you, I need to back up and explain about Garrett's dream."

"Garrett who finds lost things. Someone is lost," John mused. "What did he dream?"

Toni met his eyes across the desk. "He dreamed about Harry Rabbit. When I tried to comfort him he said that Harry was dead. He said he saw Harry Rabbit …and something big and black next to him."

John listened in silence, absorbing every word.

"The dream was the night after the sheep ran away from the living nativity, so I thought something big and black must be the sheep in the dark, or something like that. Then he found your calculator." Toni paused to catch her breath. "Last night he dreamed about Harry Rabbit again."

"We both know that Harry Rabbit is buried in your body farm," John finished for her, a fateful tone entering his voice.

"I know all this has to sound crazy," Toni said quietly, her hands so unsteady she could hardly hang onto her uneaten sandwich. "But I have to check."

"Would you like me to go with you?"

"I was hoping you would," she admitted with a whoosh of relief.

"If it's any comfort, I don't think you sound crazy. Abraham Lincoln dreamed two weeks before his assassination that there was a funeral at the White House. When he asked a soldier in the dream who was in the casket, the soldier told him the president of the United States. Mr. Lincoln told his wife about the dream later, and her response was that he would die in office."

Toni found herself being thankful for John's obsession with history.

"Mark Twain had a vivid dream where he saw his brother in a casket," he continued. "Less than a week later his brother was killed in an explosion on a boat."

"Those men dreamed that something was going to happen," Toni pointed out, finally biting into her sandwich. "That's not what Garrett does."

"No, his dreams remind me more of some in the Bible. Joseph is probably the best known dreamer, but there were plenty of others. Jacob. Solomon. Abraham. Daniel and Nebuchadnezzer."

She nodded and pressed her fingers over her eyes as he enumerated examples. "But Garrett's dreams are surely just coincidences."

John shook his head slowly. "I wouldn't discount them. I heard a minister say once that God used dreams for various reasons, like to reveal prophecy, or to encourage and to give warnings. An example of that is how the Magi were warned in a dream not to return to Herod."

Toni considered each of them. "Garrett only finds things that are missing. And he's just a kid. He wouldn't …"

John swallowed his last bite and began to tidy his desk. "Let's stop trying to analyze and go check the farm anyhow, just reassure ourselves as to whether your youngster has found something else that's lost."

The bell rang, sending Toni scurrying for the door.

"Meet me as soon as the last bell rings," he called after her, taking up his post by his door as students began to enter the room. "We won't be gone long. Your boys will wait for you."

*

By three o'clock Toni's doubts and questions had morphed into near panic. John entered her classroom and waited while she answered a question for two students who had lingered after class. As soon as they left, she grabbed her coat and pulled it on as they hurried from the room. John closed the door behind them.

"It was last year when the boys found that rabbit," she said as they exited the building. "It was around the first of October when Harry died and the class put him in the body farm. We put a milk crate over him and charted his decomposition throughout the school year. By summer the remains had skeletonized, and I put them in a box and let the boys help me bury it."

"So Garrett knows exactly where the grave is

located."

Toni nodded and traipsed across the road ahead of John. She veered into the woods behind the school. About halfway up the hill they came to a less heavily wooded area. The air smelled of wet decaying leaves—and more. They approached a crude fence constructed of plywood, the sheets nailed to posts provided by the maintenance staff. Toni raised the latch of the hinged gate and walked inside, John close behind her. As the odor grew stronger, Toni noted a dead raccoon lying about four yards from the back fence.

She held her breath and tramped past the dead animal to where a small strip of wood was nailed to a stake in the ground. White with black lettering, it bore the name HARRY RABBIT. Next to the marker was a rectangular mound of soggy leaves and clumps of dirty snow.

"There's something here, but it's probably an animal." Her hand trembling, Toni pointed toward the corner of the fence. "There's a shovel in that locker."

"I'll get it." John went to the black footlocker where the class stored large trash bags, small plastic bags, a shovel, and some small garden spades. He opened it, picked up the shovel, and returned to the leafy mound.

Gently he probed along the edge of the leaves, pushing back debris until something black appeared. "I think it's a big trash bag."

Toni watched him move the shovel again. When something thunked, she squatted and raked leaves away with her hand. A purse came to light. Trying not to be sick, she picked it up. With a terrible sense of inevitability she extracted a wallet and opened it. And stared at Marsha Carter's driver's license.

She clenched her fists against her stomach. *Oh, God, what have I done?*

Toni reached into her pocket for her cell phone and discovered she had left it in her room. That must never, ever happen again, she promised herself.

"Let's get back to my room and call the police," John said, noting her fruitless motion. "I don't have my phone either."

They began to run.

Chapter 3

Toni's hand trembled as she dialed the secretary from the phone extension in John's classroom. "Pam," she gasped as soon as she got an answer. "Please call the police for me."

"What's wrong?" Pam Wesley had been anchoring the front desk in the principal's office for over ten years and was one of Toni's closest friends.

"We may have found Marsha." Toni tried to keep her voice steady.

Pam paused, but only for a moment. "Where shall I have them meet you?"

"In the lobby."

"I'll notify Ken and have the teachers with after-school activities send their students home." The phone disconnected.

Toni hung up and raced to catch John, who had already taken off. They reached the glass walled lobby and had only waited about two minutes when two police cars swung into the drive and skidded to a halt in front of the building. Police Chief Buck Freeman emerged from the first car, Deputy Dale Brown from the second. John pushed the door open for Toni to exit the building ahead of him.

"Hi, Toni," Chief Freeman said as they met outside the door. Six foot two, white haired and broad shouldered, he had gone to high school with Toni's dad. His face grim, intelligent dark eyes under bushy eyebrows raked over them. "Tell me what you found."

"We think it's a body," Toni said, her voice strained.

"We found a mound of leaves and uncovered Marsha Carter's purse," John explained.

"You better show me," Buck said as the deputy rounded his car and joined them. In his early forties, Dale's four inches shorter height, thinning brown hair, and ruddy skin were a striking contrast to Buck.

John set off at a brisk pace, Toni and the two officers following single file behind him.

"Hey, I'll go with you." Phil Norton, the school's Resource Officer, caught up to them. "Pam called me," he explained briefly.

"Where are we going?" Buck asked as they rounded the corner of the building.

"To the body farm," Toni said, trotting to keep up with him. "It's a small, fenced plot up the hillside. My forensics class built it," she explained, noting Buck's puzzled look. "We place bodies there, in the open or buried in shallow graves, where we study and chart their process and rate of decomposition."

"Bodies, huh?" the chief grunted without breaking pace.

"Squirrels, birds, fish, a rabbit..."

Toni and John led the little procession through the gate and back to the mound next to Harry Rabbit's grave marker. She pointed. "There."

The chief and deputy knelt next to the mound, and Buck pushed more debris away from the spot

John had already cleared. Dale picked up a stick and ran it through the handle of the purse, pulling it upright.

Buck kept clearing debris until they could see that a black plastic bag covered the upper torso of a body. At the end of the bag a woman's muddy skirt appeared. As Toni recognized the blue plaid, her knees went weak. She fought to control the nausea rising in her throat.

Buck got to his feet. "Better get some help out here." He pulled out his cell phone and called, spoke briefly to someone, and ended the call.

"Don't touch anything else," he ordered. "The coroner will be here in a few minutes. And the County Sheriff." He looked up at the sky. "We don't have much daylight left. Phil, you go down to the parking lot and direct them to us. And keep unauthorized people away."

"Will do." Phil took off in a run.

Dale stood and surveyed the area. "Do you think this is where she was killed?"

Buck shook his head. "I doubt it. She's obviously been here awhile, so any signs of a struggle will be hard to find. I think this is just the dump site." He faced Toni and John. "Have you seen anything that looks like a weapon?"

"I took a shovel from Toni's supply locker and used it to check ... that." John pointed.

"I didn't notice anything like blood on it," Toni said.

"What have you touched besides the purse?"

"Everything in here," Toni snapped defensively. "It's *my* body farm."

Buck gave her a curious look, but his eyes gleamed with shrewdness. "I see. Do you notice anything else that's different, changed in any way from how you left it the last time you did anything class related up here?"

Toni studied the area around the grave and beyond. "No," she said, thinking. "Unless…"

"Unless what?"

"The trash bag." She pointed at the plastic covered torso. "We keep some like that in the supply locker. It's mostly tools, a shovel, a couple of small gardening spades, and some small plastic bags. And a few of those bigger black ones." Her teeth chattered from the cold.

"Look closer at that skirt," Deputy Brown said, pointing at a particular spot. "It's real muddy from being buried, but it looks like there's damage to it, too. Some pulled threads, like maybe she was dragged."

"I don't see any blood around here," Buck observed.

Dale took out a notebook and began to sketch. "We need to search for a hidden weapon," he said as he drew a map.

"You two stay right where you are while we search," Buck ordered, motioning at Toni and John.

The two men were working their way around the small, enclosed area when they saw the coroner's vehicle pull alongside the edge of the road at the bottom of the hill, another police car behind it. Following them was a vehicle Toni recognized as belonging to Tammy Benson, the local newspaper reporter.

By now curiosity seekers had begun to gather at the bottom of the hill, staff and students who had stayed after school and Pam had apparently been unable to persuade to leave. Phil prevented them from advancing past the edge of the parking lot.

Ken Douglas came puffing up the hillside, his authority as principal having gotten him past Phil's barricade. "What's going on?" he demanded as he reached the gate to the little farm. "Pam said you found something."

"Hi, Ken. I'm afraid we have bad news." Chief Freeman walked over and placed a hand on the principal's shoulder, preventing him from getting any closer to the grave site.

His gaze traveled past the chief. "Have you really found Marsha?"

"We can't confirm anything, but it looks that way," Buck said grimly.

Two more cops arrived. "Hi, Frank. Rod." Buck acknowledged them briefly. "Get this area secured and let me deal with the reporter I see trying to get past Phil down there." He glanced back at Toni. "You're shivering. Why don't you and John go back to your classroom and wait for me? I have to ask you more questions. I'll find your room." He headed down the hill.

Toni hugged her coat around her and trudged alongside John behind the chief. At the parking lot Phil stood guard while Buck talked to the reporter.

"Omigosh, I forgot the boys," Toni gasped, breaking into a run.

They found Garrett and Gabe sitting on the hallway floor next to the locked door of Toni's room.

They bounced to their feet when they spied her. "What's happening?" Gabe demanded, his voice shrill with fright.

Toni opened the door and ushered them inside.

"Don't treat us like little kids and try to hide things from us. We know something bad happened."

She dropped into the chair beside her desk and eyed both boys across it. "Okay, have a seat."

They sat in student desks facing her. John stood behind them.

"John and I found Mrs. Carter," Toni said quietly.

"She's dead, isn't she?" Garrett asked, his voice solemn.

"I'm afraid so. We found her buried in the … uh, the body farm."

"Next to Harry Rabbit," Garrett whispered, his big round eyes locked on her.

Toni nodded.

"Your mom and I have to wait here for the police chief to question us," John explained calmly.

"Your dad should be home by now." Toni went to the phone and dialed quickly. She was relieved when Kyle answered.

"Can you come get the boys?" She gave him a quick summary of what had happened, and he said he would be right there.

Kyle arrived within five minutes. "I'll take them somewhere to eat," he promised Toni as the boys put on their coats. "And I'll pick up something for you." He gave her a quick peck on the mouth and left.

A coldness like she had never experienced before seeped through Toni, making her feel she could never be warm again.

John leaned his head forward onto his arms on the desk. Toni sensed that he was praying. She wished she could do the same, but she couldn't think, much less pray.

It was another half hour before Chief Freeman entered the room. "Thanks for waiting." He sank into the chair John had vacated before leaving the room.

"All right, let's go over some things and see if you can help us." Buck spoke tiredly as he took out his notebook.

"It is Marsha, isn't it?" John asked as he returned with his own desk chair.

Buck nodded. "She was the administrator, so therefore your boss, right?"

They both nodded.

"Okay, so your relationship to her is clear. Now let's see if you can help determine when she was killed. Do you remember when you last saw her alive?"

"I guess that would be the last day of school before Christmas break," Toni answered after a moment of thought.

"Yes, at the staff's manda…uh, Christmas party," John confirmed.

Buck's gaze sharpened. "What did you start to say?"

John hesitated.

Buck repeated the question.

"Mandatory Christmas party," John said. "It was sarcastic. I'm sorry."

"But what did it mean?" Buck's dark gaze drilled into him.

"She announced that the Christmas party was mandatory," John explained hesitantly. "Marsha made a practice of announcing special meetings at a moment's notice and making them mandatory, because that was the only way most of the staff would attend."

"So her relationship with the teaching staff wasn't very good. What about other staff?"

"I don't think she was liked by very many," Toni said, mentally cataloguing the few who were the woman's favorites. "So if you're asking who might have wanted to harm her, you have about seventy-five percent of the staff to consider. But, as much as everyone resented her, I can't think of anyone who might have actually killed her."

Buck jotted in his notebook. "Anything happen recently that might have triggered an explosion?"

Toni and John exchanged glances as they thought it over.

"I can't think of anything specific," John said, the corners of his mouth pulled back in a grimace.

"Just the usual grumbling and dissatisfaction," Toni confirmed.

"Ever hear of any money problems?"

Toni shook her head. "I don't know anything about her personal affairs."

"Me either," John seconded.

A thought hit Toni. "You might check her computer."

Buck made a note, and then focused on Toni. "What were you doing up there in your body farm on a cold day like this? Were you working on something, or did you go up there specifically to look for her?"

"I, uh, we went looking for her," Toni stammered.

"Why?"

"I'd rather not say." She clamped her mouth shut.

"I think you have to," John said quietly.

"Yes, you do." Buck's stern order left her no choice.

Toni chewed her lower lip, still reluctant. "If I tell you, will you keep it confidential?"

He ran a critical eye over her. "It depends. Make me understand."

Toni took a deep breath. "There have been some incidents over the past few months when Garrett found things that someone lost."

"Your youngest son." He knew her entire family. He was just confirming which son.

"Yes."

Skepticism colored his expression. "Sort of a sixth sense, you mean?"

Toni nodded. "Things no one else could find. We didn't think anything of it the first time or two, but it got to be kind of a joke. If you can't find something, have Garrett look for it."

"For example, I lost a calculator and he found it," John interjected.

Buck frowned. "Are you telling me he's the one who found Marsha?"

Toni shook her head. "No, but he had a strange dream." She told him about it. "All that triggered the awful idea that I should check the body farm. I spoke to John during lunch today, and he offered to go with me."

"I should book you for lying to a police officer,"

Buck threatened when she finished. "But it's so farfetched that I have to believe you wouldn't tell me such a story if it weren't true."

"The horrible truth is that Marsha would have been found sooner or later, and probably by me," Toni said in a steadier tone. "Logical or not, it was just sooner this way."

Buck considered her statement and made more notes. "I don't see any reason to make a big deal of Garrett's part in it," he said when he finished writing. "But can either of you pinpoint exactly what time you last saw her?" He glanced from one to the other of them.

"I remember her last party activity, when she announced that everyone should take an ornament off the Christmas tree and look for a red dot on it. If you found one, you won a prize," John explained. "I don't remember seeing her after that."

Something occurred to Toni. "I don't recall seeing her after the tree ornament thing, and I know she left the gym before cleanup, but I remember seeing the light on in her office as I left the building."

"What time was this?"

"Around five, I think. It was right after a couple other staff members and I took the Christmas tree down and cleaned up the gym. Everyone else had left by then."

"I left at five," John said.

"I left about fifteen minutes after that," Toni said, remembering.

"Which exit did you use?"

Toni thought back. "The east one. As I was going down the hall, I noticed that the door to the administration offices was open, and there was a light on in Marsha's office."

Buck frowned. "Was that unusual?"

Toni shook her head. "No, she was known for being at the school at all hours. It wasn't unusual to arrive in the morning and find a note on your desk commenting on something she had found in an evening room check, so her office light was often on at night. I didn't think anything about it."

"You were likely the last person to have been near her on that date then, which was …"

"December twenty-second," John supplied. "Which would have been eleven days ago."

Toni suddenly remembered something else. "Her car was parked at the end of the building that day, instead of in her usual reserved space by the front entrance."

"She parked there because it was handier for hauling in the boxes of stuff she brought for the Christmas party," John explained.

Buck took a moment to respond. "When we found her car at the airport, the key was in the glove compartment. There were no prints on it, so someone killed her, took the key, and drove the car away from the school."

"That means she was killed in the lower parking lot," Toni said, theorizing.

Buck got to his feet. "Let's go take a look."

It was frigid and almost dark when they got outside. Buck used his flashlight to swing a bright beam around the concrete surface of the lot. When Toni pointed out the exact spot where Marsha's car had been parked, they examined the area closely.

Buck squatted where the driver's door of the car would have been. Then he leaned closer. "There have been eleven days of snow falling and melting, and then traffic through here today. It's been wiped and then tracked over, but here's a big blood stain."

"Here's a piece of glass." Toni pointed at a small shard, but didn't touch it. About an inch in diameter, it was pointed on one side and rounded at the back, a rough resemblance of an ice cream cone. She watched Buck put on a glove, pick it up, and drop it into a small envelope.

He stood. "It looks like we've found our primary crime scene. Thank you both for your help."

John turned toward the door. "Let's go home."

Toni moved to follow him, but then hesitated. "When I opened Marsha's purse to look for identification, I saw a cell phone."

Buck nodded. "I'll have her phone records checked. And we'll get a technician to look into her computer."

"I can try to find out more about her activities during that last day if you like."

Buck heaved a sigh of longsuffering. "Toni, I know you're a science instructor and the daughter of a retired trooper, but you have no business getting involved in this investigation. You found her, yes, but it's our job from this point on. Let us handle it without interference."

"So if I learn anything, just keep my mouth shut, right?"

"Don't get smart with me, young lady," he warned gruffly. "Or I'll turn you over to your dad. Furthermore, I'll never buy you another Coke."

As Toni got into her van and started it, she closed her eyes against a fresh onslaught of guilt. She had wanted Marsha gone, had even spoken those thoughts aloud to others. Honesty forced her to admit that she felt a sense of relief that the woman's reign of threats and intimidation was over. She should feel more grief. Long forgotten words from the Bible surfaced in her mind.

Whosoever hateth his brother is a murderer ...

Had she caused Marsha's death? No, she hadn't physically killed the woman. Yet an irrational part of her felt as if she had.

Toni forced her head up and put the van in motion. When she arrived home, she found the living room deserted. Exhausted, she tossed her purse and satchel on the foyer table and started down the hall—and heard the shower running. That accounted for Kyle.

As she passed the boys' room, she heard odd muffled sounds. Curious, she stopped and eased the door open a crack. Both boys sat on the floor, their backs to the door, absorbed in something on the carpet.

"I think I hear a parental unit on the premises." she heard Gabe say, mimicking a term John Zachary had been known to use in their presence.

"X or Y?" Garrett asked in a near whisper.

When Toni eased inside the door, they spun around, guilty expressions on their raised faces.

"Definitely X." Arms folded, Toni surveyed the room. Apparently they had listened more closely than she realized to a discussion she and John had one day last week after class about a lesson on male and female chromosomes. Her sons lived in a home where conversations often revolved around education, aviation, and scientific subjects. She found it amusing, even pleasing, at their retention and subsequent use of a scientific concept.

However, the sight she saw on the floor was *not* amusing. Her budding scientists had spread a newspaper on the carpet and dumped the contents of the vacuum bag onto it. But they had seriously underestimated the amount of paper needed to hold the mess. Dirt and debris littered the carpet far beyond the edges of the newspaper.

"What do you boys think you're doing?" she asked, not sure whether to laugh or cry.

"We wanted to use our new microscope, and we read in the manual about how we could learn things from dust," Gabe explained in his scholarly way.

"We wanted to see what we could find in *our* dust," Garrett added, his eyes blinking.

"We'll clean up the mess," Gabe promised, trying to wheedle his way out of trouble. Toni was too tired to mete out any discipline, and, truth be told, she was pleased at the route of their curiosity. "What did you find?"

She could almost hear the muscles relaxing in their small bodies. "Salt and pepper and talcum powder," Gabe enumerated proudly.

"And some hairs," Garrett added. "We were trying to figure out who they all came from."

"What did you have to eat?" she asked, deciding to change the subject.

"Hamburgers," they chorused, as expected.

"Be sure you clean that up. And get all of it. I'll be checking later to make sure you did a good job."

"We will," they chorused as she turned and headed for her own bedroom.

Kyle emerged from the shower, clad in a navy bathrobe. "Your lasagna and salad are on the kitchen cabinet. Eat and try to unwind. I'll join you in a minute."

"I need a shower, and I'm not hungry."

"But you need to eat," he countered, tugging her to him. "And you don't smell *too* bad."

Toni pushed away from him. "Just for that, I *will* eat before showering."

"Good." He grinned in satisfaction.

A couple of minutes later he took a seat across the table from her. "How did things go?"

Toni sighed. "I'm not sure." She went over the session with Chief Freeman and about finding the blood and glass fragment on the parking lot. The phone rang as she finished.

Kyle leaned over and grabbed the cordless receiver from the counter. "Yes, she's here." He handed it to Toni.

"Hello."

"Toni, the three of us—Ryan, Sara and myself—contacted members of the board." Her principal's voice was tense as he referred to the middle school and elementary principals. "We'll have school as usual tomorrow, but there will be a faculty meeting before classes in the library at seven-thirty."

"No problem," she said and started to disconnect.

"Uh, I trust you'll tell Loretta?"

Toni rolled her eyes. Loretta Mullins, their

librarian, was not a favorite among the staff. How her name happened to follow Toni's on the emergency call chain was a mystery. Or maybe not. She suspected deliberateness on Ken's part, because he thought she could deal with Loretta's negative personality.

"I'll take care of it." She disconnected and immediately made the call.

"What!" Loretta exclaimed in her usual whiny tone when she heard that the meeting would be held in the library. "I just got in a big order of books today. There are boxes all over the floor. I can't possibly get all those books put away, or the boxes moved by that time."

If that weren't the case, there would have been another excuse. Loretta didn't like having her space invaded, and she didn't do any more work than absolutely necessary. But she was tenured and planned to be employed there until she retired.

"Just shove a path through them, and we'll be fine," Toni said, her teeth on edge. "Whoever gets there first will help. I'll see you in the morning." She disconnected before Loretta could voice any more complaints.

Kyle wore a big grin. "Efficiently done. Ken knew what he was doing when he arranged things so you have to handle Miss Nit-Picky. He's afraid anyone else would tell her to stuff it."

"Someday I may. She's really not a bad person. She's just such a chronic complainer that no one wants to be around her."

He eyed her across the table. "Are you sure you're all right? You've had a rough day."

Toni emitted a long sigh. "I'm fine. But I'll be better when I've had a shower and some sleep."

He reached over and tipped her face up with a finger. "Be honest with me, Toni. What's wrong?"

She gulped and blinked back tears. "I feel guilty."

When her chin quivered, he got up and rounded the table. He pulled her to his chest, and she plucked at a button on his shirt. "I don't understand what happened."

With a thumb he wiped the lone tear that had escaped. "Bad things happen. The devil never rests, you know."

She smoothed the button back into place. "I know. But they don't usually happen to people I ...wanted out of my life." Her voice broke.

Kyle drew her closer. "Life has some shockers, but God will give us comfort and help."

Toni lifted her face to peer up at her husband. She hadn't realized how much stronger his faith was than hers. She didn't have the heart to tell him how weak hers had grown. "I'll try," she said softly.

"My schedule got changed today. They have me routed cross-country for the next two weeks. I hate to leave you for that long right now."

Toni fought to contain her frustration. He was gone more and more, and she had so many things running her in circles. They no longer had time for in-depth communication. They talked about urgent matters that needed immediate attention, but they no longer shared their inner thoughts and dreams the way soul mates should.

Chapter 4

Wednesday morning Toni left the boys in the elementary office where the secretary already had the children of several other teachers corralled to keep an eye on them for the thirty minutes until they could go on to their classrooms.

When Toni entered the library at seven-fifteen it was already teeming with staff. Loretta's boxes of books were stacked along one wall, and Ken stood nearby. He gave Toni an almost imperceptible wink when she looked his way. She smothered a grin and gave him a discreet nod.

Loretta came bustling through the door of her domain. Five two and slightly overweight, she had short, curly gray hair, and a small mouth that wore its usual down-turned expression.

"I would have been here sooner, but my cat took my car keys, and it took me half an hour to find them," the librarian sputtered.

So now it's the cat's fault.

Besides having excuses, Loretta was chronically late for everything. Covert glances passed between staff members, but no one uttered a word. The room finished filling as faculty and staff entered and found seats.

"We only have a few minutes, so let's get

started," Ken announced from the front of the room.

A hand shot up from a nearby table.

"Yes, Hal?"

"Wouldn't it be appropriate to dismiss school while the police are working around here, out of respect for Mrs. Carter?"

Newbies should keep quiet.

Toni swallowed the taste of dislike that rose in her, realizing she was biased against the man. She missed Rick. She had liked the young math teacher and thought he was doing a good job. But Marsha had fired him mid-semester—no one seemed to know why—and hired Hal Warren as his replacement. Hal was an odd duck who struck Toni as a know-it-all and far less competent than Rick had been.

Ken frowned, his control rigidly contained. "It's obvious that everyone has heard about the death of Mrs. Carter. The principals have met with the board and decided to proceed as normally as possible. That was to be my first announcement. I assure you no disrespect is meant, but we need to keep the students focused as much as we can."

He paused before continuing. "The second announcement is that there will be a guard posted to see that everyone stays away from the taped off crime areas. We will appreciate your help in keeping those areas clear."

He looked around the room, as if expecting questions. But it remained silent. "If you have students who are upset or have more questions than you can answer, please send them to the counselor's office. We've contacted a couple of nearby districts and borrowed counselors from them to help Kelly."

Kelly Graham was their high school counselor.

"The police will be on the premises, questioning people throughout the day. Please give them any assistance you can. Now Dennis Guthrie, our school board president, will announce the board's appointment of an acting superintendent."

Ken stepped aside for Dustin Guthrie's dad to take the floor. Dennis was a big man with thick bushy eyebrows and a thatch of wiry, dark hair cut in a military style. Toni guessed that Ken would not be the board's choice because of Marsha's open dislike of him. She was correct.

"Ryan Prewitt will serve as acting superintendent, and the other two principals will provide any assistance he needs," Dennis Guthrie announced. "The board is confident that the entire staff will assist them in any way possible."

The meeting broke up noisily. Conversation buzzed as Toni joined the line filing out of the library, her thoughts fragmented. She wondered who had killed Marsha, but she didn't have time to dwell on the possibilities now. She had classes to conduct.

The day passed slowly. Toni didn't push the students. She allowed them to just talk, or go to the counselor if they wished. When they seemed ready, she proceeded with as much of the day's lesson as their attention span could handle.

When her forensics class arrived last hour, the picture changed. This upper level class didn't require as much one-on-one guidance and would work with minimal prompting.

"Okay, students," she said when she had finished taking roll, scanning the twenty-two students who were mostly seniors. "Let's see if you can solve a crime for me. Last night someone ransacked my desk, threw supplies on the floor, and took some money hidden in one of the drawers."

"Is this another of your sim...simu..." Jodi Garrison hesitated. A junior, she was an above average student in science, but weak in language skills. It was good to see the girl present in class today. Her first semester attendance record had been a serious problem.

"Simulations," Sidney Rayford, an intelligent senior with an attitude, supplied for her.

"Yeah, one of those crimes that's just make believe," Jodi responded with a nod.

"That's right." Toni held up a plastic bag. "Fortunately, I was able to gather some evidence. In here I have a hair sample, a fingerprint, and a thread from an article of clothing. Someone in this class is the perpetrator of this crime, and it's up to you to determine which one."

"I did it!" Dustin Guthrie waved his hand in the air, obviously trying to be funny.

"Oh, be quiet," another student snapped. "You just want to show off and interrupt class."

"Focus on this case," Toni instructed firmly. "We only have a four-day week, and I want the perpetrator identified by the end of it. Now, how do you propose to begin to solve this crime? How will you analyze the evidence collected?"

Beth Price raised a hand.

"Yes, Beth."

"We should collect evidence from everyone in the class. Same as you collected from the crime scene. So we can compare it."

"That's right. Since every member of the class has access to the crime scene, you're all suspects."

Beth surveyed the room, studying her classmates. "I'll figure it out," the petite, dark haired girl promised.

Toni held up more plastic bags. "I'm going to give each of you one of these bags. You're to place a hair sample and a thread from your clothing in yours. Use a piece of adhesive tape to pull a piece of thread from your clothing, or you may snip a small thread from the inside of a garment with a pair of scissors."

"This is my favorite class," Beth said to no one in particular.

"Then each of you must submit your fingerprints for analysis," Toni continued, ignoring the comment. Beth was an average student with a hunger for attention that there wasn't enough time to supply at this moment.

"How do we do that?" Dustin asked. Tall, dark haired and dark eyed, he was poorly motivated and a regular in ISS, In-School Suspension, for disruptive behavior. He should never have been allowed to take this class, but the children of school board members were known to receive preferential treatment. Dustin wanted in the class because of its popularity. Too much money and privilege, and too little regard for the rules, made Toni fear that the boy was heading for serious trouble.

Patiently she outlined it for him. "You draw a dark pencil smudge on a piece of paper. Then you rub your fingers, beginning with the little finger on your right hand, on the pencil smudge until they're all blackened. Next, you put a small piece of clear tape on the pad of your right thumb and gently press down on it. Then you carefully remove the tape and place it on one edge of a clean sheet of paper. Repeat the process for each finger, placing pieces of tape across the sheet of paper and labeling them."

"How do we label them?"

The procedure had been discussed in class before, but this was the first time Dustin had shown any genuine interest. Maybe the repetition would result in some retention.

"Label the thumb of your right hand with a T, the index finger with an I, the middle finger with an M, the ring finger with an R, and the little finger with an L. Then repeat the steps for your left hand," Toni explained.

Dustin stared at her, apparently working on a decision. "Okay," he said at last.

The class period continued in a satisfyingly hectic fashion. The students eventually got themselves organized and busy, and the time passed quickly.

Toni glanced at the clock. "Put your things away. The bell rings in two minutes."

As she watched the students depart, she felt unbalanced. Living in a small town had insulated her from the harshness of life in many areas. Her studies in science and forensics were intriguing and absorbing, but she hadn't applied them to any real-life crime situations.

Growing up, she had always been naturally curious, loved to solve problems, and had gravitated to science like a magnet. It seemed so relevant to everyday life. After all, everyone had a body and lived in the world of air, land, and water.

She had been fascinated by the Discovery channel and loved and found humor in the animal shows. Her biggest fights with her brothers had been over the television and what to watch on the only set that had been in their home at that time. Having a mother who worked in the medical profession was probably why she decided at a very young age that she would be a doctor. After all, her favorite board game had been Operation.

Her fourth grade teacher had been color blind, and Toni wondered how things looked to him. Then in fifth grade her model of the planets and sun and their orbits had won a blue ribbon. Advancing to regional competition, she had won a second place ribbon at her first science fair—and was hooked. She considered that the real turning point of her life, and from then through high school graduation had never missed a science fair.

When her classmates began taking babysitting jobs to earn extra money, Toni did not. She wasn't comfortable with kids and didn't want to spend her life dealing with them. But that also changed. She still remembered the moment it happened.

One day while waiting for her mother in the waiting room of the clinic, a woman and young girl had sat next to her. The kid was restless and acting up, and it was easy to see that the mother felt too sick to deal with the child. About four, the little girl wore a bunch of small bracelets on both her arms.

Impulsively Toni had asked the girl how many bracelets she was wearing. When the child shrugged,

Toni began helping her count them. Then she removed two of them and asked how many were left. The little girl counted again, and the game continued, adding, subtracting, and recounting bracelets.

When the mother's name was called and she took the girl inside with her, Toni had sunk back in her chair and gasped with the sudden realization that she should be a teacher. She forgot about her plans for pre-med and earned her teaching certification, then a master's in science education, and returned to her home town to teach.

Now she faced a real life incident of violence to someone she knew personally. It was a shock that filled her with questions of who, why, and how. There was a compulsion inside her to seek answers, but she knew Police Chief Freeman was right. It was not her job. Her job was to teach science concepts to these students. She considered herself to be a scientist who taught—not a teacher who did science.

It was a relief when the last class of the day arrived. As they filed into the room and took their seats, Toni noted that Jodi Garrison was absent—again. She had hoped when she saw the girl in class yesterday that it was a new beginning for Jodi.

As soon as class ended and she had the room tidied, Toni went downstairs to the principal's office. "What can you tell me about Jodi Garrison's chronic absenteeism?" she asked the secretary. "Is there any legitimate reason for it?"

Pam frowned, her long blonde hair falling past each side of her attractive oval face and down her back. Her soft lavender pantsuit reflected her gentle nature. "She brings written excuses from her mother.

I have my doubts about her really being sick, or believing whatever other excuse is given, but it's not my decision whether they're accepted as excused or not."

Toni didn't know anything about Jodi's personal life. "What kind of home situation does she have? Do her parents work?"

"Her dad works at a manufacturing plant, and her mother is a waitress at a large restaurant, both in Poplar Bluff. With the long work hours, plus the commute, I doubt they're home much."

"So her mother probably does pretty much whatever Jodi asks of her," Toni surmised with a slow nod. "I need to call her."

Pam opened a computer file. "I'll give you a phone number."

Toni took the number and started to leave.

"Toni," Pam said hesitantly.

Toni paused at the door. "Was there something else?"

"The police interviewed several people today, including Ken." Her voice wavered.

Toni studied the secretary's concerned expression. "Are you saying they suspect Ken?" she asked, incredulous.

Pam nodded. "I think he's their number one suspect. There's no way they could talk to all the people they did and not find out about Marsha's efforts to get him fired."

Toni shook her head in disbelief. "So the police think that's a motive? If so, they're grasping at straws."

How could they believe him capable of such an

act?

"I know he didn't do it," Pam declared with conviction. "No matter what Marsha dished out, he just took it and kept his mouth shut."

"I know," Toni agreed, tight lipped. "We'll stand by him."

Pam seemed to draw some reassurance from that.

Toni returned to her room and attempted to call Jodi's parents, but got no answer. She gave up and hustled down the hall. At the gym door, she stuck her head inside and saw Gabe and Garrett gathering basketballs and replacing them in the ball rack for the basketball team members who were shooting free throws. "Let's go, guys."

They continued to chase stray balls.

"Now," she called sternly.

They each tossed a ball in the rack, grabbed their things, and trotted after her.

"I need to stop by the police station on the way home," Toni said as they climbed into the minivan.

"Can we go in?" Gabe asked.

"May we," she corrected automatically.

"May we?"

"Okay."

Toni drove left out of the school parking lot, passed their turnoff and followed the highway into town. From one end of town to the other was about a mile.

The area had been settled in the early eighteen hundreds, but fire had destroyed half the business district near the end of the century. Then a terrible flood had destroyed much of it about twenty years later. Those had been hard times, but the stubborn residents and business owners had rebuilt each time. Today the colorful Missouri Ozark community, within easy driving distance of several lakes and rivers, thrived on tourism and small businesses.

About halfway across town Toni turned right and drove a block to the police station that sat next to the city library and faced the Post Office and City Hall across the street. Inside the building, she guided the boys to chairs near the front desk. "Wait here," she instructed, and then approached the desk where officer Pete Rogers sat. "I'd like to speak to Chief Freeman."

"Hi, Toni," Pete greeted her in a friendly manner. "Hear you found a body yesterday." He had graduated from high school a couple years behind her and joined the department a few months later.

The entire force consisted of the chief, six deputies and two reserves. One of those six deputies was the K-9 officer, and one was their school resource officer. The department had no clerical staff, so deputies manned the desk.

"It wasn't my best day," she admitted.

"Let me see if he's free." Pete went to the door of the office behind him and stepped inside. A moment later he emerged. "Go right in."

"Hi, Toni." Buck Freeman stood and extended a hand across the desk. "You just caught me. What's on your mind?"

"You know what's on my mind. What have you learned about Marsha's death?"

Buck dropped back into his chair. "You just curious, or are you playing detective?"

A little uneasy about probing, but compelled to

do so, Toni raised her chin. "Chalk it up to nosiness if you like, but give me credit for having a vested interest."

The narrow eyed look he gave her was piercing. "Granted, you had a traumatic experience yesterday, but I'm not sure you should be involved."

"I don't plan to interfere," Toni assured him. "But, like it or not, this has affected me. As much as I didn't like Marsha, I can't stop thinking about how she died, or finding her like that. And my job is affected."

Buck rubbed a long finger and thumb back and forth over his upper lip. "In what way?"

Toni took the chair next to his desk, stifling the twinge of guilt niggling at her for using their relationship this way, but she needed to know what had happened to their superintendent. Buck and her dad had been pals from the time they were young boys. After graduation from high school, Russell had enlisted in the military, while Buck had gone right to work for the local police department and earned his degree in criminal justice over a period of several years. When their longtime chief retired six years ago, Buck had run for the job and won.

"I was seriously considering looking for another position, but now I don't know what to think or do. I guess I just need to know what happened. I'm positive Ken didn't do it." She added the last with utter, almost hostile, certainty.

Buck seemed startled by her adamancy. "Is this your personal or science knowledge speaking? Or is it just the fact that the guy is your friend?"

Toni held on to her temper. "I know Ken

Douglas. He's not a violent person. In fact, he's a bit of a pushover. Knowing the truth would clear him and help me make a decision about my job." She didn't mention the personal guilt underlying her motives.

"Okay, maybe you're entitled—to a point," he granted in a gruff drawl. "But if I share information with you, I have to be convinced that you'll not reveal too much or get in the way. And if you get any ideas or learn anything, you bring them directly to me."

Toni nodded. "Fair enough. Now what can you tell me?"

He leaned forward on his arms. "The blood we found in the parking lot was a match to Marsha, but we didn't find anything helpful in her computer."

"What about her cell phone?"

"Her phone log shows a call to Jack at ten-thirty that night, supporting what he said."

"You talked to him?"

Buck nodded. "We did. He said Marsha called him that night to tell him something had come up and she had to go to Aaron's."

"Her son."

"Right. Jack said he tried calling her the next day to check on her, but she didn't answer her cell phone. He tried calling Aaron, but he couldn't get an answer there either. He says he kept trying to reach both of them, but days passed and he still got no answers. He was getting worried by then but didn't know what to do. That's when he started calling friends and family members to see if anyone knew where he might find her."

"Did he ever talk to her son?"

Buck eased back in the chair. "Jack said he

finally got Aaron on the phone New Year's Day. The boy's a college student and had been on a skiing trip with some friends. He knew nothing of his mother's whereabouts."

Toni tapped a finger against her knee. "We know the rest of the story. What about the piece of glass we found near the blood in the parking lot?"

"No reports on that yet."

"Okay, thanks for leveling with me." She rose to leave.

Buck tipped his chair back, his brow creased in thought. "Maybe your knowledge of the school and the people who work there can be helpful to us. Since everyone knows you, they might share details with you that they wouldn't think to tell us."

Toni pushed her purse strap onto her shoulder. "Is that permission to talk to them?"

He emitted a long sigh. "We both know the gossip mill is alive and well, and no one can tell you not to listen to people or talk to them. I suppose it's permission to do it with a purpose."

She left quickly, before he could change his mind.

On the way home, Toni fought the tension headache that had crept through her neck and shoulders and moved up into the back of her head. The argument the boys were having in the back seat didn't help. She opened her mouth to put a stop to it, but was interrupted by the ringing of her cell phone.

Her first impulse was to ignore it, but a quick glance at the caller ID told her it was her best friend, Kara Yates, who probably wanted to discuss her wedding plans.

Keeping her eyes on the road, Toni put the phone to her ear. "Hello, Kool Kara."

"Hi, Terrific Toni," Kara returned brightly. Then her voice changed, became serious. "I heard on the news about your superintendent being killed. You're the science teacher who found her, aren't you?"

Toni drew a deep breath. "I'm afraid so."

"How are you handling the situation?"

"Angry. Tired. Guilty," she added, knowing Kara was the one person who would always understand her.

"I know you didn't like the woman, but you have no control over what happened to her."

"I wanted her gone."

"Wow. And how many others did the same? Okay, your guilt is misplaced, but I see how it could affect you. Just don't let it eat you alive. Put on your reality cap and accept that you don't have the power to wish someone dead. Oops, someone's at the door. Chin up, okay?"

When she disconnected, the wedding had not been mentioned. But Toni felt a tiny bit better. Kara always knew when she was down and could lift her spirits. Toni missed her and wished she still lived here in Clearmount.

Their friendship dated from junior high when Kara's family moved to Clearmount. One day during Mr. Hamlin's science class they had been assigned to the same small work group and given the assignment of seeing how many genetic and inherited traits they could identify that they had in common with their parents. During class they were given a work sheet with a list of common traits for them to compare with their classmates—like sticking out their tongues to see if they could curl it into a U. Then they put their hands together and interlocked their fingers to see if they were right or left thumbed.

Toni and Kara had become fascinated as they continued their comparisons and found more and more traits in common. They both had dimples. They both could spread their fingers in a Vulcan hand sign. They had the same hair color. By the time the classroom exercise ended, they decided they must be sisters and their parents just didn't know it. By that time they were besties. Still were.

After high school they attended different colleges but kept in touch—and both majored in science. Kara had been Toni's maid of honor when she married Kyle, but Toni had not been able to reciprocate for Kara, whose longtime engagement to her high school sweetheart had gone sour and been broken during their senior year. That was when Kara had decided not to return to Clearmount.

Instead, she had accepted a teaching position at a high school there in Springfield. Later she began an eBay business on the side and started attending auctions and other sales where she could find antiques or items she thought would turn a profit. When there were estate sales in the area, she came to attend, and Toni got to visit with her. During Kara's spring break in March, that long delayed privilege of serving as Kara's maid of honor was to be rectified.

*

As soon as Toni arrived at her classroom Thursday morning she called the office and asked to speak to her principal. "May I visit with you third hour?" she asked as soon as Pam put her through. Each teacher had one period free to take care of class preparation and other duties. Hers was third.

"I'll try to be here," he promised in a tired voice.

Toni understood that meant if he didn't have to deal with an unexpected disciplinary matter or an impromptu meeting. Under the circumstances, anything was possible.

Two hours later she got a Coke from a vending machine on the way to Ken's office. When she entered, popping the top of the can, she recognized dejection in his demeanor.

The office was small, with a desk in the center and a credenza behind it that held a laptop, assorted books and papers. A large bookshelf stood to the right, a smaller one on the left, leaving only enough room for one chair in front of the desk.

"Hello, Imelda," he said with a ghost of his usual spirits, eyeing her pale pink pumps that matched her pink blouse. Ken often kidded Toni about her penchant for shoes, which she had in nearly every color imaginable, although not as many as Imelda Marcos, the former first lady of the Philippines who had left behind a collection of over three thousand pairs when exiled.

Toni dropped into the chair and got right to the point. "I heard that the police gave you a hard time. Will you tell me about it so I can get some things straight in my mind?"

He shuffled a stack of discipline reports from one side of the desk to the other. Then he met her gaze across the desk. "They grilled me like they think I killed Marsha. In fact, I thought they were going to take me to jail."

"Do you have any idea who could have done it?"

He shook his rumple-haired head. "I know a lot of people who think she deserved it, but I can't imagine who really did it."

Toni knew how hard Ken had worked, commuting to night classes during regular semesters, taking summer classes, all while working on his thesis. He had also taken on extra stipend-paying duties so his wife could stay home after their son was born.

"Can we talk about it and see if we can develop any theories?"

Ken's eyes narrowed. "Does that mean you don't think I did it?"

Toni nodded and grinned. "You're too much of a marshmallow."

Ken's smile at her attempted levity was halfhearted. "Thanks for the vote of confidence. I guess it's true what they say about finding out who your friends really are when you're in trouble. The truth is, I don't think I could kill someone if my life depended on it."

"Do you remember the last time you saw Marsha?"

"Like I told the police, I remember seeing her leave the gym around four that last afternoon of classes before the break. She went out the north door, so I assumed she was headed to her office."

"Which is probably true from the look of things. What time did you leave?"

"It was somewhere around five, right behind you."

"But you went out the front door."

His troubled gaze darted around the room. "Yes, just like I always do."

"I didn't," Toni said thoughtfully. "I had parked in the end lot, so I went out the way Marsha did, past the administration offices."

Ken waited for an explanation.

"Marsha had parked down there that day. It looks like that's where she was killed, and then her body was moved across the road and up the hill. The killer had to be someone who could have been there at that time and done that. Does anyone at all come to your mind?"

Ken rubbed his forehead. "There are several people who probably feel that someone did us all a favor, but I can't envision a killer among us."

"It's a given that your personal feelings weren't exactly warm toward her," Toni said cautiously. "You did have problems, didn't you?"

Ken grimaced. "There was friction, certainly. The woman was trying to get me fired. But, as you pointed out, I'm too much of a marshmallow to kill her." The last was said in a small return of his normal spirits.

"Okay, let's see how many people we can identify who had real issues with Marsha. I know Jack has to be considered, since most murders are committed by people close to the victim."

"His wife ... ex-wife has to have some pretty bitter feelings."

"The same might apply to their children. What about staff?"

Ken shook his head slowly. "This is so hard. I've

never had to think about any of us in this way before. I know she wrote up Maxine Horner for complaining to a board member. And there was a stink when she fired Rick Montgomery last fall. And ...." He hesitated.

Toni leaned forward. "What?"

"Well, I guess you heard the rumors about a relationship between her and Jimmie Huff."

Their special services director had only been in the district the past two school years. "I've heard. The story is that she and Marsha worked together in the past, and that's how she ended up here. If Marsha brought her in for personal reasons, it didn't last long."

"The problem," Ken said, spreading his hands in a gesture of helplessness, "is that there are so many who wanted her gone. Not dead, just gone," he clarified wearily.

"Didn't she have any close friends?"

"Not that I can ..." Ken paused. "She was pretty tight with Dana Smith. They had lunch together fairly often, which is kind of strange now that I think about it. Dana is just the bookkeeper, and it wasn't like Marsha to associate with people she considered beneath her."

Toni's brain hummed. "Do you think they could have been up to some financial monkey business that turned sour?"

He rolled his eyes up at the ceiling, as if he could find answers there. "I guess anything's possible. They spent a lot of time together in those offices, so it's feasible. But even if they weren't up to anything, Dana should know Marsha better than anyone."

Toni glanced at her watch. "I need to go, but one more question first. After you left the school that day, did you go straight home?"

"I did. But later I went out to pick up Sandy's Christmas gift."

"What time did you leave and get back?"

"I told Sandy I had to attend a meeting and left right after dinner, around six-thirty. I was trying to surprise her," he explained. "I got in my old pickup and drove to the mall at Cape Girardeau to pick up the new coat I had on layaway for her."

"So you got to Cape around eight o'clock. What time did you get home?"

Ken grimaced. "I should have come straight back to Clearmount, but I didn't. I felt practically dizzy with relief that evening, knowing I had the week and a half of holiday break ahead of me when I wouldn't have to come in here and deal with whatever new problems Marsha had devised for me."

"So what did you do?"

"When I came out of Macy's I went to my truck to come home," he said, as if quoting repeated facts. "But I wasn't ready. So I locked the package in the truck and started walking. It was cold, so I stopped at a mini mart and had a cup of coffee. Then I kept going. I don't know how long I walked, but it got my circulation going. As I walked and exercised, my thinking cleared, and I finally came to a decision."

Toni didn't comment, just waited.

"I decided to update my resume´ and check the online listings. Then, after the break, I would start making calls and job hunting in earnest."

Toni grinned. "I believe we were on the same

page."

"You, too?" He seemed surprised.

She nodded. "What time did you get home?"

He raked a hand through his dark hair, rumpling it further. "Around eleven. I can't be sure to the precise minute, but Sandy had already turned off the television after the ten o'clock news. She was just coming from the shower and made a remark about it being a long meeting to run that late."

"So you can't really prove where you were around the time Marsha was likely killed. But you would have to be one quick dude to have killed her around ten-thirty, the time when she called Jack, and have made it home by eleven."

"The police seem to think there's enough leeway in the timetable that I could have done it."

"Have they talked to Sandy?"

He nodded. "Someone came by last night and questioned her."

"So she found out you weren't really at a meeting that night."

He managed a weak grin. "She thought that part was kind of funny, because we always joke about it being okay to lie around Christmas time. Secrets are fun then."

Toni grinned. "Same at our house."

Ken rubbed his temples and reached for the bottle of pills he took for the headaches that plagued him. He held it up and gave her another wry grin. "Over the break I never took one of these. I thought maybe the headaches were gone."

He shook out two pills and popped them into his mouth. Then his expression sobered. "There's a certain irony to all this. Marsha was trying so hard in life to ruin me, and now she's about to get it done in death."

"Well, we'll just have to keep that from happening," Toni said with resolve.

His brow creased. "How's that?"

"By finding out who did it." She glanced at her watch again. "I have to run, or I'll be tardy."

Chapter 5

As she walked back to her classroom, Toni's conviction of Ken's innocence grew so strong that it made her want to shout it to the police. Call her a trusting fool, but her gut said he was a victim, not a killer. But who had done it? Considering the logistics of the crime, it seemed most likely to have been a man, but that wasn't conclusive. If rumors were to be believed, Marsha had multiple intimate relationships. No one could be discounted.

In spite of Jack Rayford's seemingly upset state, could he have done it? He had a lot of clout in this small town, so the police would have to tread lightly if they were to consider him. What would have been his motive? Another woman? What kind of alibi did he have? The number of questions continued to swell.

Toni's thoughts shifted to Marsha's computer. How thoroughly had it been checked? Perhaps it held answers that the police wouldn't recognize, since they were not on a day-to-day familiarity with the education system.

Toni wasn't sure how much more help she could get from the police department—or how much she should help them. They seemed focused on Ken, and the fact that she disagreed would put severe limits on how much they would tell her.

As her thoughts crystallized, a new sense of purpose flowed through her. To prove her convictions she would have to suspect everyone, be less trusting and more observant. But she had to know the truth.

By five after three Toni's classroom had emptied, except for Beth Price, who was out collecting recyclables from containers that the science club kept in the commons and various locations around the building to collect aluminum cans, plastic bags, plastic bottles and newspapers.

The girl came through the doorway, dragging two large black trash bags that were each about three quarters full. "Here's the last batch."

"Let me help you." Toni left her desk and grabbed one of the bags. They added them to the stack in the back of the room.

For the next hour Toni graded papers while Beth sorted the stuff into proper containers. When she finished recording grades, Toni closed her grade book and joined Beth at the back of the room.

"Thanks for helping, Mrs. Donovan. You didn't need to do it, but it's fun having you work with me," Beth said as they pulled cans and bottles from bags, dumped any contents into the sink at one of the lab stations and tossed them into a different bag.

Toni smiled at the soft spoken, slightly built girl. "I know you're president of the science club, but you shouldn't have to do all the work yourself."

"Oh, it's all right, Mrs. Donovan, I enjoy it. Besides, the other kids have ball practice and things like that."

In other words, they were all too busy dating and being popular to do lowly grunt work related to academics. Beth fit on a lower rung of their social scale because she wasn't an A student or an athlete. Toni wasn't quite sure what that made her, other than invisible—unless someone needed something. Hungry for attention and importance, Beth took on a multitude of responsibilities. Toni hated to see her taken advantage of, but she didn't have the heart to risk hurting the girl by curtailing her efforts.

"Are you and Jodi Garrison friends?"

Beth dropped two cans into a bag and looked up. "Not best friends, but we get along pretty well."

"Do you know anything about her home life?"

Beth paused, a can in each hand, her face creased in thought. "Well," she said at last, "I know her dad works at the car engine plant, and I think he works a lot of overtime. Her mom also works a lot of hours. So they're not home much."

That only confirmed what Toni already knew. "Do you have any idea why Jodi misses so much school?"

"I'm not sure," the girl said quietly, tossing the cans into a bag. "She didn't used to miss at all, but this year's been different."

"Yes, it has."

Beth grew even quieter. A look of hesitation crossed her face.

"What is it?" Toni felt a tad guilty at using Beth to get information, but justified it because of her genuine concern for Jodi.

"She broke up with her boyfriend."

That could explain a lot. Teenage romances were taken so seriously that teens had even committed suicide after a break-up. God forbid that Jodi was anywhere near such a point. "Do you think her being sick so much could be related to the break-up?"

"I hope not, but I really can't say," the girl said, clearly uneasy. "Nothing's been the same lately. I mean about Jodi. We used to eat lunch at the same table and take some of the same classes. But last summer she started going steady with Randy Owens and spending all her time with him. Then, between Halloween and Thanksgiving, they broke up. She was really spaced out for a while, so I know she was hurting bad. I thought she would start hanging out with our group at lunch again, but she didn't. Then she started missing school. I'm worried about her."

"Beth, are you ready to go?"

They looked around to see Maxine Horner just inside the door. A teacher aide in the special education department, she worked with Mrs. Morris upstairs. About five two, Maxine had long curly hair that needed a trim, and she spoke with a slight lisp. She and Beth were neighbors, and Beth sometimes caught a ride home with Maxine when she stayed after school.

Beth grabbed a wire twist tie, gathered the top of the bag, and wrapped the wire strip around it. She gave it a twist. "I am now." She turned to Toni. "Kim and I will get these out of here in the morning before first period."

"Thanks for everything, Beth." They both knew she meant more than just the recycling.

Maxine lingered just inside the door as Beth left. "All anyone's been talking about is you and Dr. Z finding Mrs. Carter's body," she said, her S's hissing. "It musta been awful."

Maxine wasn't exactly the sharpest axe on the block, but her curiosity was natural and understandable. "It wasn't among my most pleasant experiences."

Maxine stuck her head out the door and called down the hall. "Go on to the car, Beth. I'll be there in a minute."

She moved closer to the desk. "Do they have any idea who killed her?" she asked, obviously hungry for juicy details.

Toni shoved her grade book into her satchel. "The police don't tell us what they think. But what about you? Do you have any idea who it might have been?"

Maxine shook her head. "No, but I know a lot of people who'd like to line up to say thanks to whoever it was. Oops, sorry," she apologized with a giggle. "I shouldn't say that."

Toni almost smirked, but caught herself. "I understand the sentiment."

Maxine frowned in thought. "Well, I guess that really was my first reaction, but a murderer running around free...well, that's just plain scary."

Toni tapped a pencil on the desk. "If you knew anything helpful, would you tell it?"

Her head nodded rapidly. "Sure, but I still couldn't say I'm sorry she's dead."

"Does that mean you had personal run-ins with her?" Toni tried to sound matter-of-fact.

Maxine snorted. "You bet it does. As you may know, my uncle's on the school board. Well, when some stuff got dumped on our department, I discussed it with Uncle Art. Marsha found out about it—he musta said something—and she wrote me up for talking to him personally about a school problem. Said it was going over her head. So I've got a pink slip in my file."

"That sounds unfair." Toni tried to sound appropriately sympathetic.

"What Marsha wanted to do, Marsha did." Maxine's head bobbed in rhythm to the words. "That woman was something else. She's not only a jerk about her job, but she dumps her woman lover for a married man. I mean *was*," she corrected. "I guess she couldn't make up her mind what made her tick."

Toni decided to continue playing dumb. "You mean she had something going with a woman on our staff?"

Maxine snorted and rattled on. "Of course. Didn't you know that Jimmie Huff came here last year from the same district Marsha came from earlier? Marsha brought her here, or Jimmie followed Marsha, one or the other. And they were real thick last year. One of the janitors, I think it was Clay, caught'em in a compromising way, if you know what I mean, in the teachers' lounge after school one day. They didn't know he saw'em, but he told it around."

"Does that mean you think Jimmie did it?" Toni sneaked a glance at her watch, wondering if Maxine would ever run down.

Maxine noticed and got the message. "I have to go. I don't know who did it, but I know one thing that gives me a lot of comfort. I have an airtight alibi," she said as she darted out the door.

Toni tried once more, without success, to call Jodi's parents. She picked up two pizzas on the way to her parents' house. When she had to stay after school, the boys sometimes rode the bus to their grandparents. If Faye had to work the late shift, like today, Russell took care of them. Toni, the boys, and Russell shared the pizzas.

*

Friday morning Toni put off the errands she needed to do during her plan period and used the time to visit the special education directors office. At the door she hesitated, unsure of her reception. Taking a deep breath, she opened the door and peeked inside.

Jimmie, seated at her desk, looked up with a smile. It disappeared when she recognized Toni.

"Are you busy, or may I come in?"

"Come in,'" she said, her tone not very gracious. Her hair was dark, sculpted around her ears, and she wore a black tailored pantsuit. Toni guessed her to be in her late forties.

"Can you chat with me a bit?"

"If it's about school, fine. If it's about Marsha, forget it," she snapped, radiating hostility.

"Does that mean you aren't interested in finding out who killed her?" Toni spoke with a forcefulness she didn't really feel.

"It means I'm tired of everyone asking questions," Jimmie replied frostily. "I know you found her body, but so what. It's not your job to find out who did it. Let the police handle it."

"You're right. I know they're working on it, and I know you've probably been questioned. But I'm worried about Ken," Toni said in a spurt of honesty. "I think they've settled on him as their main suspect, and I'm sure he didn't do it."

Jimmie studied her for a long moment, and then her shoulders sagged. "What do you want to know?" she asked, a touch of frost still in her tone.

Toni took a seat and faced her squarely. "I understand that you knew Marsha and worked with her before coming here."

"I'm sure that's not all you heard."

"No, it's not," Toni said honestly. "So was what I heard true? Did you and Marsha have a special relationship beyond academics?"

"Yes," Jimmie answered, her tone flat. "And after she got me here, she dumped me. Now you want to know if I killed her. I didn't."

"Look," Toni said softly. "I'm not trying to give you a hard time. I just don't want to see Ken Douglas get charged with something he didn't do. I hoped you might know something that could help clear him of suspicion."

Jimmie seemed to relent a bit. "I doubt that anything I know could be helpful, but I guess I can go over the history for you."

Toni was all ears as Jimmie took a thoughtful breath.

"When Marsha applied for a position here, it was because she was working on her Ph.D. and knew your superintendent planned to retire soon. She took an assistant position with plans to move up."

Which she had.

"Did the two of you keep in close touch during that time?"

"Not very. She was caught up in her new job and ambitions, and we drifted apart. She played her political game well and snagged the superintendent's job when it came open. Then this position came open, and she called me. I almost didn't apply—and shouldn't have—but I caved in and did what she wanted. It was a quick hire, and we were together again. Then she decided she wanted Jack. I guess he was in a position to do more for her."

Toni nodded in sympathy. "You were already under contract and stuck here when that happened. Did she make things uncomfortable for you?"

"We stayed out of one another's space as much as possible," Jimmie said stiffly. "Between doing my job and avoiding her, I didn't keep up with things going on around here."

"So this means you don't have any idea who killed her."

Jimmie nodded. "That's what it means. I don't know much dirt. You'd have to ask someone like Rick Montgomery that kind of stuff—if you can find him."

Toni frowned. Rick had been with the district several years when Marsha fired him in October. The reason was never made public, and Toni wasn't sure where he was now. "Do you know why he was terminated?"

Jimmie shook her head. "I'm not sure. I just remember hearing him and Marsha arguing in the hall one day, and soon after that he was gone. When I asked her about it later, she just made some comment about him being insubordinate." She paused and produced a sardonic grin. "He should have known better than to try to play hardball with a pro."

"Thank you for talking to me." Toni rose and went to the door, but then stopped and looked back.

"One more question. I don't want to make you mad, but the police will ask this if they haven't already. Can you verify where you were the evening of the twenty-first?"

"I sure can," Jimmie snapped. "I drove to St. Louis and caught an eight o'clock flight to Chicago to join my family for Christmas."

"Thank you. I appreciate your time." She left the room, certain that Jimmie would not be returning next year.

Toni used her lunch time to take care of errands, hoping to get caught up so she could leave right after school. When her final class arrived, she was happy to see Jodi present—until she took a closer look at the girl. She wore heavy makeup, but no amount of camouflage could hide the ugly bruising around her left eye. That side of her lip was puffy and cut.

Other than the black eye and split lip, Jodi's appearance was similar to the other female students. She wore hip hugging jeans and a short denim jacket over a long tailed print shirt. Large blue eyes in an oval face, with long straight hair that had been lightened, made an attractive picture. But the solemn mouth belied any happiness in the girl.

Toni didn't want to ignore something that looked like a need for help, but she didn't want to say or do anything that would draw unwanted attention to Jodi during class. She would speak to the counselor after school. Perhaps there was a reasonable explanation, and no reason to call the hot line.

Feeling helpless, Toni proceeded with the lesson on DNA fingerprinting. Here she was teaching a class involving crime-solving techniques, and she had no answers to a real crime right under her nose. Also, right there in her class sat a student she was sure was in some kind of trouble, possibly being abused. And she could do nothing about either.

When the bell rang, Toni removed her lab coat, gathered her things, and went to meet her boys. "Hey, guys," she called as they met in the cafeteria. "Wait for me here while I see the counselor. I'll only be a few minutes, then we'll go home and have a real meal."

Garrett's eyes brightened. "Can we have homemade egg noodles? May we?" he corrected before Toni could remind him.

"Okay," Toni agreed, unable to resist the little con artist.

"May we go up and invite Dr. Z and Jenny?" came from Gabe.

Toni considered for a moment. "It's okay to invite them, but if the answer is no, you accept it and don't make pests of yourselves."

"We won't," they promised, grabbing their backpacks and racing down the hall.

When Toni entered the counselor's office, Kelly looked up from her computer. "Jodi Garrison was in class today, but I'm worried about her. Did you see her?"

Kelly stopped typing. "You mean the black eye?"

Toni nodded. "Do you know what's going on in that girl's life? I've tried calling her parents about her absences, but I can't get an answer."

Kelly grimaced. "So have I. I saw the way she looked today, but I didn't spot her until after lunch. This week's history, so it'll be Monday before I can talk to her."

"If she's here." Toni gave an exasperated shake of her head. "I talked to Beth Price and learned that Jodi and Randy Owens broke up. So I assume that's not who's hitting her. I hate to think that a parent is doing it."

"Same here." Kelly reached for a pen and made a note on her calendar planner. "I'm documenting this now. Monday morning I'll ask the nurse if Jodi has been to see her, and I'll do my best to get the girl in here for a talk. Then I'll ask Ken for advice."

"Thanks. Let me know if there's anything I can do to help."

John and the boys were coming up the hall when Toni exited the office. "Can you come?"

"May we bring the puppy?" John asked, his mouth curved in a line of uncertainty.

Toni smiled. "Sure. The boys can play with him." Some of Jenny's students had given her a puppy for Christmas, a spaniel they had named Bingo. She and John were still trying to train him.

Once home, Toni tossed a load of laundry in the washer and put some chicken breasts on to cook. As she put the meal on the table an hour later, the phone rang. Toni deposited the hot dish she was carrying and snatched the receiver off the cabinet, sure it was John or Kyle. "Yes."

"I haven't asked the question yet," came a short bark.

Toni paused a second as Buck Freeman's voice registered. "So what is the question?"

"How soon can you get down here and talk to me?"

She recognized a mandate when she heard one. Buck might be a friend of the family, but he was also the head of law enforcement in this small town. "I'm just putting food on the table, and I'm expecting company."

"Then come as soon as your company is gone," he ordered, his sharp tone softening a bit.

Toni glanced at the time. It was six o'clock. "It'll be an hour or so. Isn't that too late for you to be in your office?"

"I'll be here." The click in her ear told her the conversation was over.

While she still held the silent phone, the doorbell rang. "Come on in," she called, on her way to the stove for another dish.

"What can I do to help?" Jenny asked as she and John stowed their coats in the foyer closet.

"Nothing," Toni answered from the kitchen. "It's ready. Let's go ahead and eat. Then we can visit."

She debated whether to tell them about Buck's call, because she didn't want them to feel they had to rush away, or feel obligated to stay with her boys. Not wanting to take advantage of them, she decided to wait and tell John anything he needed to know in the morning.

Jenny carried the puppy into the kitchen. "Where should I put Bingo?"

"Put him in the utility room. He should be content there while we eat. And, no," she said to the boys as they both started toward Jenny with their arms outstretched. "You may not play with him until after we've eaten."

Disappointed, they took their seats at the table.

"When is Kyle due home?" John asked a half hour later as Toni dipped ice cream over banana slices and dribbled chocolate sauce over it.

She placed the sundaes on the table before them. "Not until next Wednesday. I kind of wish he was here so I could leave the boys with him in the morning. I'd like to see if I can find Rick Montgomery and ask him some questions."

"Rick?" John's look was one of surprise. "I heard he moved to Farmington and went to work at the prison. Do you think he knows something about our murder?"

Toni grabbed the last dish of ice cream off the cabinet and returned to her seat. "I'm not sure, but Jimmie mentioned him." She related the conversation.

"I'm sure you can find him in the phone book," John said. "As for the boys, drop them at our place. They can stay with us and play with Bingo."

"Can we play with him now?" Gabe begged. "We're done."

"May," Toni corrected automatically.

"May we?"

"All right." She faced John again, frowning.

John raised a palm. "No, before you can even suggest it, we won't accept payment for watching your boys for a little while."

"But we might work a swap," Jenny suggested quietly. "I'd like to go visit my folks next weekend, and Bingo gets sick in the car. Could we exchange some sitter services?"

Toni laughed. "You've got a deal."

As soon as John and Jenny had helped clear the table and tidy the kitchen, they went home so John could grade test papers. It was seven forty-five.

"Get your coats, boys," she said as Garrett turned on the television.

Both boys turned to face her in surprise. "Where are we going?" Gabe asked.

"Buck wants me to come see him. Bring your homework if you have any."

"Can't we stay here?" Gabe pleaded.

"I don't know how long it will take, so I don't want to leave you alone. Let's go."

He opened his mouth to protest, but closed it when he read the look on her face.

*

Toni parked the boys in chairs out front before going to Buck's private office. When she entered, Buck sat back in his chair instead of standing and extending a handshake, as he normally would have done. His sharp gaze took in every detail of her appearance, as if looking for hidden secrets. Dark circles smudged below his eyes. She knew he liked her, but tonight she sensed that those feelings had been put aside. He was tough and competent, but he seemed to be calculating his approach with her.

"I have to ask you some personal questions. Have a seat."

She obeyed. "What's going on?"

He leaned forward on the desk and peered into her face. "Toni, I have to be blunt. We've been talking to school employees."

She nodded, beginning to feel a bit unnerved. "I understand. You have to do your job."

"During those interviews several staff members mentioned that you and Ken Douglas were still in the building after they left on the last day Marsha was seen alive."

"That's right," Toni answered without hesitation. "He left about the same time, but he went out a different door than I did."

"So, besides him, you were the last one to leave, other than Mrs. Carter."

"I suppose so, but I didn't actually see her. There was a light on in her office, and her car was parked outside. I already told you all this."

His eyes narrowed. "I know. But humor me. There may have been some details missed. Don't you find it odd that she was there so late?"

What was he implying? Toni went tense as cold prickles of fear inched through her. "No. She hung around all the time. She was paranoid, had to keep her thumb on everything."

"Where were you that Thursday night at ten o'clock?" His tone became a growl.

Toni raised her chin. "I went home."

He raked a hand through his thick white hair. "What did you do after you got there?"

She thought back. "I fed the boys and put away the science club's box of decorations that John, Ken, and Lisa helped me take off the tree at school. Then I took a shower and spent the evening reading."

He scribbled on his notepad and looked back up. "Where was Kyle?"

"Out of town. He had an extra run that week and didn't get home until late Friday night. Are you accusing me of having something to do with Marsha's death?" She hated sounding defensive, but couldn't help it. "Surely you're not serious. You really think I would ...."

He raised a hand in a signal for silence. "You know I have to cover all the bases, Toni. It was suggested that we talk to you."

"Why? By whom?"

"Several people find it odd that you just happened to be up there at that body farm at that particular time and found the body."

Temper rising, Toni had trouble speaking. She wanted to punch something—or someone. "You didn't tell them about Garrett, did you?"

"Of course not," he barked. "But I can't ignore it when your name keeps popping up in interviews."

"That's bound to happen, since I ... we found the body. But why would anyone think I would do such a thing?"

His brows drew together over a cool stare. "No one said you did it, but someone heard a conversation between you and your superintendent that wasn't described as amicable."

"When? Never mind," she said as a flash of memory came to her.

"You remember it," he said in an odd tone that didn't actually seem accusatory. In fact, he seemed almost as puzzled as her. "Tell me about it. Did you like working for Mrs. Carter?"

"No, I didn't. But neither did most of the staff. I was considering a job change. As were some others." She didn't want to name John.

Buck made another note. "Tell me about the argument you had with her."

Toni's head moved back and forth. "It wasn't an argument."

"Then whatever it was," he said, his eyes narrowing dangerously. "Quit stalling."

Toni clenched her hands. "All right. But I have to explain. It was more like being called on the carpet. There were a couple of issues."

He waited impatiently.

"Back in May I made out a requisition for six microscopes. Then I wrote what I thought was a very polite, persuasive letter and put with it, explaining why I needed them for my classroom."

"Which was?"

"To begin with, I only have eight, and I need more like fifteen, enough for classes of twenty to thirty students to be able to have one per two students. The eight I have are outdated and have scratched lenses and dusty internal workings that cause them to have a lot of play in them. They've already been refurbished more than once and need replacing. My budget for the year is only a thousand dollars, and new scopes cost seven to eight hundred apiece."

Buck tapped a pen on the notepad. "Go on," he prodded when she paused.

"Like I said, that was back in May. At the end of our second workshop day at the beginning of school in August, Marsha called me to her office and informed me that my requisition was being denied because there wasn't enough money. She suggested that I have my science club and the student council, the two organizations I sponsor, purchase one or two microscopes each from their fundraising monies."

An eyebrow arched, but he said nothing.

"I was steamed," she admitted. "Their service

projects are for charitable purposes. The science club recycles things and uses the money they earn to buy school supplies and Christmas gifts for needy students. The student council adopts a family from the community's twenty neediest families project and provides at least one of the family's listed needs and a gift for each child. Taking money from those organizations would be robbing from the poor to buy for myself."

His mouth twitched ever so slightly at the fervor of her recital. "So you told her that?"

"I did." Toni nodded vigorously. Then she clamped her mouth shut and sat back in the chair, arms folded across her chest.

"You said a couple of issues."

She stared up at the ceiling until she grew calmer. "By that point Marsha knew I wasn't a happy camper, so she hit me with a complaint for excessive copying."

He frowned.

"Last year Marsha decreed that we can no longer make copies for ourselves like we've always done in the past. We now have to fill out a form, attach it to whatever we want copied, and turn it in for an aide to make the copies and keep a record of them."

"Is it such a bad system?"

"I guess not. The major problem is that we're expected to allow three or four days to get our copies."

"So no last minute stuff, huh?"

"Which is a pain in the royal patoot," she sputtered. "Sometimes we need things impromptu. But the reason my copying is excessive is because I don't have workbooks to go with my forensics textbook. I have to make all my own worksheets, quizzes, and tests and have them copied." Her voice had risen again.

"I can tell you're passionate about this."

She closed her eyes, took a deep breath, and rubbed the tight muscles in the back of her neck. "One of the first things Ryan did as interim superintendent was to shut down the copy system. He didn't like it either. So does that make him a suspect?"

"Don't get smart with me, Miss Toni," he snapped. "So you were fuming when you left Mrs. Carter's office that day."

She gave him a meek grin. "Oh, yeah. I was so hot that I banged my fist on the wall as I turned the corner in the hallway. The custodian saw me. And I suspect the secretary heard the entire conversation."

He neither denied nor confirmed the statement.

"I'm in the process of writing a classroom grant, but it may or may not get approved. And it won't even be read until spring. I don't know what my chances are of getting new microscopes for next year. Do I need a lawyer?" she asked abruptly.

"I don't think that's necessary. But I'd like to speak with your boys before you leave."

She glared at him. "Only if I'm here in the room."

"Go get them."

She summoned Gabe and Garrett and sat silently as Buck asked them simple questions like what they each got for Christmas and commented about how much fun it must have been to have such a long break from school. Then he asked what they did the first night after school dismissed for the holiday. Both shrugged and told him they had stayed home with Mom and watched television, confirming Toni's story.

"Go home," he ordered gruffly, aiming the words over their heads at Toni.

Chapter 6

Saturday morning Toni dropped the boys with John and Jenny and set out for Farmington. John had found Rick's number, called him for a chat, and found out where he lived. She hoped she wasn't making a mistake in not calling and telling her former colleague she was coming—and that he would be home. But she felt that talking to him in person would be more helpful than a phone conversation.

The January landscape was barren. Raised arms of leafless trees covered the hillsides, and clumps of snow still dotted the fields and ditch lines. But Toni found beauty even in the starkness. The Missouri climate was so varied that her dad often repeated the old adage, "If you don't like the weather today, just wait a bit and it will change."

She took the Farmington exit and wound her way into the city. Located about seventy miles south of St. Louis, the town had begun in the late 1790's as a family settlement originally called Murphy Settlement. Today it was a thriving municipality with over fourteen thousand people and a solid economy.

Toni cruised through residential areas of stately homes on tree-lined streets until she found the address John had given her. When she rang the doorbell at Rick's apartment she got no response, but waited until convinced that no one was home. Disappointed, she turned and headed back to her vehicle.

"Toni?"

She whipped her head around and looked back over her shoulder. Rick stood in the doorway in his sock feet, looking sleepy eyed and rumpled. She retraced her steps. "I didn't think you were home."

"That's what I meant for you to think," he returned honestly. "Come on in. We'll have a Coke together." He gave her a weak grin.

Toni entered a simply furnished apartment that showed signs of bachelor living, but wasn't a total mess. Stacks of books rested on the end of the sofa, and there was a blanket tossed on it, indicating Rick might have been stretched out there. She perched at the uncluttered end.

"Here we go." He came from the tiny kitchen beyond the living area with a can of Coke and a glass of ice that he handed to her. "There's a coaster on the lamp table next to you." He slumped in the recliner facing her.

"You're looking good," Toni said, wondering how to broach the subject of Marsha.

"After John's little call last night, I pretty much expected a visit today," he said, his expression listless. "I just wasn't sure if it would be him or you who showed up. I figure you want to talk about our dear departed friend." He put a cynical inflection on the word friend.

"Guilty," Toni admitted with a shrug. "Wouldn't you like to know who killed her?"

"No." His response was immediate. "Unless it's to give the person a medal for making the world a better place." Bitterness colored his voice.

Toni was hard put for an answer. "I understand your feelings, but having a murderer running free bothers me. I was told that you might know things about Marsha that could help us find who killed her."

"Well, you were told wrong. Look," he said with a heavy sigh. "I screwed up and lost my job, but I can't be sorry she's dead."

"Can you tell me what happened? I never heard any details—and I didn't ask."

"I can tell you, but I can't see where it'll do you any good."

"You never know what might mean something."

At that he produced a laconic grin, his first sign of animation. Six foot one, dark haired and green eyed, he was one of the most handsome men Toni knew.

"I found out about the thing she had going with another staff member," he began slowly.

"Jimmie?"

He nodded. "Marsha and I had a confrontation one day over what she called my dereliction of duty in not turning in a bunch of paperwork. It was stuff that was redundant in the first place, and in the second place I had already submitted it. I wasn't about to do it again just because she, or someone else, lost it. Probably on purpose," he added with a touch of sarcasm. "Yeah, I know. I had it in my computer and could have just printed another copy, but I was already fed up over a lot of things. When she threatened to write me up, I told her to go ahead and do it, and I would have a little talk with the board about her personal life."

"Is that when she fired you?"

He shook his head, his fingers tapping aimlessly on the chair arm. "No, she backed off, said she'd let it go this time, but that it better not happen again."

"Did you expose her to anyone?"

"No, I thought about it, and I wanted to cause her some trouble if I could, but I didn't. I figured it would just turn into a big stink that would hurt both of us."

"So what else happened?"

"I blew it," he snorted, clearly angry with himself. "There was an attraction growing between me and ..." He paused and gave her a beseeching stare. "Do I have to say a name?"

"I don't care who it is," Toni said. "But you never know what might prove important."

He sighed in resignation. "All right. Rhonda Dollins and I were drifting into an affair, and Marsha must have seen us having lunch together and interpreted something from it. As soon as she knew there was something between us, she fired me. It's all right for her to have relationships with co-workers or authority figures, but not for anyone else."

"I don't know what to say." Toni had not realized that he and an elementary teacher were an item. "That's why you didn't fight the dismissal," she said with sudden insight. "You didn't want Rhonda hurt by it."

"That's right," he said grimly. "I took my lumps and went job hunting."

"How are things going?" she asked, truly concerned.

"Okay. I'm teaching a GED program at the prison. Education is needed by more than just teenagers."

"I bet you miss your advanced math classes, though." She forced a smile.

He shrugged. "I do. But I'm trying to do the right thing."

"You mean about Rhonda?"

"Yes. She's working at keeping her marriage together, and I'm working at learning to live with it. I've even had a couple of dates with Becky. If we hadn't been separated and looking at divorce, Rhonda would never have happened."

"I'm sorry things have been rough for you, but I'm proud of the way you're handling it. I hope you and Becky can resolve things."

"We'll see," he said noncommittally. "As for being proud of the way I'm handling it, don't be. I may be surviving, but I sure don't feel any sorrow about that woman's death. I nearly danced in the streets when I heard about it."

"I've had some of the same feelings," Toni admitted. "I'm the one who found her. Actually, John Zachary and I found her. You know that I'm too curious for my own good, so you can understand why I'm asking questions."

"Classic Toni Donovan," he said with a shake of his head, his mouth curving slightly at the corners. "Well, I think it's an interesting puzzle for you, but I still can't say I want you to catch whoever did it. You're still my pal, and you're real good at what you do. But just this once I kind of hope you fail." He wrinkled his nose at her.

She took a deep breath before spitting out her next question. "I hate to ask this, but in case the police should question you, can you prove where you were the night she was killed?"

He leaned forward. "You mean December twenty-first, right?"

"Yes."

He thought about it a moment. "I was at the prison. We did a special evening class that week."

"Good. Thanks for your time." She raised her glass. "And the Coke."

Toni took care of her shopping, and then headed home. As she drove, she wondered if Rick was right. Maybe she should just leave it alone. All she seemed to be doing was spinning her wheels, and she understood Rick's feelings. She should forget the whole thing.

That resolve lasted until she picked up the boys.

As soon as they arrived home she called the police department and asked the deputy who answered if she could speak to Chief Freeman.

"He's not in right now. May I help you?"

"Is Dale Brown available?"

"Hold on just a minute. I think he's in the back."

"Hi, Toni," the deputy's voice came on the line at last. "What can I do for you?"

"I've been thinking about the phone call Marsha Carter made to Jack Rayford the night she was killed."

"You know about that?" Surprise tinged the question.

"Buck talked to me," she explained, hoping it would make him more forthcoming. "Did her phone log show that she called him at home or on his cell phone?"

"I'd have to check."

"Would you please?"

He was gone only minutes. "The number on the log is for their apartment land line."

"Thanks. I guess that means he was at home then, like he said."

*

Sunday morning Toni woke with her to-do list running through her mind. Lesson plans had to be made, letters written, and a dozen other tasks awaited her attention. She didn't have time to go to church. But Kyle wasn't here, and the boys would be disappointed if they missed their Sunday School class. She crawled out of bed and got dressed.

After church Toni took the boys to the Sunday buffet at the Zinger Restaurant. Cooking didn't appeal when Kyle was gone, and this would save her time and energy.

"Hey, there's Grandma and Grandpa and Chief Freeman," Gabe said as they entered the restaurant.

Sure enough, the chief's regal frame was seated next to Toni's dad. Buck and Russell's friendship had cemented even further since Buck's wife had lost her battle with cancer months earlier. Toni felt a twinge of unease over her last meeting with the police chief, but she pushed it aside, knowing it had been a professional necessity. She hoped for another opportunity to speak with him, but not as a suspect.

"Hello, boys." Faye Nash stood and gave each of them an exuberant hug. Then she looked back at the men. "We've ordered, but let's move to the round table."

The front section of the restaurant had a counter

along one wall, with a window behind it through which orders were dispensed from the kitchen. Small square tables occupied the rest of the room, with a large round one in the corner that would accommodate larger groups. A buffet and salad bar were located in the rear of the restaurant.

Buck and Russell shoved their chairs back, picked up their tea glasses, and moved to the bigger table. Gabe and Garrett quickly claimed seats next to their grandpa. Toni slipped her coat over the back of the chair between her mother and Buck.

"Hello, Chief. Are you and Dad getting the problems of the world solved?"

"Not exactly." He leaned over and whispered into her ear as she slid into the chair. "I know you have questions, but let's wait and talk out front after we've eaten."

Toni nodded and smiled. "Thanks."

The waitress brought menus and glasses of water. "What'll it be, Mrs. Donovan?" Her teenage smile flashed with braces. Toni knew her from school, but didn't have her in class.

"Buffet or burgers?" Toni asked the boys.

"Buffet," Gabe responded. "And iced tea."

"Burger and fries," Garrett said, as expected. "And I want a Coke."

Like mother, like son.

The meal was solid country fare—fried chicken, mashed potatoes, broccoli casserole, rolls, and banana pudding for dessert.

"Why don't you let the boys come over for the afternoon?" Faye suggested when they had finished eating and settled their bills.

"Please?" Gabe shifted from one foot to the other in impatience.

Toni peered at him, then at Garrett. "Do either of you have homework to do?"

Both assured her they didn't.

"All right." She buttoned her coat, shoved her purse strap up onto her shoulder, and followed the group out the door.

Chief Freeman leaned against the door of her minivan. "Do you mind if we get inside? It's freezing out here."

"You bet." Relieved that their relationship seemed to be back on solid footing, Toni unlocked the doors and climbed behind the wheel.

Buck slid into the passenger seat. "Are we good?" were the first words out of his mouth.

Toni nodded. "You had to question everyone who had close contact with Marsha. That included me."

He just nodded. "Russell seems to think you have a good head on your shoulders."

She started the engine and turned on the heat. "We both know he's prejudiced, but it's a nice thing to hear."

"Tell me who you've talked to and what you've learned."

"Then do I get to ask questions?"

He turned to face her. "That's the deal."

Toni glossed over her talk with Ken, not wanting to stir any open opposition at that point. Then she told him about her visits with Jimmie Huff and Rick Montgomery.

Buck's expression became pensive. "I suppose

that gives us a little more insight into Mrs. Carter's life, but I'm not sure if any of it's going to help."

"I know. That's why I didn't call you. I wasn't sure you'd even be interested."

"I'm interested." His mouth curved ever so slightly. "I'm also aware that you checked Jack's alibi."

She shrugged. "I needed to know."

He heaved a sigh. "I guess you did."

"I also need to know if Rick and Jimmie's alibis hold up. Rick says he was working at the
prison the night Marsha was killed. Jimmie said she took an eight o'clock flight to Chicago. Will you verify those?"

He studied her for several moments, and then seemed to come to a decision. "Okay, I can do that. And here's what I can tell you at this point. The technicians verified that the piece of glass was probably from some type of large flashlight."

"Do you think that's what was used to kill her?"

"I think it's possible. The autopsy report came in. Mrs. Carter was beaten to death, multiple blows to the head and some to the liver. The markings around the liver area look like they could have been made by such a weapon. The deterioration of the body leaves some room for doubt, but my gut says that's what it was."

"Were the head injuries on the left or right side?"

A flicker of surprise crossed his face. "The left."

"Then the killer was probably right handed."

"Probably," he agreed after a moment's consideration.

"Are you aware that Ken Douglas is a lefty?"

He stared at her a long time before speaking. "Look, I know Ken is a friend of yours, but we had to question him."

"You did some very intense questioning," she accused. "I think you've decided he's your best suspect, and I'm convinced he didn't do it."

"Now, don't get all hot and bristly with me, Toni Donovan," he snapped. "We have to question everyone, and …" He paused. "No, I didn't realize he's a lefty. But it may mean something, and it may not."

Toni felt certain the chief was wrong, but she didn't want to lose this line of communication. "I understand," she said, her resolve to defend Ken strengthening even more. "Has the body been released?"

"If it hasn't, it should be by tomorrow. I need to be going." He opened the door.

"Thanks for talking to me," she said to his back.

*

Toni didn't have time Monday to do any investigating. Before first hour she went to the office and submitted an announcement for the morning bulletin reminding Student Council members that they were to meet in her room for a working lunch. They had to make work schedules and assignments for the next night's ballgame. The concessions were one of the best fund raising projects in the school, but they were a lot of work.

She and two students who could get out of their study hall spent her third hour plan period transporting boxes of candy bars, chips, hamburger and hot dog buns to the concession booth, unpacking and shelving them. The meats would be brought in tomorrow night. Soft drink canisters and the popcorn machine would be prepared right before game time.

The concession room, located down the hall from the gym, had a high front counter, with only enough room for three or four workers to move around inside comfortably. Candy bars were displayed on shelves above the back counter that held hot dog and hamburger containers. Along the wall next to the gym were a soda dispenser and a popcorn machine. Supplies were stored beneath both counters and under the soda dispenser.

Tomorrow should be one of their best nights of the year financially because it was a three game night. Typically there were two games, with the Junior Varsity and Senior Varsity teams playing. But two or three schools had to come from so far away that they only made the trip once a year. So they started earlier and played their boy and girl games on the same night, the girls first, followed by the boys Junior Varsity, then the boys Senior Varsity. Maybe it wasn't balanced, but that's how the districts did it.

During seventh hour a student office aide entered Toni's classroom, handed her a sealed memo, and left.

"Just follow the instructions and finish this exercise on your own. I'll help if you get stuck," she instructed the class as she opened the memo.

Staff:

We will dismiss classes right after lunch Friday so anyone who wishes to attend Marsha Carter's funeral may do so. It will be

> *at 3 p.m. at Mountain Methodist Church. Staff members are encouraged to attend, but it is not mandatory.*

Toni swallowed a chuckle and tucked the memo into her purse. *Chin up, my friend.* She returned her attention to her class.

Schools were institutions of learning, true; but there were inner dynamics just like in any profession. Dynamics extended even beyond that. Teachers were expected to carry out administrative mandates, however unpopular. Yet they had to keep the welfare of the students first. Students, creatures of habit that they were, loved to push the rules to the limits, and beyond if they could. Discipline was a constant problem that drove some teachers from the profession.

Some rookie teachers had difficulty distinguishing where to draw the line between adult behaviors and trying to be friends with their students, and falling into their patterns of behavior. Then there were older teachers who had settled into humdrum routines that they didn't want to change or work to improve. But there were others who constantly looked for ways to improve and increase learning.

Toni found fulfillment in teaching, but it wasn't without its trials. She had a genuine desire to be effective, and she considered most of her colleagues worthy of their hire. But teachers were human. Some hated paperwork and did their best to avoid it, while others knew every trick in the book to dodge supervisory duties. Overall, though, she thought the Clearmount teaching staff functioned well as a team.

Dissatisfactions and strain in recent months were primarily attributable to the top administrator. Although Marsha's death was tragic, Toni hoped that working conditions and morale would improve under new leadership.

*

Tuesday was hectic. Toni went straight home after school, fed the boys a hurried meal, and rushed back to the school. She let them go inside the gym and find seats to watch the games.

As mothers of students arrived with their pots of burgers and hot dogs, Toni set their crock-pots in place on the back counter. Students checked the soda tanks and got them ready to go. A large jar of dill pickles was placed at one end of the counter, with a supply of pickle sticks and napkins beside it.

From the gym door Toni watched people fill the bleachers, while the visiting team ran drills on the floor. Jenny Zachary had chairs set up on the stage for her pep band. They would play the national anthem just before the first game, and then pep songs between games and at halftimes. Toni knew this was one of Jenny's favorite after-school duties. It also provided a way for some of the non-athletic students to be involved in a sport activity—and got them into the game free.

Everyone stood at attention while the band played the anthem. Then the noise resumed. Toni watched the beginning of the first game from the doorway.

"Mrs. Donovan, where is the extra butter for the popcorn?" A student's call drew Toni back to her post.

At halftime she checked to see if the students needed any help with the concessions. They only had a small rush of business, but Toni knew things would pick up later in the evening. When play resumed, she returned to the doorway to watch more of the game—and her sons.

She scanned the crowd. Gabe and Garrett still sat behind the home team bench, and it looked like they were having a good time. As the cheerleaders turned handsprings, did back flips and led cheers, the boys added their part to the racket.

On the floor Lisa Baker paced in front of her seat, coaching the girls through their plays and weaving them on and off the floor.

Lisa and Jordan each coached two sports. In the fall she coached volleyball, and he did baseball. In the winter they both coached basketball. Then he had baseball again in the spring. They both lived within a mile of the school, which was fortunate since they spent so much time there. Jordan had a home in the estates, not far from Toni and Kyle. Lisa lived in the new Middlebrook subdivision below the main junction at the east edge of town.

As soon as the game ended, with a close win for the home team, Toni hurried back to her students and worked alongside them as they got busier.

By the time the Junior Varsity game ended and the Senior Varsity game began, Toni was so tired that all she wanted was for the night to end. At halftime they had another rush of customers, the biggest yet.

"I need a cold soda," Lisa Baker's husky voice announced at the counter, her face flushed and her expression angry. The assistant coach, a junior high social studies teacher, stood behind her. Lisa reached into the pocket of the team jacket she wore over a dark green tailored suit, in accordance with their dress code for coaches at games. "Tommy Hill was hot dogging again. Hanging on the rim got us a technical foul that may cost us the game." She pulled some bills and coins from her pocket and slammed them down on the counter.

Coins went bouncing off the countertop onto the floor, and Toni turned just in time to watch the assistant coach make an awkward grab at a spinning quarter. Her elbow jerked and hit the pickle jar, sending it into a slide along the counter.

Lisa, seeing the jar move, made a grab for it, but missed. When it crashed on the concrete floor, glass shattered, sending pickle juice and pickles flying everywhere. Lisa slipped in the liquid and fell to her knees. People around them jumped back quickly.

Hissing an expletive through clenched teeth, Lisa grabbed her left hand with her right as blood dripped onto the floor. She squeezed the hand and darted a quick look around to see if anyone had heard. Toni pretended she hadn't read her colleague's lips.

"Shannon, find a janitor." Toni buttonholed the nearest student as she ran out the door and around to the front of the counter where Lisa was getting to her feet.

"Do you need a doctor?" she asked, trying to get a look at Lisa's hand.

Lisa got to her feet and opened her palm. "No, it's not bad." She examined where a cut ran in an arc across the fleshy area below her thumb.

Toni reached over to the concession counter and

grabbed a handful of napkins. "Here." She placed several over the bleeding cut and pressed down. "This should protect it long enough for you to get to your first aid kit."

"Thanks." Lisa held the napkins in place as Toni removed her hand. Lisa glanced around at the mess and grimaced. "Sorry about this. Order another jar and let me know the cost. I'll pay for it."

Toni shrugged it off, also surveying the mess. "Accidents happen. Everyone stay back," she ordered as spectators gathered to gape.

She turned back to Lisa. "Go on and take care of yourself. I'll deal with this."

Just then Phil Norton appeared. "I'll take care of it," the resource officer said to Toni. "You take care of your students."

Looking up the hall, Toni saw Shannon returning with one of the night janitors. About five four, Clay was slightly plump and balding, and had several teeth missing. He was pushing an industrial mop bucket.

Within minutes Clay had everything clean and shiny. He had worked silently, but Toni was confident he would find an opportunity at some point to fill her ears with his opinion of students or staff who went out of their way to create extra work for him. She made a point of thanking him effusively before he could get going on that.

When the janitor headed back the way he had come, Toni walked over to where Phil Norton still kept watch. "Thanks for the quick help. You're a handy guy to have around."

He grinned. "Glad I was here."

By the time the game ended and they had the

concession stand tidy, Toni was bone weary. The boys waited at their usual place by the door when she finally headed out of the almost empty building, one arm wrapped around a crock-pot and the other hand gripping a bag of soiled kitchen linens.

"Let's go home," she said unnecessarily as Gabe and Garrett caught up to her. "Gabe, will you carry this for me?" She handed him the crock-pot.

He took it and followed Garrett out the door.

Toni looked out over the parking lot that was a huge concrete apron fronted by an asphalt roadway and saw only four or five cars left out there, highlighted by streetlights at the main entrance and a few strategic points.

A lone car backed out of its parking spot at the west end of the lot. It stopped, and then rolled forward very slowly. Garrett was a few feet ahead of Toni and Gabe when suddenly the car accelerated with a lurch and a scream of rubber. It headed straight toward Garrett.

Chapter 7

With only a second to react, and oblivious to her own safety, Toni dropped her purse and the bag of linens. "Garrett!" she screamed, running at him and shoving him forward in a flying leap. He tumbled into a heap, and Toni landed behind him in a bone jarring crash on her elbows and knees. Her head jerked forward, cracking her forehead on the pavement as the car roared past. She saw stars and nearly blacked out, but a moment later she managed to lift her head enough to look out over the parking lot.

Her eyes widened and her heart squeezed in horror as she watched the car skitter across the concrete surface. The driver braked, sending a spray of loose gravel flying, and made a U-turn. Then the car accelerated again. It veered and came back directly toward Garrett.

Terrified she wouldn't reach him in time, Toni stumbled to her feet and half crawled, half ran to where Garrett had staggered to his feet. Dimly she heard someone scream as she propelled her body forward and gave him another shove that sent him rolling end over end across the hard concrete. The car fender clipped Toni on the hip and sent her rolling after him. She hit the surface with such force that the wind was knocked completely out of her. She lay stunned, every bone in her body screaming in pain.

Her vision so blurry she could hardly see, Toni fought for breath and forced her eyes open. Dimly she registered a dark blur swerving and screaming out of the east exit of the parking lot into the street. It sped toward town.

"Are you all right?" A well-dressed gentleman knelt beside her, a woman standing behind him. He started to touch Toni's arm, and then drew his hand back. "Should I call a doctor?"

Toni held up a hand, struggling for breath, her head pounding till she could hardly see. When she finally managed a gulp of air, she whispered, "No," and pushed herself upright.

Phil Norton skidded to a halt beside her. "Toni, what happened?"

"Garrett," she gasped. "Where is he? Is he all right?"

"I'm okay, Mom." Garrett came crawling to her side and wrapped an arm around her, his little body shaking.

Toni squeezed him to her, unable to speak past the tears choking her. Finally she eased her youngest son back to examine him through the haze of tears. His face was scratched and bleeding, and he held one arm cradled to him.

"A car came from down there." The older woman behind them pointed, her voice shrill. "It sped up and came right toward the little boy. This lady pushed him out of the way. Then it turned around and came back and tried to run him down another time. She pushed him out of the way again."

"Can you describe the car? Which way did it go?" Phil pulled a cell phone from his pocket as he spoke. Bareheaded and gloveless, he seemed oblivious to the bitter cold.

The woman nodded but held her tongue until he had thumbed through his cell addresses, called the police, and requested assistance at the school.

"It went back toward town." The woman spoke again as soon as he broke the connection, pointing that direction.

"It was a dark blue Taurus or Sable," the man, apparently her husband, added. "It was kind of beat up, and the rear passenger window had strips of duct tape on it."

"What about the driver?"

The husband shook his head. "I couldn't see a face. It looked like there was something over the driver's head."

By now Ken Douglas had joined them, and a smattering of spectators had gathered, drawn by the commotion. "Did anyone else see anything?" Ken asked, scanning the small group.

"I heard squealing tires and burning rubber," came from a young woman holding a baby. "But I was on the other side of my car and didn't see what happened."

Since not many people had been left in the parking lot, the only good description of the car came from the couple who had been behind Toni.

"We came to watch our nephew play ball and had left a few minutes earlier," the husband explained. "But Gloria missed her gloves, and we came back to look for them. We found them under the seat where we sat during the game."

"It was when we were leaving for the second time that we saw that car try to hit the little boy," the woman interjected. "It was terrible."

An hour later the police report had been written up, and the police told Toni that she and the boys could go home.

"I'll call an ambulance." Ken pulled out his cell phone.

"No, don't do that," Toni nearly shouted, her teeth chattering. "Call my mom. She's a nurse practitioner and perfectly capable of taking care of us."

He considered for only a moment. "What's the number?"

She quoted it.

He made the call. Apparently Faye didn't waste time on questions, since he disconnected immediately. "She's on her way. Stay home tomorrow. Use some of the sick time you have accumulated. I'll get someone to cover your classes."

"Don't bother. I'll be here," she said, fighting the pain in her head and hip. "I'll be fine," she assured her principal when he started to argue.

Reading her determination, he shook his head in resignation. "Have it your way."

But she didn't refuse her mother's comfort and medical attention when Faye arrived and took them to the clinic.

*

"Grandma Faye took good care of us," Garrett said softly as Toni tucked him into bed later that night. His eyes drooped from the sedative he had been given. "You saved me, Mom."

"I love you, Son." She sat on the side of his bed, struggling to hold back tears, and the rage that had her about to explode. How dare someone try to hurt her son.

She held his small hands in her own, palms out. "We're quite a pair."

He grinned wanly at their matching scrapes and scratches. There was an elastic bandage wrapped around his left wrist, and another bandage covered a cut on his jaw. Toni had a big purple bump on her forehead and a hip that was stiffening.

"Let's get some sleep now," Toni said, hoping they could. She needed another of the pain pills her mother had given her.

"Okay." Garrett's eyes closed.

Toni left him and went to her own bedroom. Gabe waited on the edge of her bed, his expression troubled.

Toni sat next to him, realizing that he wanted to talk to her without Garrett hearing. "What's bothering you?"

Gabe started to speak, but hesitated. Then he tried again. "Do you think the person who killed Mrs. Carter tried to hurt Garrett?"

Toni wasn't sure how to answer. Behind her headache the same question nagged. "What do you mean?" she asked, stalling.

"Well, Garrett finds things," he said slowly. "Do you think that person is afraid Garrett will find him?"

Did she?

"I don't know," she said carefully. "I don't see how the person could know such a thing. But there's something I *do* know."

His big brown eyes fastened on her. "What?"

"The rules around here have to change. From now on I want you and Garrett to stick together like glue. I can't pull you out of school, but I can keep you with me more. I'll drop you at your building each morning, and then you're to wait inside the building or by the door for me to pick you up after school. No more walking around anywhere on your own. Okay?"

His ten-year-old frame seemed to swell with responsibility. "Okay. I'll take care of Garrett."

"I'll go over it with him in the morning. I don't want you worrying. Remember, it may not be anything like that. But it won't hurt for us to be extra careful for a while."

"Should we call Dad?"

"I don't think so," Toni replied after a moment's hesitation. "We're fine, and he has a busy schedule that we shouldn't interrupt."

Seeming satisfied, Gabe slid off the bed and went back to his and Garrett's room, his shoulders erect.

Toni took two pain pills and crawled into bed. Fierce anger and a sense of urgency sizzled inside her. Someone had deliberately tried to hurt her child. Finding Marsha's killer was no longer just a matter of curiosity or the challenge of figuring out a puzzle. She had to protect her son. At last she fell into a drug-induced sleep.

It seemed only moments later when the lights flashed on, blinding her. Toni squinted up at the sight of Kyle standing in the bedroom doorway. "What are you doing here?" She pushed upright in the bed. The digital clock on the nightstand read four a.m.

"Checking on my family." He dropped his overnight case and came to sit by her on the bed. "I had to see for myself that you're all right."

"The brat called, huh?" Her voice muffled against his neck when he pulled her to him.

"Of course," he said gruffly. "Gabe knows the right thing to do, whether you do or not."

Toni drew back to examine his face. "I didn't want to worry you. I truly didn't think it was necessary to call you, because I was afraid you would feel you needed to …"

"Come home," he finished for her, his expression somber.

She had no argument. "I don't understand what's happening. I'm mad."

He brushed her hair back to examine her bruises and scrapes. "You have reason to be."

"Why are these things happening?" she wailed, clinging to him in an uncharacteristic display of helplessness.

He eased back and peered into her face. "I don't know. But I know God cares what happens to us. We need to pray for His guidance and protection."

She frowned at her husband. "I didn't know you had taken up preaching."

He grinned. "I've had some experiences in the air that have forced me to rely more on prayer."

It unsettled her to think of him getting in trouble while flying an airplane. She needed to question him more about his work, and those experiences. It sank ever deeper into her how much they missed in one another's lives. Kyle wasn't the only one spending too much time at work and being too absorbed in things beyond their home life. He wasn't the deficient one here. The acknowledgement sent guilt zinging through her.

His eyes narrowed. "Gabe tells me you plan to go to work in the morning."

Toni nodded. "I told you I'm fine."

"You need to stay close to the boys—and out of the murder investigation."

"How can I?" she snapped, bristling. "Someone tried to hurt Garrett. Whoever it was has to be stopped."

"But it's not your job," he pointed out. "Your priority is the boys."

"Right. And that means protecting them, stopping someone from hurting them."

He drew a deep breath and looked up at the ceiling. "You're being stubborn," he said when he looked back at her a few moments later. "But I see your point."

"I appreciate that you're concerned, but I can't just hide in the house with them. I'll be careful," she promised.

He got to his feet. "I'll go peek in on them and be right back."

*

It took some doing, but Toni finally convinced Kyle to return to work the next morning. She promised to call him if she had any problems, and outlined her plans for safety measures regarding the boys. She moved very carefully because of her bruised and stiffened hip.

First hour was barely underway when Ken Douglas stepped inside her classroom. "I'll watch your students for a few minutes," he said softly, facing her with his back to them. "Chief Freeman is in my office, and he wants to talk to you."

Toni addressed the class. "Students, finish reading the chapter and answer the first set of questions. I'll be back in a few minutes."

She entered Ken's office to find Buck seated behind the desk, the only spot he could be comfortable in the tiny office. He grinned. "The bruise and knot on the head match the shoes."

Her pumps were a plum color that matched her wool blazer, and her slacks were black. She gave him a sheepish grin. "Thanks. The students seem to like them."

His expression turned solemn. "I suppose they've asked a lot of questions?"

Toni eased her sore body onto the chair facing him. "Of course. And I told them the truth. I just didn't tell them I think it was deliberate."

He leaned back, making Ken's chair squeak. "We got enough of a description of the car, right down to the taped up rear passenger window, that we've found it. It's Tom Keller's."

Toni's mouth dropped open. "Was he drunk?"

"We don't think he was driving it. He was at his usual spot last night."

"People know he practically lives at the Railroad Bar."

The chief nodded. "That's right. I talked to the bartender, and he says Tom was pretty full by eight o'clock last night. He got busy after that and didn't pay much attention to the man."

"It was about nine-thirty when the car tried to run

Garrett down," Toni said, thinking aloud. "If Tom was already loaded by then, could he have gotten some kind of crazy idea in his head and driven a mile and a half to the school to harm a child?"

"I suppose there's a slim chance," Buck admitted. "But when I talked to him he seemed clueless. Plus, the bartender remembers seeing him go in and out of the bathroom several times."

"If the man felt sick, that would make it even more unlikely he would be driving around in his car."

"He has a little trouble keeping track of it," Buck said. "A couple of weeks ago he called us and said his carburetor was missing."

Toni didn't understand. "Missing as in malfunctioning, or missing as in gone?"

The chief chuckled. "Gone. One of my deputies, Dale I think, went to the bar and checked the car. The carburetor really was missing."

Toni shook her head slowly back and forth. "That doesn't make sense."

"We've had other reports of missing car parts," Buck said matter-of-factly. "We figure Tom was just an easy target for kids pilfering stuff to fix their own jalopies. Tom's drunk so much he doesn't know what's going on around him. I think someone borrowed that car."

Toni agreed. "Not to change the subject, but do you think someone could have tried to hurt Garrett because of his dream?"

Buck rubbed a hand over his chin. "I've been wondering why in the world anyone would attack a child, but I never mentioned what you told me to anyone. It's more likely that someone is trying to stop you from snooping. I hope you got the message. This is dangerous."

"But could anyone know about Garrett?" she persisted.

His expression turned troubled. "I made a note in my report. I didn't mention it when we discussed the case, but it's in the file," he repeated in a voice gruff with concern.

Worry built in Toni. "I wish I knew who all has seen that file."

"I'll do some checking," he promised. "The connection is a long shot, but it's all we have at this point. I promised Kyle that I'll keep a closer eye on you while he's gone."

"I told him I'm fine. He shouldn't have called you."

"He's concerned, and he's right to be," Buck said without smiling. "I wanted to see you this morning and assure myself that you're really okay."

"I am," Toni said with emphasis. "But there are a couple more things I'd like for you to check if you would." She gave him her best puppy-dog face. "Can you find out whether Rick Montgomery was working the night of the twenty-first like he claims? I would also like to know what Jimmie Huff was doing that night. Right now I need to get back to my class."

"I'll check," he promised with a sigh of resignation.

On the way back to her room Toni began to shiver, unable to prevent the visions of that car coming at Garrett, and wondering why someone had tried to hurt him. She didn't dare let him out of her presence beyond school hours. She debated about calling his teacher, but decided she would wait and talk to her after school.

Third hour she took some more pain pills. Seventh hour she took two more as the forensics class filed into the room.

"Today we're going to start a unit on blood," she informed the students once they were seated, relieved to see Jodi present again.

When she had covered the chapter, she asked, "How many of you know what type blood you have?"

"I have hot blood," Dustin blurted with a snort of laughter.

"Yeah, he thinks he's a big hot lover," someone muttered sarcastically.

"Maybe he's a cold blooded lady-killer," another student wisecracked.

The room went silent.

"I'm sure that was meant as a joke," Toni said as calmly as she could. "Let's get back to our focus here. I repeat, how many of you know in which blood group yours belongs?"

Only three students raised their hands.

"How many of you would like to know what type you have?"

This time all hands lifted.

"Good. In today's lab we'll be doing just that. Here are all the materials you need. You may work in pairs. Be sure you wear gloves and place all used items in the bio hazard bucket." She slipped off her blazer and replaced it with the lab coat draped across her desk.

Toni facilitated the students as they worked. While helping Beth prick her finger, she glanced up and saw Dustin blowing up a latex glove like a balloon. "Dustin," she snapped. "This is neither the time nor place for horseplay. Put that glove on your hand, and let's find out what kind of blood you really have."

She moved over by him. "Here, I'll help you." She waited for him to put on the glove. Then she massaged and swabbed a finger.

He made a big production of enduring pain when he pricked his own finger, but then he settled down and completed the lab, determining that his blood was Type A.

After school Toni hurried to the elementary building and explained to Garrett's teacher that she didn't want the boys walking anywhere alone before or after school, that they were to wait inside the building or by the door for her to pick them up each day. When she arrived home with them, she put a casserole in the oven and made phone calls while it cooked.

First she called Sam Brinkman, the school board member she knew best, and arranged to visit with him after supper. Then she called her parents and explained that she needed to leave the boys with them for a while.

"Why don't I just come to your house and stay with them," Russell offered. "That way I can be sure they're in bed on time."

Toni accepted.

*

An hour later Toni sat on Sam Brinkman's couch facing him. A tall, lanky farmer, Sam wore western jeans, shirt and boots. A dark mustache adorned his upper lip.

He sat in a worn leather recliner. "Susan and the kids are in the basement rec room. Now what can I do for you?"

Toni took a deep breath. "I'm not sure where to begin. I'm looking for any information that might help identify Marsha's killer."

Sam leaned back in the chair. "I understand that. I just don't know how I can help."

"I don't want to breach any ethics or rules of confidentiality, but if there were any major problems brewing, it would help to know about it so we could look for a connection."

"I'm afraid I have to say that the district was never trouble free from the time Marsha took over," Sam admitted in a raspy tone, his shoulders sagging. "I know you found the body, and I heard about the incident in the parking lot, so I understand your feelings. But I don't know anything that would help."

"Do you know who benefits the most from her death?" Toni asked. "I mean like insurance money."

Sam leaned forward and pinched the bridge of his nose. "Marsha had the same group policies as the rest of the staff. I wouldn't know about any extra ones."

Toni made a mental note to ask Buck if he knew about any life insurance policies. "What about money problems? Do you know if she had any unusually big debts?"

Again Sam shook his head. "I know nothing of her personal finances. As for the school district, it's common knowledge that we're facing some serious budget constraints. Naturally those have been under discussion. Marsha had been preparing a plan for some staff reductions and reassignments."

Who did she plan to terminate or reassign?

Do you have any written reports on that yet?"

He shook his head. "She was supposed to present one at the next board meeting. It was shaping up to be an interesting session."

Toni heard something in his tone that made her interest sharpen further. "What do you mean?"

"Well, this is confidential," he said, rubbing his neck with a hand. "But now that we don't have to worry whether to fire her, I guess there's some justice in this world after all."

So the board had been considering firing Marsha. "Things were that bad?"

"There were just too many conflicts. I'm not even sure what the board vote would have been."

"So there was division even there," Toni mused, meeting his gaze. "Do you think …"

Sam read her mind. "I can't see anyone on the board getting into a fight with her and killing her."

Toni studied the grim line of Sam's mouth and decided to not push any further. "Thank you for talking to me." She stood to leave.

Sam came to his feet and extended his hand. "I hope you have better luck elsewhere."

On the way home Toni pondered everything she had learned over the past week. Jack's alibi seemed airtight. The police still suspected Ken, which to her way of thinking was way off base. It would be more reasonable to think that a student had done it. Could someone have talked a student into doing it for them? Bribed or paid them? She couldn't fathom that, but she had to consider all possibilities.

Marsha had made enemies, firing and threatening people. She had brought her lover to the district, only to dump her. Those acts would have caused anger. But to the point of murder?

Were Rick's and Jimmie's alibis sound? Were the police finding any prints or other evidence as to who might have been driving Tom's car? Would Buck search Marsha's computer again, this time looking for anything that looked like reports meant for the school board?

The questions were getting tangled in her brain. As Toni went over and over the facts, only two of them were clear to her. One, whoever had killed Marsha was strong enough to beat her to death and drag her body up the hill. Two, that person now seemed to have targeted Garrett.

Chapter 8

All day Thursday Toni struggled to stay focused. By seventh hour she felt a little better about life in general. But when she had to mark Jodi absent again she lost that sense of comfort. Whatever was going on in Jodi's life was not good, and she was helpless to do anything about it.

In elementary school a teacher had the same twenty-five to thirty students all day, providing numerous opportunities for interaction with them. It became more complicated in middle and high school. Teachers now had one hundred fifty or more students circulating through their classes each day. Communicating with parents also became more difficult.

Toni kept trying to reach Jodi's parents though. As soon as her last class ended, she made another futile attempt to call them. Then she checked to see if the counselor had been any more successful. Kelly had not.

Toni picked up the boys and stopped for pizzas on the way home. As soon as they finished eating, she delivered them to her parents and drove to Janet Rayford's house. It was just turning dark when she rang the doorbell of the modest brick home situated at the back of a subdivision. Sidney opened the door.

"What are you doing here?" she asked, her tone not exactly welcoming. She made no move to admit Toni.

"I want to talk to your mother."

"She's not feeling well."

"Who's there, Sid?" Janet's too loud voice came from behind the girl.

A pained expression crossed the teenager's face. "It's Mrs. Donovan from school," she said over her shoulder.

Janet's face appeared behind Sidney's shoulder. "Why, it sure is," she declared, her voice slurred. "Please come in." She stepped back and swung her hand in a sweeping arc.

When Sidney opened the door wider, Toni stepped inside. The house was neat enough but lacked an air of loving care. A partial bottle of whiskey sat on the coffee table, a half full glass next to it.

Janet plopped onto the sofa and reached for the glass. "What can we do for you, Missus … Teacher?"

Sidney gave Toni an apologetic look and the slightest of shrugs, conveying that she had tried to spare them this embarrassment.

Toni debated whether it was a mistake to talk to Janet, but decided that a loose tongue might not be a bad thing. "Would you mind talking about Mrs. Carter?" she began carefully.

"Now why would I mind talking about dear Mrs. Carter," Janet said in a sarcastic slur, rolling her eyes. "The woman was a saint. Saints are dead. She's dead. That makes her a saint, right?" She laughed harshly at her own black humor and nearly spilled her drink.

"Mom, you don't have to do this." Sidney scooted onto the sofa next to her mother.

"It's okay." Janet sat up straighter and patted Sidney's knee. "Mrs. Carter was a friendly woman, more friendly than most of us. She had friends everywhere. For instance, she had her friend Jimmie." Janet paused to hiccup. "'Course, that didn't last long, 'cause she got to be better friends with Jack. Now they were some great friends, those two. Good old Jack and Marsha."

"Mother, please." Sidney cast another embarrassed glance at Toni.

Janet ignored Sidney and raised her glass in the air. "Don't you think Mrs. Carter was a friendly woman, Mrs. Donovan?"

"I'm sure she was," Toni said evenly.

"She was real friendly with the bookkeeper, too," Janet prattled on. "I used to wonder if there was something kinky going on there, but I guess ole Dana was just playing up to the woman because of her paycheck."

Something in that last statement grabbed at Toni. "You found their friendship unusual?"

"I sure did." Janet sloshed more whiskey into the glass and took a gulp. "Dana is just a bookkeeper, and Mrs. Carter," she put a sneer on the woman's name, "didn't make a habit of being friends with people lower than her." She emphasized the word lower. "So the ole gal musta been up to somethin' with Dana, is how I figure it."

This was probably just the reasoning of a woman scorned and turning to the bottle, but it was the best she was going to get. Toni stood. "Thank you for your time. I'm sure you have things you need to do, and Sidney probably has homework."

"I need to read tomorrow's chapter for your class," Sidney said, and then hesitated as a new thought struck her. "I guess I won't have your class tomorrow."

Toni nodded. "That's right. We're being dismissed early for the funeral, so the afternoon classes won't meet."

"Sidney really likes your class." Janet started to get up, but slumped back onto the sofa. "She talks about it a lot." She gave her daughter a sappy smile.

"I enjoy having her in the class. Did she tell you how she helped me with a lab just before Christmas?"

Janet drew back, her expression blank.

"We do some simulated crimes and try to solve them in the class. Sidney played the part of the criminal in one of our labs. I appreciate the way she handled it." Toni gave Sidney a smile meant to convey encouragement as she buttoned her coat. "I'll see myself out."

When she was in the van, Toni called her parents and asked them to have the boys meet her in the driveway in five minutes. As soon as they were home and the boys had gone to their room, she called Sam Brinkman.

"Hello, Mr. Brinkman," she said when he answered. "This is Toni Donovan. I'm sorry to bother you again, but I want to ask a favor. I don't have proof of anything, but more than one person has mentioned how chummy Marsha was with Dana, the bookkeeper."

"I believe I recall a comment or two along that

line myself," Sam responded. "What are you suggesting?"

"I think an audit of the district's finances would be a good idea."

There was a long silence. "You realize that's not a decision I can make by myself, don't you? The best I can do is bring it up in board meeting. Of course, if you think it's urgent, I guess I could call Guthrie and see if he thinks we should call a special meeting to discuss it."

"I don't know how urgent it is," Toni admitted. "I do know that we have an unsolved murder, and money seems to be at the root of most criminal cases."

"I'll call him," Sam promised in resigned acceptance.

She thanked him and disconnected.

Sleep didn't come easily that night as Toni wrestled with the thunderstorm in her head. A tempest of questions raged like a tornado. What if she had not gotten to Garrett in time? What if he had not had that dream? How could she go to that funeral?

God, please protect Garrett. I can't be with him every minute. You're the only one who can do that. I'm sorry I wished Mrs. Carter gone, but I don't want to go to that funeral tomorrow. But I will if you'll ...

Her prayer trailed to a halt as she realized that God would not bargain with her. At the same time, conviction grew in her that it was important she attend the service. Once she accepted that she must go, she fell asleep.

When Toni entered the church the next afternoon, she saw that the service was well attended.

No matter what Marsha Carter's status had been at the school, her death was a big local story. Even though this was not the church Toni attended, she recognized most of the people present. She spotted a group of school staff sitting in a back section of pews and joined them. Marsha's son and daughter, and a man she assumed to be their dad, sat on the front pew at the right side of the center aisle. Jack Rayford sat alone on the opposite side.

Just as the service started, Chief Freeman slipped into the church and took a seat in the very back pew. Deep wrinkles formed brackets around his mouth and etched frown lines between his eyes. When he turned his head, his gaze met Toni's.

She raised her eyebrows in what she hoped he recognized as a signal that she wanted to speak to him later.

The service was a solemn affair. There was some recorded music and a message delivered by the older, heavyset and balding minister. As he spoke, Toni fought her burden of guilt. She knew her feelings toward Marsha had not killed the woman, but the guilt persisted anyhow. When the minister finished speaking, the organ began to play. People formed a line to file past the casket and out of the room.

Toni eased into the line a few feet behind Buck. At the exit he stepped to the left of the door and waited for her to join him. "I got the impression you want to speak to me."

"I just want to know if you've had a chance to check Jimmie Huff's and Rick Montgomery's alibis."

"They both check," he said briefly.

"Would it be possible for me to get a look into

Marsha's computer?"

His frown lines deepened. "What would you be looking for?"

"Anything that would indicate proposals she meant to present to the board about budget or staff cuts. Also anything to do with insurance policies she might have had besides the standard district group policy."

He nodded. "Let me think about that and get back to you. Are you going to the graveside service?"

She shook her head. "No, I've done my civic duty. I wasn't exactly close to the woman."

Toni had left the boys with her parents again after school. Once she picked them up and arrived home she decided to take the evening off and just relax. She was exhausted, both physically and emotionally.

After bowls of chili and crackers, Toni took a shower and curled up on the sofa with a book. But she couldn't read. Her body ached, and depression weighed her down. It had now been a week and a half since finding Marsha's body. There was a killer out there, and she had no idea who it was.

"Hey, Mom!" Garrett slid to a stop in the doorway. "Gabe's high on pot!"

"What?" Toni sprang to her feet, flinching with pain and grabbing her hip as she did so. "Where is he?"

"In here," Garrett called over his shoulder as he raced toward the bathroom.

When she reached the open doorway, Toni stopped abruptly. Gabe stood on top of the closed lid of the toilet stool, waving his arms. "I'm high on pot," he crowed. "I'm high on pot."

"You brat," Toni sputtered, crossing the room and wrapping her arm around the kid's neck in a headlock. With her other hand she reached around and grabbed Garrett in a similar hold. Then she rubbed their heads together in a playful scuffle. "You two are in big trouble."

The three of them wrestled their way across the room and ended up in a heap on the hallway floor.

"I'll teach you two to scare me like that." She gave each of them a kiss on the cheek. Then she sat upright and looked from one to the other of them.

Gabe was still laughing, but Garrett had quieted.

"You know what I think you boys are doing?"

They both shook their heads and chorused, "Huh uh."

"I think you're trying to cheer me up."

"Did it work?" Garrett asked quietly.

She took a deep breath. "I believe it did. But I still think you deserve punishment. I think I'll just refuse to let you grow up and leave me."

Gabe laughed.

"How will you do that?" Garrett wanted to know.

Toni grinned. "I'm still working on that."

*

Monday started out gloomy and stayed that way. The overcast sky presaged more snow and dampened student morale. Toni breathed a sigh of relief when the last class ended. She stood by the doorway until the hallway cleared, and then went to get the boys, leaving the classroom unlocked for Beth Price. When she returned, the boys went to seats in the back of the room to do their homework, and Toni put a CD into the player on the bookshelf near her desk. A rousing band march from the collection Jenny had given her for Christmas filled the room. She turned the volume down.

"Hey, I like that." Beth entered the room, dragging a big trash bag in each hand. She sashayed rhythmically to the rear of the room and deposited them. Then she looked back and spotted the boys. "I could sure use your help, guys," she called as she began to tie newspapers into bundles. "Gabe, why don't you start on that bag of cans?" She pointed. "Garrett, you can help me with these papers."

"It's okay," Toni told them. "You can finish your homework later."

While Beth and the boys worked and chattered in the back of the room, Toni made a test for later in the week. When she finished, she gathered her grade book and papers and shoved them into her satchel.

Beth approached the desk. "Mrs. Donovan," she said quietly. "You asked me about Jodi Garrison the other day."

Toni put the satchel down. "Yes, I did. I care about her."

"Well," Beth began uncertainly. "I told you that she broke up with her boyfriend."

"Are you saying you were wrong?"

Beth shook her head. "No. I mean yes. She did break up with him. But I heard she has a new boyfriend. I don't know his name, but it's supposed to be an older boy, someone who graduated two or three years ago."

"That's interesting. I appreciate you getting back to me about it."

"If I hear anything else, I'll let you know." Beth put on her coat and left the room.

Oh, the angst of teenage love. Toni remembered it well. Her childhood had been a happy one, and growing up with two younger brothers had taught her a certain amount of responsibility, as well as self-defense. But she had not escaped the pangs of romance.

She had known Kyle Donovan casually as they grew up in a small town and attended many of the same school activities, but in seventh grade everything had changed. One night at a high school basketball game she had lost her purse. It hadn't contained much of value, but she wanted a Coke, and her allowance was in the purse. As she looked for it under the bleachers, Kyle had come by and helped her in the fruitless search. Then he took her to the concession and bought Cokes for the two of them. At that moment she fell in love with him, sure that her heart would burst, and that she would never be whole without him.

The next day Toni had been devastated to learn that he already had a steady girlfriend, and thought her thirteen-year-old heart would break. But her despair turned to joy later that week when Kyle stopped her in the hall, asked if she would sit with him at the next game, and assured her that he no longer had a steady girlfriend.

They were sweethearts from that time forward. When Kyle graduated from high school two years ahead of her and left for college, Toni thought she would die of loneliness. Kyle wanted to get married when he graduated, but she had not wanted him to support her through her last two years of college. So he went to work for the airline and saved money while waiting. They married right after her graduation, and she signed a contract to teach at Clearmount.

They had weathered some rough times in those first years of marriage while Toni was trying to balance teaching, working on her Master's degree, and having babies. But they had worked through things, and she had found satisfaction in teaching. When schools began offering forensics classes, she had been among the first to seize the opportunity to incorporate crime solving into her curriculum.

"Let's go, Mom." Garrett tugged on his coat.

Toni returned to the present and gathered her possessions. On the way home she debated whether to leave the boys again. She hated to, but she wanted to talk to Tom Keller.

As she pulled into the driveway, Toni's cell phone rang. She picked it up and noted the Zachary ID. "Hello, John."

"It's me, Jenny." Her voice sounded tense. Dejected.

"What's wrong?" Toni turned off the motor, but didn't get out of the warm van. The boys sat tight also.

"Michelle is sick."

"Is it serious?" Michelle Turner taught art at the school.

"I don't think so, just the flu. But she's supposed to go with the band tomorrow."

Suddenly Toni understood. All-District Band auditions. "You're short a chaperone for your trip tomorrow," she said, thinking fast.

"Because we have to haul our instruments as well as the students, we're taking two buses," Jenny explained. "If you could possibly go on the other bus in Michelle's place, John would be happy to look after your boys. He'll even come to your house so they can sleep late in the morning. I'm desperate, Toni." She had reached the point of pleading.

Toni drew a silent sigh as her entire Saturday slipped away from her. Jenny would do as much for her, though. She knew that. "Kyle is still out of town, so that'll work fine."

"Oh, thank you, thank you." Relief came across the line in waves. "He'll take them out for pizza, or wherever they want to eat."

Treat them like little princes, Toni thought with a grin.

"You ready for the bad part?" Jenny asked.

Toni went still.

"We have to be at the school at four a.m. to load the buses and get on the road."

Now she laughed. "I thought you were going to say I had to sit with the tuba."

Jenny's laugh was almost a giggle. "Thanks," she repeated before disconnecting.

The next morning Toni packed her book satchel to take with her so she could grade some papers during the lengthy ride. Still sleepy eyed, she left right after John arrived and reached the school exactly on time, not one minute late, but certainly not early.

The day was a carefully orchestrated event. They arrived at the host school at seven-fifteen, registration began at eight, and the judges began auditions at nine.

By early afternoon the students had been shepherded through the process, and they headed back to their buses.

"Winners will come back for rehearsals and a concert the first weekend of February," Jenny said as she and Toni watched the students carry their instruments back onto the buses.

"I enjoyed the day, but I won't mind if Michelle is able to come next time," Toni said with a teasing grin.

It was five o'clock, with dusk beginning to fall, when they arrived back at the Clearmount School. Anxious to get home, Toni curbed her impatience while waiting for the students to store their instruments in the building and drive away or catch their rides.

"See you in the morning at church," Jenny called as Toni sprinted for her van. She started the motor and was letting it warm when her phone rang. She shivered from the cold as she answered it.

"Toni, this is Sandy Douglas." The voice of her principal's wife was low and hoarse, unrecognizable.

Toni frowned. "Are you okay?"

"No, my car quit, and I can't get it going. Ken's not home. Can you come get me?"

"Where are you?" *Please let it be close.*

"I'm at the lake campground, near the spillway. And I'm freezing." Her voice sounded unlike her, quavering and almost indistinguishable. She must be scared as well as cold. And Toni found it odd that she would be out at the lake.

Toni glanced at her watch. "It'll take me ten minutes to get there."

She put the van in motion and dialed her house. Gabe answered. "I'm in town, but I have to run an errand on my way home."

"That's okay. We're playing carom with John. Bye." It was their favorite board game, played much like pool, with plastic donut-like caroms that they knocked into corner pouches by finger flipping a shooter carom at them.

Toni made it to the campground entrance in nine minutes. She reduced her speed and turned left, and then slowed to a crawl as she followed the road through the park, keeping watch for Sandy's car, a blue van if she remembered correctly. She rounded the final curve to the spillway and peered ahead. The area was deserted.

A loud burst of sound and impact on the side window behind her startled the wits out of Toni. Without conscious thought she slammed on the brakes. As the van skidded, another explosion came, and the vehicle careened to the edge of the paved surface. For a moment she thought it was going into the water, but she held onto the wheel with a death grip and managed to bring it to a full stop at the very edge of the lake.

Someone was shooting at her. Toni hunkered down in the seat and pushed the door partially open. She waited a couple of seconds, and then risked a peek through the bottom of the door glass. Across the grounds she saw a lone figure dart from behind a tree and take off across the campground, running and weaving through the trees and campsites. The person wore a dark hoodie and a dark bulky jacket.

Toni glanced back and saw that a hole had been

blown through the rear window of the van. The glass was cracked in a huge web all around it, and her left rear tire was flat. Filled with rage that someone had lured her out here with a phony call and tried to kill her, she leaped from the van and ran after the assailant. She lost sight of the fleeing figure for a moment, but then spotted the person leaping from the ditch to the paved surface.

Pushing with everything she had, Toni raced that way. The figure stumbled once, but then took off across the roadway and disappeared behind the check station. By the time Toni got across the ditch, she saw the person fleeing into the trees up the hillside.

Gasping for breath, she drew to a halt and stared as the last flash of color disappeared. No way could she catch him or her. In defeat, she took several deep breaths and then started back across the empty campground. When she reached the van, she crawled inside and dug her phone from her purse. She called the police station, thankful she had the number saved in her phone.

"Deputy Dale Brown. May I help you?"

Toni rattled off what had happened, fighting for control.

"Stay put. Someone will be right there."

Like she was going anywhere with a blown out tire—and the January cold and wind filtering through the hole in the window. She started the motor and turned the heat up full blast. Then she sat there, her fists clenched so tightly that her nails bit into her palms, trying to get warm and calm down.

How could she be calm? Someone had tried to hurt her child. And now her. Rage boiled in her.

Minutes later a police car came flying up the road, siren screaming, and swung into the campground. When it slid to a halt beside her, Buck Freeman emerged from it.

"Tell me what happened," he ordered gruffly as Toni opened the van door.

Toni repeated what she had told the deputy, but added details she had been unable to articulate earlier. Buck's gaze followed the line of her aim when she pointed to where the shooter had disappeared.

"Toni," he barked, looking back at her. "Don't you realize how dangerous that was, chasing someone with a gun who had been shooting at you?"

She swallowed the knot in her throat. "I was mad. I wanted to catch the monster and strangle him. Or her," she added, visualizing the figure again. She had no idea who it might have been. And that enraged her even more.

"Okay, calm down," he said, his voice gentling. "A couple of deputies will be here any minute. I'll have them search those woods and examine your van. When they're done, they'll have it towed to whatever garage you prefer."

"Take it to Wally's," she said, her body threatening to melt into a puddle.

"I'll take you to the station and get your statement. Then I'll take you home," he said as another police car swerved into the grounds.

By the time he delivered her home, Toni had grown calmer. But she was still ripping mad. "Thanks for everything," she said as she stepped out of the cruiser.

Buck nodded and drove away.

As Toni made her way up the driveway, the garage door began to grind upward.

"Hey, Mom. Dad came home, so John left," Gabe announced from the doorway of the utility room at the back of the garage. "Where have you been? Why did the police bring you home?"

Her gaze landed on Kyle's truck parked next to where her van should have been. "I didn't expect your dad until Wednesday. And Buck brought me home because I had some trouble with the van." She didn't want to tell the boys about the shooting.

When Gabe turned, Toni followed him through the utility room into the kitchen. Kyle stood in front of the stove, stirring something in a big pot.

"What are you doing here?" she asked, her anger momentarily forgotten.

He put the spoon down and pulled her to him. "My boss adjusted the schedule."

Toni stepped back and narrowed her eyes at him. "Oh, yeah? His idea or yours?"

He shrugged. "A little of both. He knew I was concerned about you, so he juggled some things, and here I am. I have a run scheduled for Friday and Saturday, but that leaves me free to goof off for three days."

Toni tipped her head to study his expression, not sure whether to be upset with him or to love him to death for his concern. It would be good to have him here to help with the boys. Maybe they would even find a way to spend some time alone. She didn't want the romantic part of their marriage to be over.

He returned to the stove and resumed stirring the pot. "I have spaghetti about ready. "What were your plans for tonight?"

Her anger and frustration returned in a rush. "I want to see if I can find Tom Keller and talk to him."

The slightest flash of irritation crossed his face. "Your dad's right. He says you're burning the candle at both ends. You should stay home and rest."

"You mean forget about finding who attacked our son?" Her voice rose. "And probably killed Marsha Carter?" *And tried to kill me.*

She closed her eyes, recognizing her fault. Running off to talk to Tom was exactly the opposite of spending time with her husband. But she had to go. She might learn something helpful from the old man. When she opened her eyes, she was calmer.

"Where's the van, Mom?"

Gabe's question made Kyle's gaze intensify. "Yes, where is it? Why are you so late? John told us Jenny was home over an hour ago."

Toni turned around, fighting to keep her voice steady. "You boys go wash up for supper while I help your dad get his spaghetti on the table."

As soon as they left the room, Kyle gripped her arms and studied her grim expression. "All right, what did happen to the van? I take it you didn't want to tell me in front of them."

"I was shot at tonight," she said through clenched teeth.

By the time she finished her story, Kyle's eyes were stormy. "You're telling me someone shot at you, and you actually ran after him?"

The question suddenly made Toni feel foolish, so lacking in judgment. "It was instinctive," she defended, the entire incident finally catching up to her. "I didn't think. I just wanted to stop the person and …" She stopped, not knowing what she would have done if she had caught up to the culprit.

Kyle heaved a deep sigh. "I'm glad I came home. I'll go to Wally's in the morning and see what the damage is to the van and contact our insurance agent. You need to stay here and see to yourself and the boys."

Toni shook her head. "I already told you I planned to go talk to Tom. Now I have to. I have to do something. Don't you see?"

Kyle went silent, gazing into her face and seeing the tears threatening to spill. "Toni, I'm trying to understand," he said at last. "I think I do, but I'm afraid for you. Someone has attacked my family, and I don't know what to do about it other than try to keep you home where you'll be safe." He wrapped an arm around her shoulder and pulled her back to him. "I can't force you to stay here, as much as I want to, and I understand that you have to deal with things as you see fit. I just don't want anything to happen to you," he added in a softer tone.

Toni sighed and gave him a hug. "I know. I understand your position, too. I don't want to upset you, but I have to find out what I can, which means I still want to talk to Tom tonight. I'll be careful."

"I'll keep the boys," he said, an edge of frustration still in his voice. "But let's eat together before you take off. And if you're not home in an hour, I'll come looking for you."

Gabe returned to the kitchen. "Is supper ready yet?"

"We're hungry," Garrett chimed behind him.

Toni hurriedly went about setting the table.

After supper she shrugged into her coat and headed for the door. "You boys do your homework and get ready for bed."

She drove downtown and turned onto Elm Street, passed the newspaper office, and went slowly up Second, watching for a dark colored Chevy with duct tape on the rear passenger window. When she found it at the end of the street in front of the Railroad Bar, she was relieved. In a bigger town, it probably would have been compounded. She parked in the small lot behind the building and walked around to the front.

It was a two-story brick building with four apartments upstairs and the bar downstairs. The streets outside were poorly lit, and the bar was known for roughness. But it was right there in the heart of the small town in which she had grown up. Even though she had never been inside the place, Toni felt safe.

When she entered, she glanced around quickly. The big roughly finished room was smoky and dimly lit, but she spotted Tom Keller at a small table near the west wall. She marched directly to it and sat across from him.

"Hi, Tom. I'll have a Coke," she told the waitress who had followed her.

Tom peered at her blankly. "Hi yourself." He hiccupped, emitting a powerful alcohol breath.

"How have you been?" Toni asked, trying not to inhale deeply.

"Fine," he replied thickly, staring at her through eyes hazy from drink. Suddenly his expression brightened with recognition. "Well, if it ain't Toni Nash," he pronounced slowly, jabbing an index finger at her. "No, that's not right. You married that Donovan boy. Toni Donovan," he repeated, proud of himself.

"That's right." Toni hoped he wasn't too fuzzy to answer questions. "I understand that your car has been playing tricks on you."

His face crinkled in confusion. "My car?"

"Yes, your car," she repeated. "It's been identified as the one that tried to run over my son after the basketball game last Tuesday night."

The waitress returned and set a Coke on the table. Toni nodded and mouthed a thank you.

Tom scratched his head. "Yeah, the cops asked me about that. I don't think I was driving it. I can't 'member."

Toni felt kind of sorry for Tom. He had once been a successful businessman, but drink and divorce—she wasn't sure which spawned which—had eventually led to the bankruptcy of his business. He was an intelligent man who had lost his way.

"Do you remember where you parked it that night?"

"Musta been there on the corner," he muttered, jerking a thumb toward the street. "That's where I always park."

"Do you remember anything different about that night?" she persisted. "Did anyone ask for your keys? Chief Freeman said there was no evidence that the car was hot-wired."

Tom's eyes darted around the room. He took a drink from the bottle in his hand before answering. "Wasn't any different from any other night." He wiped his mouth on his sleeve. "Just like I told the police, I always come down early so I can get my parking place. Sometimes I drive home later, and sometimes somebody takes me."

"Could someone have taken your keys without you knowing it?" Toni watched his face and sensed he was lying. What he was lying about, or why, eluded her.

"Like I said, wasn't nuthin' different that night," he repeated, sounding like a child who had memorized his lines and was determined to stick to them.

Toni asked him a couple more questions and was met with the same response. Recognizing the futility of her efforts, she finished her Coke and got to her feet. "Thanks. Have a good evening." She paid for the soda and left.

Tuesday morning during her free period Toni went to the administrative offices to see the bookkeeper. "Good morning, Andrea," she greeted the receptionist.

Ryan Prewitt emerged from the superintendent's office, an empty coffee mug in his hand. Blond and athletically built, he looked in need of caffeine. But he smiled when he saw Toni.

"Good morning. Would you care for a cup?" He waved the mug in a friendly gesture as he went to the coffee pot on the counter in the small nook that served as their lounge.

"No, but thanks. I just dropped by to speak with Dana."

"I'm sorry, she's not here," the receptionist said. "She called in sick this morning."

"Okay, I'll check back tomorrow."

Toni returned to her room. At the end of the day she was preparing to leave when the librarian bustled into the room.

"Oh, good, I caught you," Loretta huffed, breathing heavily. She wore a blue pantsuit that stretched tight over her ample waist, and carried an armload of newspapers. "Here are last week's papers for recycling. Where do you want them?"

"Just dump them on the floor in the supply closet." Toni nodded toward the back of the room. "I'll have a student bundle them and take them out tomorrow."

Loretta walked in her odd loping way to the supply closet, tossed the papers inside, and returned to Toni's desk. "I have a bag of soda cans at home that I'll bring tomorrow."

Toni smiled. "Thanks, we appreciate it. The students are proud of the success of their service projects."

"I know you use the money they earn to buy school supplies and Christmas presents for students who can't afford to buy their own. That's why everybody saves stuff for you."

Toni finished putting on her coat. "I'll walk you out."

They fell into step down the hallway. "I stopped by to talk to Dana this morning," Toni said conversationally, hoping Loretta's penchant for gossip might prove helpful. "The secretary said she's out sick, but she didn't say what specifically is wrong."

"I'm not surprised," Loretta said in her slightly grumpy tone. "She's probably worn out."

"I know she's divorced and a single parent." Toni fished for more information.

"It's bad enough that she has a handicapped child, but that older boy of hers is an even bigger problem."

"The younger boy is about fourteen or fifteen, isn't he?" Toni asked.

Loretta's gray curls bounced as she nodded. "He just turned fifteen, but he has cerebral palsy and requires total care. The older boy is nineteen and can't keep a job. He has an illegitimate baby with some girl he got pregnant and dumped. She had a paternity test that proved it's his baby, and he's supposed to be paying child support. My guess is Dana pays any support that gets paid. That, plus extra expenses for the fifteen-year-old, has to be enough to keep her tired and depressed. The flu's been going around, and she's so exhausted she probably caught it."

"You could be right. I'll see you tomorrow. Thanks for the papers."

They parted ways in the parking lot.

Chapter 9

Wednesday morning Toni tried again to see Dana. When she learned that the bookkeeper was still out sick, a tightening formed in her gut.

On the way back to her classroom, she stepped into John's room and told him about the shooting incident and the newspaper report that would hit the streets that evening. "Dad picked me and the boys up and brought us to school Monday and Tuesday. I got my van back yesterday after school."

"Toni, you have to let Buck and his officers handle this from now on," he said in alarm, clearly shocked at her story.

"No, it's more important than ever now that this person be caught," she insisted. "Garrett and I will never be safe until that's done."

He scratched his head, his face clouded with perplexity. "I had no idea how stubborn you are."

She mustered a half grin. "Well, now you do. Gotta go."

When seventh hour dismissed, Beth Price hung back near Toni's desk while the rest of the students exited the room. "Mrs. Donovan, I heard something about Jodi," she said softly when they were alone. "If you're still interested, that is."

"Of course, I am." Toni sat down so the girl

didn't have to look up at her, hoping it would put her more at ease.

Beth seemed to relax a bit. "Her new boyfriend is Donnie Fisher."

Toni's heart sank. Donnie had graduated three years earlier, by the skin of his teeth. He was smart enough, but he had never cared about anything but girls and cars and did just enough school work to eke by. He had also spent a lot of time in ISS, mostly for fighting, if she remembered correctly. "Do you know what he's doing these days?"

Beth wrinkled her small nose. "I'm not sure, but I think he's been in some trouble with the police. I don't know what for. I think Jodi could do better than him."

Toni took a deep breath. "I hope she's not in trouble. Thanks for the information, Beth."

"You're welcome. Good night." The girl left.

The next morning Toni wasn't surprised to learn that the bookkeeper was still out sick. Since she still had a little time before class, Toni went upstairs to the resource officer's little cubbyhole of an office. Surprisingly Phil was there, visible through the glass door pane. He looked up and motioned her inside. "Have a seat. What can I do for you?"

Younger than Toni by six years, Phil seemed competent. His work was split between the school and the local police force. He was at the school Monday through Friday, but he worked occasional weekends for the department when they were shorthanded during school months, and full-time during summers.

Toni took the seat at the end of his desk. "I'm

concerned about a student."

"Which one?"

"Jodi Garrison. She's been missing a lot of school, and this past week she showed up with a black eye and a split lip."

"What can I do about it?" Phil shoved his chair back at an angle and propped one leg over the other knee.

"Probably nothing directly, but I hoped you might know something helpful. I heard she broke up with her longtime boyfriend and has a new one—Donnie Fisher."

"Aah," he drawled in understanding. "You want to know what Donnie's been up to and if he's beating up on her."

"That's about it. I don't know that it'll do any good, but if there's any chance she's being abused by him, knowing about it might help the counselor decide how to approach her."

"I'll see what I can find out," Phil promised. "Is there anything else I can do?"

Toni sighed. "I wish there were. So much goes on that's beyond our control."

"Let me check around. Maybe we'll get a brainstorm."

When her last class ended, Toni rushed down the hall to turn in some paperwork before going to get the boys. Dismay hit her when she entered the office and saw a police officer posted by Ken's door.

"Here are those forms I promised you." She leaned close enough to whisper into Pam's ear as she placed them on the desk. "Are they questioning Ken again?"

"Yes," Pam whispered back, shooting a sideways glance at the officer. "Thanks," she said aloud, taking the papers. "I need to buy some breath mints from the vending machine." She reached into a bottom drawer of her desk.

Toni realized Pam wanted to see her privately.

Pam took some money from her purse, and they went out into the commons. "The police found out that a friend of Ken's was a candidate for the superintendent job back when Marsha was hired, and now that she's dead, the guy has applied again." She dropped coins into the slot and fished out the packet that fell into the bin.

Toni's jaw dropped. "You mean to tell me they think Ken killed Marsha so a friend of his could have her job? That's insane."

Pam glanced back at the office. Through the plate glass window they could see the cop still standing behind her desk. "I don't know what they think. I just know they've been in there for over an hour."

"Thanks." They exchanged grim looks and parted ways.

That night after supper, needing to unload, Toni summarized to Kyle everything that she had done and learned since finding Marsha's body.

"I don't have any answers for you," he said quietly, putting the television remote on the coffee table. "I wish I did. I understand that you have to do everything you can to protect Garrett, but don't forget to protect yourself. I have a very bad feeling about this whole thing."

"I'll be careful," she said, repeating her earlier promise.

Just before he went out the door early the next morning, Kyle made Toni repeat that promise yet again. "I'll be home late tomorrow night, but I'll spend the weekend here at home."

With her promise in mind, Toni did no investigating that day, other than to confirm that Dana was still out sick and to call Sam Brinkman before going after the boys.

"Are there any plans for an audit of the district?" she asked when she reached him.

"I've only been able to get hold of about half the board members so far," he replied in a tone lacking urgency. "But I read about what happened to you Saturday. I hope you're staying where you'll be safe."

Toni told him she was fine and gave him the same assurances she had been giving all week to those who commented or asked about it. As soon as she could, she steered the subject back to the matter of Dana's extended absence from school.

He responded with more concern. "That sounds bad. I'll press for a decision and get back to you."

Toni disconnected and reached for her purse.

John stepped inside her classroom doorway. "Is it still okay for the boys to look after the puppy this weekend?"

"They're looking forward to it. Do you want us to pick him up?"

"We'll bring him by sometime after supper tonight."

After Toni and the boys got home, she graded papers, and then made hamburgers and fries. John and Jenny arrived about seven o'clock.

"Here are Bingo's things," John said as he toted a

large cardboard box through the doorway. "His toys, food and water bowl, some canned dog food, and a supply of newspapers." He emphasized the last.

Toni laughed. "We'll put something across the kitchen door for a barrier and keep him in the utility room."

Jenny followed him inside, the puppy cradled in her arms. "We're working on the training, but we have a long way to go."

Garrett trotted into the room, his shirt unbuttoned and his arms outstretched. "Let me have him."

"Okay, but be sure you put him in his box every forty-five minutes so he'll go to the bathroom there and not on the floor," Jenny instructed as she handed him the puppy.

"We will."

"Let's take him to our room," Gabe called from the hallway.

John took Bingo's box to the utility room and put it between the dryer and pantry. Then he filled the water dish and set the dog food on the dryer.

"Can you stay and visit?" Toni asked when he was done. "There's supposed to be a good special on the Discovery Channel that might provide an idea or two for labs."

He glanced at Jenny.

"Could we make popcorn?" she asked with a grin.

Toni laughed. "Of course."

About halfway through the science special Gabe came slinking into the room. "Mom?"

"What's the matter?" Toni could hear the puppy yipping from their room.

"Uh, we forgot," he said so low it was hardly audible. "We have a little mess."

"Oh, no." Jenny bounced from the sofa, horrified. "I'll clean it up."

"No, you won't," Toni said firmly. "I'll get some cleaner, and they can have the joy of cleaning it. They didn't take him to his box like they promised."

Jenny started to protest, but Toni cut her off. "If they're going to keep him all weekend, this will make them more responsible."

After John and Jenny left later that evening, Toni took a shower and curled up on the couch, restless in the peace and quiet with the boys in bed. For someone known for having both feet firmly on the ground, she felt mighty unsteady. She thought she had learned to handle the constant shifts between mother and teacher, but these past two weeks had knocked the props from under her. She picked up the phone and called her principal's home number.

"Hello."

"This is Toni. I know it's late to be calling you, but I've been thinking."

"Uh oh," Ken said, trying to sound jovial and failing.

"On the night of December twenty first you said you were at the mall in Cape during the time Marsha was killed. I know this is a long shot, but why don't we drive over there and trace the route you walked, look for anyone who can identify you, and verify that you were there?"

"I guess it's worth a try," he said wearily. "Can you hold a moment?"

She heard him talking to his wife in the

background, and then he returned. "Tomorrow morning would work. Sandy says she'll come over and babysit your boys, along with Tanner, if that would suit you." Tanner was their two-year-old son.

"That would be better than having to drag the kids along. Oh, the boys are puppy sitting for the Zachary's this weekend. Will that bother her?"

"Just a moment."

There was more speech in the background.

"She says that's no problem. Tanner will love playing with a puppy."

"Okay, what time can you meet me here?"

"Eight o'clock."

*

Ken arrived at five till eight the next morning, dressed in jeans and a heavy coat over a warm blue sweatshirt. Toni's attire matched, except that her sweatshirt was red. "I'll drive," he insisted. "It's my problem, so the trip should be made on my gas."

About ten o'clock they reached the mall in Ken's small station wagon. "Park where you did that night," Toni instructed. "Then let's walk the exact route you took, including your shopping. We'll keep track of the time and see how long the whole thing takes us."

Ken seemed content to follow her lead, appreciative of her support. "I went to Macy's first." He opened the vehicle door.

"So far, so good," Toni said when they got to the sidewalk. She glanced up at the front of the store. "There will be a record of the payment you made for your wife's Christmas gift. The problem is that it wasn't late enough in the evening to prove you couldn't have been back in Clearmount by the time of the crime."

"I didn't come straight out of the building," he said, looking both ways as they went inside. "I wound around by the jewelry department, debating about getting her something from there. But I decided I shouldn't blow our budget any more than I already had."

As they paused by the jewelry counter, Toni pointed at a surveillance camera overhead. "We could check with security about that, but the time frame still isn't late enough to help us."

They moved on. At the end of their tour of the store, they retraced their steps to Ken's station wagon. Toni looked around. "Which way did you go from here?"

"That way." He pointed north, and they set out again. Outside a mini mart he came to a halt. "I stopped here for coffee. How about a Coke?"

Toni grinned. "You know I never turn down a Coke—or in this case a chance to get warm. I'm freezing."

Inside the store, Ken took two sodas from a cooler and paid for them. He handed the Coke to her and kept the root beer. "My headache is getting bad." He reached into his pocket and pulled out a bottle of pills, extracted two tablets, and popped them into his mouth. He washed them down with root beer.

"What time do you think you were here?"

He gazed upward, thinking. "It was about eight when I got to Macy's. I probably wasn't in there over a half hour, so it would have been about eight-thirty or eight-forty-five, I think," he added uncertainly.

As Toni scanned the interior of the store, her

eyes stopped on a surveillance camera mounted over the north corner of the room, up near the ceiling. "Here's another place you might have been videoed."

"But the time would still have been too early to clear me," he pointed out.

"Okay, let's go."

They walked the rest of the route Ken remembered, ending up back at his vehicle. "Well, that's that." He spread his hands in a gesture of defeat.

Toni rubbed the back of her hand over her eyes, waited while he unlocked the car, and pulled the passenger door open. Shivering from the cold, she crawled inside and leaned back, staring upward through the windshield as Ken started the engine. Suddenly she froze.

Ken started backing out of the parking space.

"Stop!"

He slammed on the brakes, jolting them both nearly out of their seats.

She pointed upward. "Look."

Ken stared for a moment. "That camera overlooks the exit-entrance of the parking lot." His voice rose with hope.

"It should have caught you driving out of the parking lot." Her voice also rose. "Let's go back to the mini mart."

He looked puzzled.

"Maybe someone there can tell us how to contact mall security."

Back inside the mini mart, they approached a clerk and asked to speak with the manager. When they explained who they were and what they needed, the young man who presented himself as the manager called the head of mall security for them, explained what was needed, and then gave them directions to the security office.

"Ask for Monty," he instructed. "He said he'll try to find what you need. Good luck."

"Thanks a lot." Ken produced a genuine smile for the first time in a long while.

They followed the clerk's directions to the security office and were met at the door by an older, uniformed man. "We only keep those tapes for a few weeks," he explained once introductions were made. He led them inside the office and closed the door. "What was the date you said you're looking for?"

"December twenty-first," Ken supplied eagerly.

"Have a seat. I'll be right back." He disappeared through a door behind the desk.

"I'm afraid to hope," Ken muttered, dropping onto the chair next to the door.

About ten minutes later ruddy-faced Monty reappeared. "Boy, are you guys lucky," he announced in a near growl. "We only save these routine surveillance tapes for thirty days. Then we erase and reuse them. Today is the twentieth, so sometime this week our secretary would have recycled this batch. I think this is what you want." He held up a tape. "It's a six hour tape of the six to midnight hours."

"May we have it?" Ken held out a hand.

"As far as I'm concerned you can, but I better not give away company property," the security guard said, pulling it back. "And I don't have time to play it for you."

Ken's hand dropped. His shoulders sagged.

"If you'll pay for the cost of a blank tape and wait for me, I'll get my boss's approval to make you a copy of it. It can run while I finish what I was working on."

"You bet," Ken reached for his wallet.

"We'll watch it when we get home," Toni said.

Ken nodded. "I'm hungry. Let's stop for a burger on the way."

*

Puffs formed in front of their mouths as they exited the station wagon about one-thirty. Sandy opened the door, and they hustled inside.

"How did it go?" she asked Ken as he scooped a charging Tanner into his arms.

"Good, we hope." He hugged Tanner and gave her a quick kiss. "We have a surveillance tape we need to watch."

Sandy's eyes widened. "You think it shows you on it?"

His worried expression held a hint of eagerness. "We don't know, but we're hoping. It's from the spot overlooking the entrance-exit of the mall parking lot." He put Tanner down, and the toddler took off down the hall.

"The boys are in their room, so the living room television is free," Sandy explained. "I'll go check on them."

Toni and Ken put their coats away, and then Toni took the tape to the entertainment center. She was just putting it in the player when they heard a shriek from the boys' bedroom. "What have you boys done?"

Toni dropped the tape and ran down the hall, Ken at her heels. At the bedroom doorway they stared in disbelief at the small puppy in the middle of the room. Bingo had been stuffed backward into a plastic bread sack. His feet stuck out through small holes in the plastic. A ribbon looped around his neck and tied in a bow at the back of his head held the sack closed. His small head resembled a Mr. Potato Head. As for the sack, it looked like a huge balloon, sagging with the weight of yellowish liquid.

Toni was horrified. "What is the meaning of this?" she demanded, kneeling by the poor dog. She reached to release the ribbon, and then stopped, realizing what would happen.

"He has accidents," Garrett said quietly. He squatted on the floor near a pile of Legos, his eyes huge and round.

"We didn't want him to have another accident on the carpet," Gabe explained.

"So you …so you …" Toni sputtered, unable to describe what they had done. Then her voice changed to fury. "You were supposed to take him to his box every forty-five minutes."

Garrett hung his head. "We were afraid we might forget again."

"Young men," Toni said low and evenly. "You will take that puppy into the bathroom, and you will give him a bath, and then we'll …"

"I'll take care of this," Sandy interrupted. "It's my fault. It happened on my watch."

Toni took a deep breath, and then another one. "Maybe you're right," she said when she could speak again. "Not that it's your fault," she corrected quickly. "But you should see that they take care of it, because I'm afraid of what I might do to them." She glared at her offspring.

The boys sat perfectly still, recognizing the depth of the trouble they were in.

"You and Ken go ahead and watch your tape while the boys and I take care of Bingo," Sandy ordered.

Toni slowly turned around. But Ken, who had been right behind her, was gone. She went out into the hallway, then to the living room. He was not there. Puzzled, she crossed the kitchen to the utility room. From there she saw the door to the garage standing open. She went to it and peered out.

There stood Ken, propped against a wall of the garage to keep from collapsing. His arms were wrapped around his waist, clutching his gut, as he laughed so hard that tears rolled down his cheeks. She watched him sink to a sitting position and lean back against the wall with his knees up to his chest.

She stepped out into the garage, hands on hips. "So you think it's funny, do you?"

"I think it's f-f-f-funny," he choked. "But it's even funnier to see ... to see the unflappable Toni Don...Donovan...flapped." He went off into another spasm, wiping his eyes and slapping his stomach. "Oh, it hurts," he moaned.

Toni stared at her normally staid principal, sprawled on her garage floor out of control.

"It's just what I needed," Ken managed to say between gasps.

Toni thought about it. "Maybe it is," she allowed, her mouth twitching. "But they have to be punished. They didn't live up to their responsibility and promises."

Ken took a deep breath and slowly relaxed against the wall. "I know you're right, but please don't be too hard on them. It was just the pressure release I needed."

"Okay, maybe I won't kill them." She held out a hand. He took it, and she gave him a boost to his feet. "The trouble is, I don't know what punishment would be appropriate. Let's watch the tape, and I'll think about it."

They went back to the living room, and Toni put the recording in the player. Then they settled on the sofa with the remote. "Monty said there are six hours recorded on this," Toni said as she turned on the television. "But it's dated and shows the time. Let's fast forward to about eight-thirty."

"Bingo is spic and span again," Sandy announced from the doorway. "I'll stay with him and the boys while you two watch that."

"Okay," they both mumbled absently, glued to the grainy images on the screen. At first it wasn't too bad, watching the traffic flow in and out of the parking lot, but it soon became tedious and boring. Toni was just about to nod off when Ken jerked forward. He pointed. "There. That's my truck, and the license number will prove it."

Toni hit the pause button and checked the bottom of the screen. "Look at the time. It says nine-sixteen. It's over seventy miles between here and Cape."

"Crooked, winding miles," Ken added with a wry twist of his mouth.

Toni knew what he meant. "Marsha's phone log showed a call at ten-twenty-eight, so she was probably killed about ten-thirty. It takes me close to an hour and a half to make that drive. My brothers drive it faster," she added with a roll of her eyes. "But you would have had to be flying to have driven from there to here and committed a murder in an hour and twelve minutes."

"My old truck won't go over seventy miles an hour," Ken pointed out with a wry twist of his mouth.

Toni drew a deep breath of relief. "This should satisfy Chief Freeman."

"Thanks for everything." Ken retrieved the tape and tucked it under his arm.

When he and Sandy were gone, Toni fixed a quick meal for her and the boys. While they ate, she didn't mention the incident with the dog. Later that evening she went to their bedroom and peeked inside. Both boys were in bed, but she was sure they were feigning sleep. Her heart surged with emotion. They were so precious to her. But they had to be punished. "I know you're not asleep," she said softly through the doorway. "But it's okay. We'll discuss things in the morning. Good night."

She closed the door. Let them sweat. That was a form of punishment in itself.

Just then she heard Kyle's truck pull into the drive. She met him at the door and gave him a hug. "How was your flight?"

"Smooth." He deposited his bag on the floor to remove his coat. "How have things been for you?"

"Interesting. Are you hungry? I've got leftover meat loaf and …"

"A meat loaf sandwich sounds good," he cut her off. "I'll take a shower while you fix it."

Toni made the sandwich, got out some chips, and

poured a glass of iced tea. When Kyle came from the shower, she sat at the table while he ate and brought him up to date on her efforts to clear Ken of suspicion. Then she told him what the boys had done to the puppy.

Kyle stopped eating when she told him about the dog. "They did what?"

"You heard me." Toni tried to maintain a stern demeanor.

His mouth twitched. "What did you do about it?"

"I let them and Sandy give the dog a bath." Her tone dared him to laugh. "As for them, I haven't done anything yet. I'm letting them sweat."

Kyle did laugh then. "Are you going to beat them to death?"

She couldn't prevent a grin. "Believe me, I've considered it. But I guess I'll give them a lecture and suggest that they write notes of apology."

"Apologize, huh?" He grinned and went back to eating.

Later that night, Toni lay wide-awake in bed. "You awake?" she whispered.

"Barely," he mumbled. "What's wrong?"

She snuggled closer to him. "A little classroom problem won't let me sleep."

He rolled over and nestled her in the curve of his arm. "Same student it's been all year?"

Toni nodded in the dark. "Dustin's attitude is getting worse. He really pushed the boundaries this week."

"Have you written him up?"

"Not yet, but I guess I'm going to have to. He doesn't exactly refuse to work. He just makes it clear in devious little ways that he considers the class a waste of time. He ignores instructions and spends more time finding ways to flirt with Sidney, or other girls, than doing his work. I can't watch him every second," she said wearily. "I have other students who are willing to work and need my attention. I think Sidney is more hung up on him than he is on her."

"Are you afraid to write him up because his dad's president of the school board?"

"No," she answered without hesitation. "That shouldn't matter, even if it upsets Dennis. The boy thinks the rules are for everyone but him. He also thinks he's a Romeo."

"Do what you have to do. Don't worry about your job."

Chapter 10

The next morning Toni got up a few minutes earlier than normal for a Sunday and went into the boys' room. When she turned on the light, they both opened their eyes. Their beds occupied opposite sides of the room. Gabe's coverlet was a fluffy red one with a Superman design on it, Garrett's blue and featuring Spiderman.

"Time to talk."

They both sat up, and Toni pulled a chair away from the computer desk. She positioned it between their beds and sat, wearing her sternest schoolteacher face. "Do you two realize what you did wrong?"

Garrett nodded, his eyes huge and dark in a solemn face.

"We promised to take Bingo to his box every forty-five minutes so he could go to the bathroom, and we didn't do it," Gabe confessed quietly.

"Why was that wrong?"

"Because we broke a promise?"

"That's right. Anything else?"

"Was it bad for Bingo?" Garrett asked, his chin quivering.

"Well, I'm sure it wasn't good for him," Toni allowed. "It made him, uh …"

"Stink," Garrett supplied solemnly.

"That's true. He shouldn't have been forced to get messy that way, and that sack was probably hot and sticky."

"I'm sorry," Garrett mumbled.

"Me, too," Gabe echoed.

"Are you really?" She looked from one to the other.

They both nodded.

"Good. I want you to write a note to Mr. and Mrs. Zachary. Explain what you did and why it was wrong. Then you should apologize. Can you do that?"

"You mean we write a note together?" Garrett asked hopefully.

She shook her head. "No, I mean you each write your own note. And I want them ready when the Zachary's come to get Bingo this afternoon. Now go clean his box and fill his food and water bowls. Then we'll eat and get ready for church."

The sermon that morning compounded Toni's guilt. The pastor talked about how people let themselves be caught up in their demanding schedules and spend so much time doing good for others that they didn't spend enough time with their own families. His admonition to slow down and spend time with God and their families struck deep inside her. She wanted to block out his words, pretend they didn't apply to her. But she couldn't.

She poured her energies into hobbies, pleasures, activities, her job—all good things—but fruitless if her own family was neglected. Yet, when she tried to evaluate the busyness of her life, she didn't see what she could eliminate or do differently. She worked hard to take care of her family. She was here in church with them. What more did God expect of her?

Tears of frustration welled in her eyes.

I'm doing all I can, God. Please don't ask any more of me. I have responsibilities. I have to protect Garrett.

*

After church they ate at the Zinger. When they got home, Kyle took his truck to the car wash, and the boys went to their rooms to write their notes. They were still there when John and Jenny arrived at four o'clock.

"We can't stay. I have papers to grade," John said when Toni offered to take their coats.

"Gabe. Garrett," she called down the hall.

The boys crept into view and stopped at the edge of the living room.

"Hey, what's the matter?" John asked at the sight of their solemn faces.

"Here." Gabe stepped forward and handed him a sheet of paper. "I'm sorry."

Garrett did likewise. "Here." His note was folded into a small square. "I'm sorry, too."

"May we be excused?" Gabe asked politely.

Toni studied their discomfort. "For now."

They wasted no time escaping back to their room.

Puzzled, John opened Gabe's note and began to read. When he finished, he handed it to Jenny and unfolded Garrett's. He read it and looked up at Toni. Then he placed a hand over his mouth and began to sputter. He passed the second note to Jenny.

Fighting for control, he eyed Toni. "Did you read

these?"

She frowned. "No. They just finished, so I didn't have time to do that."

"Garrett says what they did was wrong because he would not want to be in a bag of pee like that."

Jenny, who had just finished the notes, began to shake in silent laughter. "Tell the boys I'll be checking with them in the future about puppy sitting. It sounds like they've learned not to take shortcuts."

"I'm embarrassed, and I'm not sure you should do that," Toni said apologetically. "But thanks for being good sports."

John headed for the utility room. "Let's take the rascal home."

Soon after they left, Kyle returned. "I'd like to see if I can catch Dana Smith at home," Toni told him as soon as he entered the house.

His accusing look made her feel guilty, but not enough to change her mind.

"All right, I'll watch the boys," he said in resignation, reading her determination.

She grabbed her coat and left. Having a pretty good idea how to find Dana, Toni drove to a housing development about ten miles from town near the river and stopped at the fire house she knew served as the community information center. It didn't take long to get directions to Dana's house.

There were four homes on the block to which she was directed. Toni parked in front of the one at the end of the street. There were no vehicles there, but she got out and went to the door anyhow. She knocked and waited. When no one answered, she knocked again.

A car occupied the driveway next door, so Toni went over and knocked on the door of that house. An elderly lady, white haired and wearing thick glasses, answered the door. She squinted out at Toni. "May I help you?"

"I'm looking for Dana Smith, but she doesn't seem to be home. Do you have any idea where I might find her?"

"I have no idea where she is," the woman said. "The last time I saw her was back early in the week. She put several suitcases in her car and left. I haven't seen her since."

Toni's suspicions ramped up another notch. "Thank you." She returned to her minivan.

*

Monday morning Toni was working at her desk when Phil Norton poked his head inside the doorway. "Got a minute?"

"Sure." She motioned the resource officer inside. "Have a seat."

"Thanks." He dropped into the chair near her desk. "I checked the schedule and saw that you don't have a class this hour. I don't have much, but I wanted to let you know that Donnie Fisher is working as a mechanic at Lonnie's Garage and Body Shop."

"Did you learn anything about his behavior?"

Phil tilted his head. "If you mean how he treats other people, especially girls, the answer is yes. The person I talked to says the guy likes to knock his girlfriends around."

Uh oh. "That's often a power thing. He controls the relationship. A girl can't break up with him if she wants out, because he has to be the one who ends things."

Phil nodded. "I think you're right. The girls won't report the abuse because they *love* him, or they're too afraid of him to do it. If they *do* report it, they end up dropping it."

"The counselor needs to know about this. Maybe she can get Jodi to talk to her."

Phil glanced at his watch. "You have class in a few minutes. Would it help if I talk to the counselor?"

"Thanks." She was glad for the help.

*

Two figures slipped through the doorway into the dark room. One of them switched on the light while the other locked the door behind them. Then, giggling, they embraced.

There was a small, almost imperceptible click.

One of them froze. "What was that?"

They listened and heard only silence.

"It was nothing," the other said. The embrace resumed.

"We better go," one of them whispered later. There was another click, but neither of them heard it.

They put things back in order and left the room.

*

Tuesday morning Kyle left early, telling Toni and the boys good-bye well before time for them to head for school. He had promised to be in sometime Saturday evening.

"Can we go eat Chinese tonight?" Gabe asked as he climbed into the front seat of the van.

"May we," Toni corrected automatically.

"May we?" he amended, rolling his eyes at the injustice of being the son of a teacher.

"Hm, that does sound good. All right."

He beamed. "Do you think we could walk down to your room after school today?"

Toni shook her head. "No, nothing's changed." She looked back to include Garrett in her statement. "I want to be sure you're safe."

"I understand," Gabe said, but his tone indicated he was beginning to feel restricted.

"You think someone is trying to hurt me, don't you?" Garrett's question from behind them was barely audible.

Toni turned in the seat to face him and tried to be honest. "It's possible, and I'm not taking any chances. I know you want to be free to do things like you always have, but I need to keep you where I can feel that you're safe." She hoped he understood.

His expression was sober. "Is it because my dream made you find the body?"

"That's a possibility," Toni admitted, wishing it were not true. She wanted to hold him and assure him, but knew he would resist such coddling.

Toni believed she had a special bond with her children, but there was a new strain since the incident in the parking lot. She didn't want to smother them, but she simply had to keep them safe. Neither of the boys had become argumentative or belligerent, but they were quieter and less spontaneous, obviously worried and trying to not show it.

She and Kyle had told them about the attack on her at the lake, but had made as light of it as they could, implying that it was probably a hunting accident. They had hidden the section of the newspaper that contained the story about it and cautioned their friends and colleagues to not discuss it in front of them. Hopefully they would not hear about it from their classmates. If that happened, she would have to figure out another way to keep them from feeling more worry than they already did.

Toni shifted in the seat so she could make eye contact with both of them. "Listen, guys, I know you don't like the way things are, and you probably feel you're being treated like babies, but your safety is very important to me. I hope it won't last much longer."

"I think Dad is worried about you—about us," Gabe said in his grown-up manner.

"He is," Garrett seconded, his brown eyes troubled.

"Which is another reason for us to be careful. He needs to know that we're taking care of one another." Toni glanced down at her watch. "Uh oh. We're about to be late."

The day began in a normal fashion. During third hour Toni went to confirm whether or not Dana was back on the job. When she entered the administrative office, the secretary grimaced. "If you're looking for Dana, she's still out sick." She grabbed a ringing phone.

A man and woman, both wearing dark business suits, emerged from the bookkeeping office. Ryan Prewitt, looking harried, came from the superintendent's office next door. "How about some coffee?" he asked the visitors as they met near the secretary's desk. "We have a pot in the lounge."

"No thank you," the woman said. "We're just going to the car for some more boxes."

Ryan watched them go out the door before he noticed Toni. His navy blue suit and pristine white shirt looked sharp, but his tie was askew. He tugged at it. "This is stressful."

Toni gave him a sympathetic smile. "I understand." Inwardly she was elated. Unless she missed her guess, those two visitors were auditors. If so, it meant something was actually being done. "If there's any way I can help, let me know."

"Maybe you and your students could clone me, so I can be in two places at once," he quipped, taking the coffee pot from its perch and filling his mug.

"I think you're doing fine," she said, wanting to encourage him. "Maybe things will settle down soon and the board will hire a replacement superintendent."

"I sure hope so." His sigh was heartfelt.

Toni returned to her classroom, and the day proceeded fine after that—until seventh hour. While distributing materials, she noticed Dustin Guthrie and Sidney Rayford sitting in adjacent desks near the back of the room. They wore angry expressions and were not flirting as usual.

Jodi sat two rows in front of them, staring silently ahead. Her eye had turned a veritable mixture of colors—green, yellow and purple. The swelling had gone down in her lip, though.

Toni went to the white board and picked up a colored marker. "Here is what you should see in the microscope." She began a simple drawing of a dividing cell and hoped they were paying attention.

They were not. Sidney turned and hissed in Dustin's face, her expression one of fury.

"Hey, knock it off, you two," Robbie Detheridge

snapped, not bothering to whisper. "Some of us want to hear what Mrs. Donovan is saying. We don't need to listen to you two arguing about a broken date."

Dustin shot to his feet, anger reddening his face.

Robbie also stood, and they faced off in hostility.

"All right, that's enough." Toni raised a hand in a cop-like signal.

"They started…"

"No arguments," Toni snapped before Robbie could say more. "There will be order in this class, or the matter will be taken up with Mr. Douglas in the office. Do I make myself clear?" She glared at one, then the other.

"Yes, ma'am." Robbie eased back into his chair.

Dustin weighed the matter for several moments before slowly resuming his seat. Sidney sat back in her chair, arms folded over her chest, and sulked in silence.

"Now, as I was saying," Toni said, resuming her lecture and demonstration.

She wasn't sorry when the class ended and the students left. Why did kids have to be so rude to one another?

"Hi, how was your day?" John greeted her from his doorway across the little foyer between their rooms.

"Don't ask," she said with a grimace and started back into her room.

He followed her. "That bad, huh?"

"Just the last hour."

The phone rang, startling them both.

Toni snatched the receiver. "Yes." There was no need to identify herself, since whoever was calling her extension knew who they were calling. There was no caller ID.

"Hi, Toni," Kelly Graham's voice greeted her. "Do you have time to stop by my office for a chat before you go home?"

"Well, "Toni hesitated. "I need to pick up my boys."

John tapped her on the shoulder. "I'll go get your boys if you need to do something."

"Just a moment." She pulled the phone away from her ear. "Kelly wants me to stop by. Are you sure you don't mind?"

"It's no trouble," he assured her.

She returned to Kelly. "I'll be right there."

"I'll bring them to my room," John said, heading up the hall while Toni went the opposite direction.

"Hi, Toni. Thanks for coming." Kelly sat at her desk, hands folded in front of her, as Toni entered her office and took a seat.

"What's up?" Toni asked.

"I caught up with Jodi Garrison today, but I'm not sure it did any good. I spoke to her about her excessive absences and the effect they're having on her grades. She insists she really has been sick and that the black eye is from a fall. I suggested she see the nurse, but of course she refused."

"Are you aware that her new boyfriend is Donnie Fisher?"

There was a moment of silence. Then Kelly spoke deliberately. "I wasn't. I thought she was being abused. Now I'm sure of it."

"I don't think she'll ever admit it. She's afraid."

Kelly nodded agreement. "I've talked to Ken,

and I've assured the girl I'll help her in any way I can if she'll just come to me. We have no choice now but to call Protective Services."

Toni rubbed her forehead in frustration. "So many students live with broken or dysfunctional families, neglect and abuse, to say nothing of the peer pressures they face."

Kelly emitted a weary sigh. "I know. We help where we can, but it never seems to be enough. I wish we could do more."

"I appreciate your attempt at intervention." Toni stood to leave.

"Let's keep an eye on her. Maybe one of us will get an opportunity to help her."

Toni hurried to John's room and found him and the boys enjoying Popsicles and playing tic tac toe on the white board.

"Great stress release," John quipped, drawing a line from corner to corner of the diagram.

She grinned. "You boys ready to go?"

They threw their sticks in the trash can. "We are now," Gabe said for both of them. He gathered his backpack and trombone.

Toni faced John. "We're eating at the Chinese Buffet. Can you and Jenny join us?"

"That's funny," he said with a grin. "She said just this morning that she wanted to eat out tonight rather than cook. What time?"

"Why don't we meet there at six?"

"We'll be there."

*

When Toni and the boys set out for the restaurant at a quarter to six, the weather had turned worse. The temperature was dropping, and snow flurries whirled in the air. It looked like it was gearing up for another snowstorm. She hoped it didn't get bad enough to cancel school. Disrupted schedules caused problems, and any days missed had to be made up later.

"I'm having cashew chicken," Garrett announced from the passenger seat beside her. Gabe was taking his turn in the back. Toni had rejoiced when they stopped bickering about who got to ride in the front and started taking turns.

"Crab Rangoon and honey chicken." Gabe smacked his lips loudly behind them.

John and Jenny were just pulling into a parking spot when Toni turned in at the restaurant. Once inside, the adults settled at a table by the east window, and the boys sat at the next one. They all placed their orders for iced tea, filled their plates at the buffet, and then sat down to enjoy themselves. They rounded out the meal with dishes of ice cream.

John put his spoon beside his empty plate and looked across the table at Toni. "You started to tell me about your last hour class. What happened?"

"It looked like Dustin and Sidney were getting close to a physical fight. Either of you have any idea what's going on there?" She looked from John to Jenny.

"I might." John raised an index finger. "I had lunch duty today, and I overheard Sidney tell some friends that she and Dustin were supposed to go out last night, but he broke the date."

Jenny flinched. "I bet Miss Rayford was hot. She's not one to tolerate being stood up."

"Well, I wish their private romance didn't affect

their behavior in class," Toni said.

"By tomorrow it will probably all be water under the bridge," John predicted.

Toni shook her head, her thoughts churning. "I don't know. Sidney seemed pretty upset with him. I feel like there are invisible vibrations going on all around us, and I can't read them. I know that's not scientific," she admitted, waving her palms.

"I'd call it sensitivity," Jenny said softly. "You care about the students and what happens to them."

"That's a good thing," John added. "But don't let it drag you down. It's important for you to maintain control to be effective as a teacher, but you can't solve all their personal problems, as
much as you might want to."

"We're ready to go, Mom," Garrett announced from the neighboring table.

"Okay, in a minute," she said, tearing the paper off her fortune cookie. When she read *Your innovative nature will help you come up with a solution*, she laughed.

"What's so funny?" Jenny asked.

Toni handed the strip of paper to her.

She read it aloud, and John chuckled. Then he leaned forward and spoke in a low voice. "Listen, I know you're trying to keep your boys with you all the time because you're concerned about their safety. Any time you need help picking them up after school, just let me know and I'll go get them for you."

"Or I can if you're both busy," Jenny volunteered.

"Thanks, I appreciate the offers," Toni said, meaning it. "If today is any example, I'll probably have to take you up on it."

"You can always swap some puppy sitting," Jenny suggested, trying to keep a straight face and failing. When she laughed outright, John joined her.

"What's so funny?" Gabe asked, pausing in tugging on his coat.

John sputtered. "Your mom got a Chinese fortune that was funny."

Satisfied, the boys each shrugged and headed for the door. Toni did the same. "I'll see you in the morning. And I really do appreciate that after school offer," she said to both of them.

*

As soon as they arrived home, the boys raced to their room. Toni changed into jeans and curled up on the sofa with the phone. She called the police station and asked for the chief.

The television blared from the boys' room.

"Turn it down," she called.

"Hi, Toni," Buck said as the volume lowered. "What can I do for you?"

"Have you had a chance to view the video Ken gave you?"

"Yes, and it looks like you've won your point. The time frame would require some pretty incredible movement."

"I didn't win a point. I just wanted to defend a friend I'm convinced is innocent."

"Okay," he conceded with a huff. "It looks like your friend is in the clear."

Toni breathed a sigh of relief. "What about the person who shot at me? Have you had any luck figuring out who it was?"

His heavy sigh came over the line. "No, we haven't. Apparently he—or she—parked up the hill somewhere around the dam. There's no sign of a trail, and the bullets we dug out of your van are too smashed to be of any use."

Toni swallowed her disappointment.

"Maybe this is a good time to ask a favor of you," he continued, sounding reluctant, and a little agitated. "We're getting an increasing number of reports from people with missing car parts. It's turning into a real headache. My opinion is that it's small potatoes. The number and type of parts is too limited for a big operator to bother with, so we're wondering about kids. Could you put your ears to the ground? Let me know if you hear any talk, especially if names are linked. We have a couple of ideas, but no proof."

A thought formed and quickly crystallized in Toni's mind.

"Do you know something?" Buck asked when she took so long to respond.

"I'm not sure," she said carefully. "I have a student I've been concerned about. She has a new boyfriend, and she's missing a lot of school. Recently she showed up with a black eye and split lip, making me think the boyfriend is abusing her. But, like you, I have no proof. The boyfriend is a mechanic."

"Does this boyfriend have a name?" he barked.

"Donnie Fisher." She hoped she wasn't making a mistake and saying too much.

"That's a name we've considered. He works at Lonnie's, doesn't he?" The chief sounded world-weary.

"I don't know that he's involved in anything like that," Toni cautioned. "I just know he was in trouble a lot when he was in school, and I heard that he's not kind to his girlfriends."

"He's familiar with my facility. We've had him in here several times over the years, but he wiggles out of things. His folks always manage to scrape up enough money to pay his fines or get him a lawyer."

"Sounds like a possibility then."

"We'll start keeping a closer watch on him and do some checking on part numbers, if Lonnie will cooperate with us." He didn't sound real certain of Lonnie's helpfulness. "Got another call."

"Thanks," Toni said to a silent phone.

Chapter 11

Anxiety and a growing sense of urgency had Toni nearly jumping out of her skin all day Wednesday. It had been a month since Marsha's death, three weeks since finding her body. If her killer wasn't caught soon, odds were that the crime would never be solved.

Jodi entered the classroom seventh hour just ahead of Sidney and took a seat near the window. She opened her textbook. Sidney went to a desk at the back of the room and sat in brooding silence instead of joining her work group.

As Toni circulated about the room, checking progress at each workstation, she leaned over and whispered in Jodi's ear. "You don't ride a bus home, do you?"

Jody shook her head.

"Can you stay a minute or two after class?"

Jodi raised questioning eyes. "Okay," she said after several moments.

Toni moved on, but stopped at the phone just long enough to ring John and quietly ask him to pick up the boys for her. Then she went to the table where Sidney still sat in idle silence. Toni slid onto the seat next to the stony faced girl and spoke softly.

"Something is obviously bothering you. Would you like me to write a pass for you to go see the counselor?"

Sidney just shook her head.

"Is there anything I can do?"

"No," the girl snapped. "I don't feel well."

Toni glanced up at the clock. She doubted there was any physical ailment, but even if there were, not enough time remained to send her to the nurse. The bell would ring in ten minutes.

"Okay, just rest. I hope you get to feeling better."

When the bell rang, Toni stood by the doorway as the students exited, and then returned to her desk where Jodi stood waiting. She smiled, hoping to put the girl at ease. "Would you like a soda?"

"I don't have time," Jodi said. "I have to be at work by four."

It was now three-fifteen. Time to cut to the chase. "Jodi, I know you don't want teacher interference in your personal life. I have no desire to meddle, but I do want you to know that I'm concerned about you and would try to help if you ever indicated that you were in trouble and wanted my assistance."

Jodi stood rigidly for long moments, and then she seemed to wilt. "Thank you, Mrs. Donovan," she said quietly, sinking into the nearest seat. "I appreciate your offer, but you can't help me. No one can." Her shoulders sagged and her eyes glistened.

Toni decided to be forthright. "Jodi, I think you've gotten involved with someone who's mistreating you, and who may be involved in some dishonest activities."

Jodi hung her head, and tears trickled down her

cheeks. "You're right," she said so quietly Toni could hardly hear her. "I ran into Donnie a few days after Randy and I broke up, and he asked me out. I'm not sure why I said yes." She shook her head in misery.

Wishing she could hug the girl, Toni said, "You were vulnerable after a breakup."

"I guess," Jodi admitted. "Anyhow, I went out with Donnie, and we had a good time. So I said yes when he asked me again."

"But it turned ugly," Toni guessed.

Jodi nodded. "He got possessive and told me I was his girl now and would do whatever he said. When I told him I didn't belong to him, he... he hit me."

"And you were caught," Toni finished for her.

Jodi nodded again and raised her head. "I think he's stealing stuff," she said faintly.

"Car parts?"

Startled, Jodi's eyes rounded. "Yes. He works in a garage, and he steals parts to put in the cars he fixes on his own after work hours. At least that's what I think he's doing."

"You're afraid to report him or break up with him. You're a smart girl, Jodi, and you deserve better. Will you let me help you?"

Jodie shook her head adamantly. "You can't."

"Jodi, it's only a matter of time until the police get him. They already suspect him."

Jodi gasped. "Are you sure?"

Toni nodded. "I'm sure. All I want is to see you safe. Can you possibly avoid Donnie for a few days?"

Jodi considered for a moment. "My boss at the restaurant might let me have some extra work hours.

That would give me an excuse for not meeting him some evenings."

Toni gave her a conspiratorial grin. "You might also have a teacher who requires that you stay after school to do makeup work."

Jodi returned a wan smile. "That might help me turn down dates."

"Good. I know you need to leave, so run along. But if your parents aren't home and you need a place to go, will you come to my house? I live in the estates, the last house on the left, and here's my phone number." She jotted it on a piece of paper and handed it to Jodi.

"Thanks, Mrs. Donovan." The girl straightened her shoulders and left.

Toni went next door where John and the boys were having their usual Popsicles. "I think I made progress with Jodi." She outlined her conversation with the girl to John.

"Are you going to tell Buck about it?" he asked, shrugging into his coat.

"Right now." She picked up his phone and made the call. When she had related the confirmation of their suspicions about Donnie, she disconnected and took the boys home.

*

The next day Toni noticed an unusual amount of behind-the-hand whispering and snickering during her afternoon classes. When the final bell rang, she stood by the door and placed a hand on Beth Price's arm as the girl walked past her. "Got a minute?"

Beth dropped back and waited. When the room emptied, Toni closed the door. "Do you know what the students found so amusing this afternoon? If so, is it something I should know about?"

Beth's face reddened, clearly uncomfortable. "I'm not sure I should tell you."

"Is it something that could cause harm to someone?" Toni wasn't sure why she was pursuing this, but some instinct was driving her to do it.

"I don't think so. I'm not sure," Beth amended, gnawing on her lip. "But maybe you should know," she decided after a moment of worried indecisiveness. "A bunch of the kids got an e-mail with a...an...odd picture in it." She gave Toni a pleading look. "Will you promise not to tell who told if I show it to you?"

"I won't tell unless it's something that I have no choice about. That's the best I can promise. But I'll do everything I can to keep your name from getting back to the students."

Beth drew in a quavery breath. "I have a hotmail account and can't access it at school."

Toni pushed her desk chair to the work desk where her computer sat. She had network rights that the students didn't. "I'll log on and monitor you while you open your account."

Beth put her books on the desk and took the chair. Within a minute she had a file open.

Peering over the girl's shoulder, Toni saw a photograph of Dustin and an unidentifiable female. Only the back of his bare upper torso was displayed, but he was clearly recognizable. Only a bare arm and leg of the girl could be seen.

"Do you know where this was taken?"

Beth didn't look up. "No."

If someone had taken this off school grounds,

probably nothing could be done about it. If it had been taken on school property, or worse yet, during school hours, that spelled trouble.

"Will you forward a copy of that to my e-mail address?"

Clearly Beth didn't want to, but after another hesitation she relented and did it.

As soon as Beth left, Toni went next door to John's room. "Can you wait here until I get the boys? I have something to show you."

"I'll get them for you." He grabbed his coat.

Toni didn't argue. Back in her room, she called the technology director. "Hi, Dillon," she greeted him, thankful he was at his desk and answered. "Can you trace the source of an anonymous e-mail for me? It's been forwarded a couple of times, and I'd like to know its original source."

"Forward it on to me, and I'll see if I can work backward to an IP address."

"Thanks. I'll do it right now." She disconnected and rushed back to her own room. She had just finished sending it when she heard John and the boys coming down the hall. "In here," she called. "You boys may go to John's room for your Popsicles," she said as they entered the room. Then she looked at John. "That's all right, isn't it?"

"Sure." His narrowed eyes told her he understood her wish to talk to him privately.

She put the file back up on her screen.

"That should be reported," John said when he saw it.

"I've already asked Dillon to trace the source. Do you think I should tell Ken about it?"

John didn't hesitate. "I think that would be smart."

"I remember Ken mentioning that he'll be in a departmental meeting after school today, so I'll call him from home tonight." She shut down the computer and grabbed her things to leave.

By the time she and the boys got home, Toni felt too drained to fix more than hot dogs and macaroni and cheese for supper. After they ate and the boys had gone to their room, she curled up in the recliner to grade papers, the cordless phone at her side. She had just read the first report when the phone rang. She answered absently. "Hello."

"This is Sam Brinkman. There will be a special meeting of the board and the principals after school tomorrow. It'll be in the library, and we'll be discussing the results of the audit we just finished. Since you're the one who wanted one so badly, I thought you might like to attend."

"Yes, I would. Thank you for including me."

"It seems you've been included in a lot of things lately," he drawled. "And you seem to be the one looking the hardest for answers."

As soon as Toni disconnected, she called Ken about the e-mail circulating among the students.

"I have a doctor appointment in the morning, but I'll look at it when I get to my office. Oh, will I see you at the meeting after school?"

"I'll be there."

Next she called John. "I told Ken about the e-mail. He said he'll look at it tomorrow."

"Good. He needs to know. We've covered ourselves."

"One more thing," she said before he could disconnect. "Sam Brinkman just invited me to a meeting after school tomorrow. The board and the principals are going to discuss results of the audit they've been conducting the past three days."

"That sounds serious. I hope they found something helpful. Why don't Jenny and I take the boys home with us after school so your parents won't have to go after them."

"But you've looked after them so much," she protested.

"Because I want to. We want to." His tone changed, became almost pleading. "Toni, I haven't said anything, but Jenny and I aren't having any luck at starting a family. Borrowing your boys is a chance to have kids around."

"Then of course you can borrow them," she said, overcome by a rush of sympathy. She knew they had both been in their late thirties when they married, but she hadn't known of their struggles to have a baby.

*

Friday after classes Toni got a Coke and hurried to the library. She found a seat at the long table next to Betty Devore. Betty turned and peered at her through the thickest glasses Toni could ever remember seeing. "Not a coffee drinker, huh?"

"Coke-aholic." Toni popped the tab and reached for a Styrofoam cup from the stack on the table. She poured half the Coke into it and took a thirsty swig.

Betty chuckled, her large body overflowing the chair.

Sam Brinkman was the last of the seven board members to arrive. The three principals filed in after him and sat across the table from Toni and Betty. The atmosphere was grave.

Dennis Guthrie stood from his seat at one end of the table. "Okay, let's get started. I'm not a financial expert, so Mr. Prewitt, our acting superintendent, will explain to us what the auditors found." He resumed his seat.

Good move.

The board members were all decent people and reasonably successful in their respective jobs, but none of them were public speakers or financial advisors.

Ryan shuffled papers in front of him and remained in his seat. "As you all know, we've had a team of auditors here this week examining financial records of the district. Their report is not good." He glanced from face to face around the table. "There are some irregularities."

"What kind of irregularities?" Dennis asked brusquely.

Ryan cleared his throat and swallowed hard. "To begin with, our enrollment figures have been inflated, meaning we've been receiving more state money than we should."

Toni could almost hear the silent groans in the room.

"Will we have to pay back a bunch of money?" one of them asked.

"That's what I would anticipate," Ryan answered, his voice not quite steady. "And we're not solvent enough to absorb a big payback."

"I thought we had a healthy cash reserve," Sam interjected, clearly upset.

"There have been some irregular payments," Ryan hastened to explain. "The auditors found records of several payments to a consultant who doesn't exist—sizable payments."

"Doesn't exist! What do you mean?" Betty Devore demanded.

Ryan raked a hand through his already rumpled hair. "I mean checks were written to a consultant who exists only on paper, so the money could be pocketed by the person behind the scheme."

There was silence. "You mean Marsha Carter," Sam Brinkman muttered in weary finality.

Ryan grimaced. "It looks that way. The Chief of Police has been checking into her personal records. He was initially looking to see if she had any insurance policies that would provide a motive for someone to murder her. He didn't find anything like that, but he did find what he called a really fat savings account."

"Don't payments like that have to be handled by more than one person?" Betty asked, glancing around the table at each troubled face.

Ryan nodded. "They were approved by Mrs. Carter and the checks issued by our bookkeeper, Dana Smith."

"But why would Dana do that?" Sam yelped. "Was she just going along with a scheme of Marsha's to protect her job?"

"There was a little more to it than that." Ryan shuffled papers again and located a particular printout. "The auditors ran a check of personnel against payroll and found that salary checks were being issued to Dana's son."

"I don't remember hiring her son," Betty snapped.

Ryan shook his head. "We didn't. He was getting a check, but he doesn't work here."

"We're guessing that was Dana's payoff for processing the payments to the non-existent consultant," Ken Douglas explained, his speech strained.

Toni felt as if she had just been dunked in icy water as the implications hit home. There had been no money to buy decent equipment and books for students because the greedy woman had been siphoning funds for her personal use.

"Then why aren't you arresting her?" Betty demanded, her thick glasses giving her a wild-eyed look.

"We don't know where she is," Ryan explained. "She called in sick last Tuesday and hasn't been back to work since. That's why I supported Sam when he asked for the audit."

"I started making calls after Toni Donovan came to me with questions and the suggestion that we should do an audit. A rather pointed suggestion," Sam added, directing a grim smile at Toni. "That's why I wanted her invited to this meeting."

Lost in her angry thoughts, Toni suddenly became conscious of eyes focused on her, as if they expected her to say something. Years of standing before classes, mastering her emotions and maintaining control while working to hold the attention of students, helped her marshal her thoughts now.

"I found it out of character when more than one

person mentioned Mrs. Carter being pals with Dana. Then I made several trips to the office to talk to Dana and found that she wasn't showing up for work. From all that, I developed a feeling that the records should be checked."

"I knew you were looking for Dana, but I didn't know why," Ryan said. "By chance have you contacted her away from school?"

"I tried, but didn't catch her home." Toni glanced around the table. "I drove out to her house Sunday afternoon. All I wanted to do was talk to her," she explained defensively.

"It's all right," Dennis Guthrie said, a scowl making his bushy eyebrows slant. "You don't have to apologize. We're glad someone was trying to find some facts. Apparently the police haven't been all that successful."

"They've been working hard." Toni didn't want any negative feelings to develop toward their local law enforcement. "Chief Freeman has let me exchange some information with him."

Dennis nodded approval. "That's good to know. I take it you didn't catch up with our missing bookkeeper."

Toni shook her head. "She wasn't home, so I spoke to her next door neighbor. The woman said she saw Dana load some suitcases into her car earlier in the week and leave. She hasn't been home since."

Another spell of silence greeted that statement. Ryan finally spoke. "As soon as we finish this meeting, I think I should have Chief Freeman look for her."

Sam nodded. "Good thinking."

"I have a written report here, and I'm going to give each of you a copy of it to take home and read." Ryan picked up a sheaf of papers and walked around the table distributing them. "I know you must have a lot of questions, but the truth is I don't have any more answers right now. We're going to have to assess the damage and meet again to decide how to deal with everything. I'll talk to the Commissioner of Education and assure him that we'll make things right as soon as we can."

Heads nodded around the table.

"I want to thank Toni for pointing us in this direction," Ryan said to the group. Then he directed his words to her personally. "We realize that you got involved in this thing in a rather grisly way, and that your follow-up has resulted in a personal attack on you. We appreciate how you've persevered."

"If any of us can do anything to help you, I want you to let us know," Sam added.

"Well, there is something I'd like to see," Toni said, recognizing a golden opportunity.

"Name it," came from Sam.

"I told Chief Freeman I'd like to look at Marsha's computer, and he said he would have to think about it and get back to me. I'd like you to tell him you approve of me seeing it."

Ryan studied her. "You're thinking that an educator might possibly see significance in her correspondence and reports that the police wouldn't, aren't you?"

Toni shrugged. "It's a long shot, but that's my hope."

He addressed the group. "Anyone object to my

telling Chief Freeman that we want him to let Toni give that computer a look?"

No one objected. "I think it's a good idea," Sam declared.

Ryan focused back on Toni. "I'll ask him to bring it by or let me pick it up. Check with me first thing Monday morning."

She smiled. "Thanks."

Sam pushed his chair back and got to his feet. "If that's it, let's all go home so you can get on the phone with Freeman."

The room emptied without anyone lingering. Toni was more convinced than ever that she needed to talk to Dana. And she wanted to beat the police to her.

When she got to the Zachary house, John met her at the door. "There's a Coke in the fridge with your name on it. But you have to drink it here while you tell me about the meeting."

"Hi, Toni." Jenny appeared behind John, shrugging into her coat. "I'm going to pick up a pizza. How about I get two, and you and the boys eat with us."

"Only if you let me pay for ours," Toni said, stepping inside their living room.

"Oh, all right, if that's how you're gonna be," Jenny grumped. "The boys are in the den."

Toni dug out some money and handed it to her. "I'll save my Coke to go with the pizza."

While Jenny was gone, Toni settled in their comfy glider with her feet propped on the ottoman, and recapped the meeting for John.

"I really would like to hear Dana's story," she

said at the end of her recital. "I'm afraid the police will find her and talk to her first, and I'll just get second hand, possibly incomplete information."

John sat up straighter on the sofa and tapped his forehead. "Just a minute." He went to the kitchen and returned with a large phone book. "I think I remember that Dana's maiden name was Harris. Or was it Harrison? Anyhow, right after she got the job here at the school I remember her saying something about her mother moving to Poplar Bluff after her dad died." He flipped through the pages as he spoke.

"Okay, here we go." He ran his finger down the page. "None of these Harris names sound right," he muttered, flipping the page. "Andy Harrison... Richard Harrison... Rodney Harrison." He stopped. "Rodney Harrison. That has to be it. Dana's son's name is Rodney, probably named after her dad."

Toni dug a pen and small notepad from her purse. "Give me the address and phone number."

"Pizza's here," Jenny called from the doorway as he read them to her.

Toni wrote down the information, stuffed the notepad and pen back into her purse, and went to help Jenny in the kitchen.

"I have an idea," John said minutes later as they sat around the table munching pizza. "Why don't I drop Jenny at your house early in the morning to babysit—or young man sit, if you prefer—while you and I go to Poplar Bluff."

Jenny's face brightened. "I'd be happy to do that. I mean it," she repeated to convince Toni. "That way you won't have to get the boys out of bed early on a Saturday morning."

Toni smiled at Jenny's earnest expression. "Okay. Maybe we can get lucky and beat the police to the punch."

On the way home later, Toni's cell phone rang. She flipped it open without looking at it. "Hello."

"Hi, Terrific Toni," Kara's voice greeted her. "I know I shouldn't call while driving, but I'll keep it short. I just want to let you know I'm on my way down for the weekend."

"I'm on the road, too," Toni said, turning right off the highway. "Can we get together while you're here?"

"There's an estate sale I want to attend in the morning. Mom called and let me know that the Richardson heirs are selling a collection of their parents' furniture and small items left after each sibling took what they wanted now that both of their parents are gone.

"Can you come over after the sale?"

"It's a big one, so it may be late afternoon or early evening, but I will definitely get there," Kara promised.

Toni wasn't sure, but she thought she detected something in her friend's voice, something not quite right. "I'll look for you. We can visit and catch up on girl talk."

"Thanks. See you."

*

They met in the early morning cold at the edge of the woods. He carried his hunting rifle, and she carried a rolled up sleeping bag. He placed the gun on the ground near a tree, and they embraced.

"Here, let me do this," she said, pulling away

from him. She spread the sleeping bag on the ground next to the rifle and sat on it, leaning back against the tree. "Now," *she whispered, beckoning for him to join her. Within moments they were entwined in one another's arms.*

"Just a moment," she whispered, scooting away from him. "I have a surprise for you." She pushed him back up against the tree and kissed him. "Now close your eyes," she murmured, backing away.

Seconds later there was a shot. Another followed moments later. She placed something in the pocket of his jacket, picked up a shell casing, and walked away.

Chapter 12

By eight o'clock the next morning, with John navigating, Toni pulled into the driveway of what they hoped was Dana's mother's house. "There are two cars here," John noted. "Maybe one of them is Dana's."

They hiked up the short sidewalk to the small frame structure that looked like it would welcome a coat of paint. Toni knocked on the door.

When it opened, they were startled to find themselves facing Dana in person. Her face devoid of makeup and her brown hair straggling around her face, she looked hollow-eyed and haggard. Wearing a faded pink bathrobe and non-matching blue house slippers, she stared lifelessly at them.

"You may as well come in. I've been expecting someone to show up," she said at last, her voice raspy, her manner defeated. She widened the door opening.

They stepped inside.

"This is my mother's house, as I'm sure you know by now. She and the kids are still in bed." Dana pointed them to a rocker and occasional chair that looked like they had been around for more years than she had.

The rest of the room was fairly neat, but with an air of haphazardness. The sofa had a pillow and rumpled blanket on it, suggesting that someone had slept there. Dana shoved the bedding to one end and sat at the other.

"You probably know what we want to talk about," Toni began.

Dana nodded in weary defeat. "I've been waiting for the other shoe to drop ever since I got here. I just couldn't work up the courage to face it."

"Face what? Marsha's death?"

Dana's head jerked up, her eyes rounded in horror. "No! I had nothing to do with that. I meant the money."

"Why don't you tell us about it?" John said gently.

Dana's gaze rotated to him. "I might as well. I don't know what else to do. I knew you two found Marsha's body and that Toni had started asking a lot of questions. It was only a matter of time until everything came apart. I panicked and ran."

"How did you get involved?" Toni asked.

Dana shrugged in misery. "I was already struggling to get by after my divorce. My younger son is severely disabled, and I didn't want to put him in an institution. I get a little disability check on him, but it costs a lot for other care. But I was making it. Until Rodney got into more trouble."

"Rodney's your older son."

Dana nodded. "He's nineteen, four years older than Robin. He's had several jobs that haven't lasted long, but we were still scraping by—until he got a girl pregnant and was ordered to start paying child support." She pushed at flyaway strands of hair as her voice trailed to a quavery halt.

"Marsha came along and made you an offer," Toni prompted.

Dana's face crumpled, and she dissolved into tears, her head bobbing admission.

They waited for her to regain a semblance of composure before Toni spoke again. "Why don't you tell us about it from the beginning."

Dana pulled a tissue from the pocket of her robe and wiped her eyes. "When Marsha first took over as superintendent she hardly gave me the time of day. I wasn't worthy of her notice."

"How did that change?"

Dana bit her trembling lip. "She needed me. I don't know exactly why, but for some reason she needed—or just wanted—a chunk of money. She called me into her office one day and handed me a payroll voucher in Rodney's name. I didn't understand, but she said she realized I was having a difficult time and was putting in more work hours than required. She said she wanted to make things easier for me, that the check would pay me for those extra hours, and there would be another one each month."

John made an odd sound under his breath. "You believed her?"

The frightened bookkeeper shrugged. "I don't know what I believed. I looked at that check and thought about the bills I needed to pay, and…" She paused, her hand over her mouth. "I took it," she finished, her voice unsteady.

"And from that time on you processed any

payment she submitted and didn't ask questions." Toni watched her eyes.

"I didn't ask questions," Dana repeated. "She got friendly with me, and the money took off some pressure. But I felt guilty. And scared," she choked.

"Why were you scared?"

"Of getting caught for one thing." Dana blurted, and then paused before continuing. "But one day, around the first of December I think it was, I overheard Marsha talking on the phone to someone about a job interview. I think she was getting ready to take off and leave me to take the blame for everything. I don't know what other schemes she had going. I didn't want to know."

"You must have been under a lot of pressure." Toni spoke without condemnation. She would leave the accusations and judging to the law.

"I was." Dana twisted her hands together in her lap. "But the night she was killed I was nowhere near the school."

"You'll need to prove that," Toni said bluntly. "Where were you?"

Dana rubbed a hand over her forehead. "I went to see Dean, my ex-husband. We got into a fight. He should tell you that."

"Where is your ex-husband?"

"He's staying with his sister in Brownville," Dana whispered hoarsely, her eyes brimming with tears. "He hasn't been helping with Robin like he's supposed to. I was handling that, but I needed him to help with Rodney. He refused and started blaming me for everything and yelling at me. I guess we both got to yelling." She took a ragged breath and wiped her eyes again. "He hit me, and that's when I got out of there."

"Was his sister home at the time?"

"No, she was at work. She works the night shift at the nursing home. She's divorced and has a five-year-old kid. She leaves Brian with a babysitter."

Toni vaguely remembered Dean Smith as a hard drinking guy who was no stranger to trouble. He had been a few years older than her, but she remembered seeing his name in newspaper stories more than once for running a meth lab.

"Are you aware that the police are looking for you?" John asked when Toni went silent.

"No, but I'm not surprised," Dana answered shakily. "I knew it had to be just a matter of time."

"What do you plan to do now?"

Dana stared at him and drew an uneven gulp of air. "Go back and face it, I guess."

"Thank you for your candor," Toni said at last, getting to her feet. When they stepped outside into the frigid air, she pulled her cell phone from her purse. "The Chief made me promise to tell him when I find out anything," she said, scrolling through her saved numbers and pressing one. She opened the door of the van and climbed behind the wheel as the phone rang. John scrambled into the passenger seat.

"What's up?" Buck Freeman answered personally, obviously having seen caller ID.

"John Zachary and I located the school's missing bookkeeper," she said in a rush. "I assume you've spoken to Ryan Prewitt about the meeting at school yesterday."

"He called and told me about it."

"Sam Brinkman invited me. I had asked Sam to request the audit, so he thought I should get to hear the results."

"Where are you?"

"We're in Poplar Bluff, not far from the Industrial Park, and we're getting ready to head home. Dana Smith is at her mother's house, and we've talked to her."

There was a heavy silence before he spoke. "Toni, you're going to land yourself in more trouble if you aren't careful."

"I *am* being careful," she retorted. "I didn't come alone."

"You wanted to talk to her before we caught up with her." Buck barked the accusation.

A guilty silence was her answer.

"Okay, okay, give me the address."

Toni recited it. "Dana says she's coming home to face the music."

"We've heard that before. Maybe she will and maybe she won't. I'll get someone on the way right now." The phone went silent.

Toni winced, tossed the phone back in her purse, and backed out of the driveway. Once they were across town and rolling north on the highway, John spoke. "I feel kind of sorry for Dana."

"I can't let myself do that. I think she killed Marsha."

John swiveled his head around to stare at her. "You do?"

Toni nodded without taking her eyes off the road. "Dana was right about one thing. Marsha was getting ready to hang her out to dry—and did. I think the pressure was getting to be too much for her, and Marsha knew it. When she left the Christmas party, Dana probably met her with the intent of telling her she wanted to end the arrangement—or maybe even quit her job. But Marsha was an aggressive person and probably threatened Dana."

"So you think Dana panicked and hit her, and it ended up in murder."

"I'm afraid so."

"But what about her alibi? She said she was with her ex."

"Who's totally unbelievable as a witness or alibi," Toni pointed out. "Dean Smith won't want to admit hitting her, and he may clam up altogether. I seriously doubt that the timeline will fit. They were probably together sometime that evening, but it's only fifteen miles from his house to the school. My guess is that the fight with Dean left her more upset and stressed than ever, and she came to see Marsha in a state of extreme agitation that resulted in violence."

"Do you think she'll come back on her own?"

Toni shrugged. "I don't know. I think she's defeated and ready to tell her story. On the other hand, if she gets packed and in the car, she might just take off in the opposite direction."

"Well, we'll never know what she would have done on her own, because there'll be someone down here to pick her up before she can pack and get out of there with a handicapped child. She won't leave him behind."

"I think you're right."

Big loose flakes of snow began to fall and stick to the windshield. Toni turned on the wipers. "I'm already tired of winter and being cold."

"But you have to admit this is a beautiful scene." John scanned the hillside.

"It is."

The barren forests each side of the highway glistened with a powder of white snow. Predominantly oak and hickory, interspersed with cedar, elm, and ash, those tall barren monuments would fill the air with green in the spring. Dogwoods and redbuds sprouting and blossoming below the taller growth would create a breathtaking panorama.

Toni glanced over at John. "How about brunch when we get home?"

"Sounds good."

About halfway home, they met a Clearmount police car speeding south. They exchanged glances of acknowledgement but said nothing.

A sense of relief washed over Toni. Now that it looked like the murderer was caught, Garrett would be safe. But that relief was short lived. As she drove, second thoughts rose to plague her.

Under stress and panicked, Dana had done something she would never have been capable of doing in ordinary circumstances. But what about the later incident in the parking lot? Could Dana really have done that? Certainly she could have committed the murder, but did she have the cold-blooded determination to have carried out such a lowly attack on a child, or attempt to shoot someone? Toni couldn't see Dana in that light, couldn't shake the doubts that niggled at her, weakening her theory.

After brunch, John and Jenny left, and Toni made the boys help her tidy the house. They weren't thrilled about it, but they cleaned their room, took out the trash, and helped her put away their clothes from the laundry she had managed to get done.

"How about running over to see Grandma and Grandpa for a little while?" she suggested when they finished. Restless and needing to get out of the house, she knew Kara would call before coming over. She could be back home in ten minutes or less to meet her.

As expected, her suggestion brought an enthusiastic response. And of course her parents were pleased to see them. They had a pleasant visit and returned home about five o'clock.

Still restless, Toni went to the kitchen and mixed up a chocolate cake while the boys took their showers. She was putting it in the oven when the doorbell rang.

Toni was startled when she found Chief Freeman standing in the doorway. Apprehension shot through her. Was she in big trouble for locating Dana and talking to her before notifying the police? "Hello, Buck. Come in."

He stepped inside the foyer. Solemn faced, with hat in hand, he followed her silently into the living room and eased his tall frame down onto the sofa. Toni sat in the rocker facing him.

Gabe bounded into the room. "Hey, we've got company."

"Hello, young man," the chief said, his smile seeming forced.

Garrett joined them. "Hi, Mr. Freeman."

"Hi, yourself." Buck extended a hand to Gabe, and then to Garrett.

"You two go on back to your games," Toni instructed after the greetings, her gut tight at the sure knowledge that the chief had not knocked on her door on a Saturday afternoon with good news.

"What's wrong?" she asked as soon as the boys left, dreading an answer but needing to get past whatever was bothering him.

Buck inhaled slowly, his face grim. "I have some bad news. Toni, I don't know what's going on at the school, but...well..."

"What is it?" she demanded, his hesitancy terrifying her now.

"Dustin Guthrie is dead," he said raggedly.

Toni was too stunned to speak. "No," she wailed in harsh denial. "He's just a kid. He can't be dead. What happened? Was there a wreck?"

"It looks like he committed suicide." The words were torn from him.

Toni covered her mouth with a hand as horror filled her. A sob worked its way up through her insides and shook her body. "This can't be happening," she whimpered. "I don't believe you."

"It's true," the chief insisted. "He left a note." He pulled a plastic bag from his pocket. "I haven't been to the station yet to submit it as evidence. It says he killed Marsha Carter." He waited for Toni to regain her composure.

She struggled to keep from fainting and blinked against the tears already leaking down her cheeks. "Maybe it's my fault." Her voice was as ragged as Buck's.

His brow furrowed. "How could it possibly be your fault?"

Toni took a deep breath and released the chair arm to swipe at her eyes, fighting to remain steady. "I saw an e-mail someone sent to some students. I should have done something."

"What e-mail?" he demanded gruffly.

Haltingly she explained about the e-mailed picture.

"What more could you have done?" he asked when she finished.

"I don't know," she moaned, shaking her clenched fists in the air.

"Mom, what's wrong?" Gabe peered around the doorway, Garrett behind him.

"I had to tell her that someone has died," the chief explained.

She swallowed and spoke to the boys as calmly as she could manage. "I'll be all right. Go ahead with what you were doing. I'll talk to you later."

They hesitated.

"It's okay," Buck assured them. "I need to talk to your mother some more. Then she can talk to you."

With reluctance they went back to their room.

"Tell me about it," Toni ordered, her voice a tiny bit steadier now as she fought for composure.

Buck exhaled heavily. "Dustin got out his rifle this morning and told his parents he was going squirrel hunting, which was not an unusual thing for him to do on a Saturday morning."

Toni knew that to be true. Kids around here hunted from the time they were big enough to hold a gun. In fact, hunting was so popular in the area, among both men and women, that their school was one of the few that still closed for the beginning of deer season. During turkey season they also had a high rate of absenteeism. Many locals paid no attention to those seasons, but hunted whatever and whenever they wanted. They didn't consider it poaching. To them it was just survival and everyday living.

"Dennis said Dustin usually comes in about lunch time," Buck continued, professionalism taking over and clearing his speech. "Today the boy didn't show up by noon, but they weren't concerned. When he hadn't shown up by three o'clock this afternoon, they began to worry. Fearing that he could have had an accident, they went searching for him."

"They probably know his favorite hunting spots."

The chief nodded. "They do, and they went to the usual places. At the third one, about four or five miles out of town on the highway, they found his black Ranger pickup parked next to the Bressler barn. The boy was about a hundred yards from the truck, sitting…" Buck's voice strangled and failed.

Toni waited for him to regain his composure.

"He was sitting up against a tree with the rifle in his hands. It's a terrible thing, but I thought I should give you an early notification."

"What about the parents? How are they?" Toni asked.

"The mother is in the hospital under sedation. She was hysterical."

"And Dennis?"

The chief shook his head. "He's just sitting there next to his wife, like he's frozen. He's the one who called us to the scene. He had his cell phone with him."

"Who found the note?"

"I did. It was in the pocket of Dustin's jacket." He held the plastic bag so that the words were visible. On a half sheet of paper Toni read two short sentences.

I killed Mrs. Carter. I'm sorry.
Dustin

Toni's heart bled as she thought of poor Dennis and his wife. "Dustin was spoiled and troublesome in class," she stuttered aloud, "but he shouldn't have ended up like this. For that matter, Marsha Carter—demanding, autocratic and manipulative as she was—didn't deserve to die the way she did either."

Startled by the dinging of the stove timer in the kitchen, Toni bounced to her feet. "I have a cake ready to come out of the oven."

Buck stood as well. "I have to get going."

Toni hurried to the kitchen and pulled the oven door open. Tapping the cake lightly with her finger, she determined that it was done and set it on top of the stove burner to cool. She rushed back to where the chief stood at the door, his hand on the knob.

"Thanks for taking time to come by and give me an advance notification. I appreciate it."

"I know how close this whole thing has been to you. And you've kept me informed. I thought you deserved the same." He put his hat on and left.

Toni pulled herself together enough to go tell the boys that one of her students had been found in the woods dead of a gunshot wound. Thankful they hadn't known Dustin personally, she was able to tell them about it without details. Sensing her state, they didn't ask too many questions, and she let them assume it was a hunting accident. They would soon hear differently, but maybe she would be better able to talk about it by then.

After their talk, Toni fixed sandwiches, frosted the cake, and fed the boys. But she couldn't eat. Sitting there watching them, it suddenly hit her that she should call her parents and John and Jenny Zachary. The story would spread quickly, but she knew they would appreciate a personal call. She picked up the phone, but before she could call, it rang. It was Kara.

"I'm on my way out," she said when Toni answered.

Toni gripped the phone so tight that her knuckles whitened. She wanted very much to see her friend, but she didn't know if she could control her emotions enough to visit. "Great," she said, forcing the word past her numb lips, and relieved when Kara disconnected immediately.

She sat down and dialed her parents.

"We know about Dustin, if that's why you're calling," her dad said when he answered.

"Yes," was all she could say. As a retired law enforcement officer, he had seen and heard so much over the years that he knew how to put up an emotional barrier when necessary, an ability Toni had not learned.

"Try to get some sleep," he ordered, his voice gruff.

That would be impossible, but Toni didn't argue.

"We'll talk later," he said and disconnected, understanding her inability to speak.

She dialed the Zachary's number. John's shock

equaled her own when Toni haltingly told him what had happened. They only spoke a couple of minutes, since they both found it hard to talk without crying.

Toni debated whether to call Kyle. She needed to hear his voice, but he would be home later tonight, and she didn't think she had the strength to make another call right now. The sound of a car pulling up outside made the decision for her. She would wait and talk to him in person. Toni took a deep breath and did her best to compose herself before going to the door.

"How was the auction?" she asked Kara as soon as she opened the door, speaking fast over the lump in her throat.

"Great." Wearing a warm smile, Kara stepped inside and caught Toni in a warm embrace. "It was held inside the big building behind the home where the Richardsons used to have their family business. Most auctions are held in the summer, but Mr. Richardson died last spring, and Mrs. Richardson in September. Their kids wanted to go ahead and get the house emptied and sell it, rather than have it sit vacant through the winter."

Kara's rush of words stopped abruptly as she backed up and got a good look at Toni's face. "What's wrong?"

Lips trembling, Toni placed a hand over her mouth. As the tears spilled from her eyes, she shook her head, unable to speak.

Kara took Toni's cold hands in her own and squeezed them. "Let's sit down." She led Toni to the sofa and guided her down onto it. "Now tell me about it," she ordered tenderly.

Toni heaved a steadying breath. "Police Chief

Freeman came by a few minutes ago to tell me that Dustin Guthrie committed suicide this morning."

Kara froze in shock, and then her arms came around Toni. "That's more terrible than I could have imagined. Dennis and his wife must be beside themselves."

With Kara still holding her, Toni choked out the story. When she finished, Kara was crying with her.

"Thanks for listening," Toni said finally, giving her eyes a wipe. "Now it's your turn. I detected on the phone yesterday that something is bothering you. Can you talk about it?"

Chapter 13

"It seems so trivial in light of this," Kara said with a wan smile. She released Toni's hands and went to stand in front of the entertainment center and stare at Toni and Kyle's wedding picture. "I'm getting really scared," she said in a soft voice.

Toni understood now. Kara feared another breakup near her wedding date. "Are you questioning your love for Logan, or are you afraid he'll change his mind at the last minute?"

Kara turned to face her. "I know I came close to making a huge mistake ten years ago. But now I've been independent so long that I'm afraid I won't be able to handle the give and take of marriage. I thought I loved Logan so much that we could handle any problems, but now that our wedding is only weeks away, I'm scared silly." Her gray eyes filmed over with tears.

"Come here." Toni patted the cushion beside her.

Kara resumed her place. "Yes, Momma," she said in an attempt at levity.

Toni managed a slight grin. "Will it make you feel any better to know that you're not the only one to ever go through this?"

Kara stared at her. "Not you. You and Kyle were

sweethearts forever."

Toni bobbed her head. "That's right. But when the wedding got close, I developed the shakes. At this point I can't even remember why I was so scared. I knew I loved Kyle and wanted to spend the rest of my life with him, but taking that big step into marriage was still scary."

Kara considered Toni's words. "But you went through with the wedding and found happiness with him."

"I did. I won't try to tell you that it's always been easy, but we've learned to work through our problems and learn from our mistakes. At least most of them," she qualified, thinking of their current lack of togetherness. "Marriage is work. But it's worth it."

For the next hour they talked, sharing their thoughts and feelings. The visit seemed to provide something they each needed. It lifted Kara's spirits and helped Toni hold thoughts of Dustin's death temporarily at bay.

"How long has it been since you talked to that fiancé of yours?" Toni asked when the conversation came to a lull.

"A couple of days. He was going to come see me last week, but something came up at the fort and his leave got cancelled."

Logan was stationed at Fort Leonard Wood and thinking of making a career of the military. He and Kara had met when he attended a workshop on fingerprinting that Kara had conducted at the college about four years ago. He had stayed after class to ask some questions, and a conversation had developed. Logan was a Springfield native, and, since the town was within the fifty-mile radius he was allowed to travel from the post when on leave, he was able to visit his parents and some of his old high school chums regularly. He had begun to contact Kara during those visits.

Their friendship had been interrupted by a year's deployment to Korea, but when he returned, it had blossomed into romance.

The sound of the William Tell Overture erupted from Kara's purse. When she pulled out her cell phone and checked the ID, a smile lit her face. "It's Logan."

"I'll fix us something to drink," Toni said as Kara greeted her fiancé. She waggled her fingers and left the room. To give Kara some privacy, she took her time in the kitchen, fixing mugs of hot apple cider and a tray of chips and salsa.

When she returned to the living room minutes later, Kara was ending her call. Toni set the mugs on the coffee table. "How about sustenance?"

"I'm not hungry, but the cider smells and looks good," Kara said, her spirits much improved.

"Did talking to him help calm your jitters?"

Kara nodded and inhaled a deep breath. "I feel much better. The first thing he said was how much he's looking forward to being married to me. I guess I just needed to hear him say that."

She paused, as if gauging her next words. "I told Logan about Dustin's suicide. His first response was sympathy, of course. But his next comment was to point out how, on crime shows, anytime you hear of a suicide, foul play is suspected."

Toni started to brush off the observation, but

hesitated. "Those shows create distrust and suspicion at everything," she said after a moment. "Buck didn't sound suspicious when he showed me Dustin's note. But he didn't say he was satisfied with the conclusion, either," she added slowly.

"Logan asked a lot of questions that I couldn't answer," Kara continued. "He wanted to know about the position of the gun, gunshot residue, things like that. I told him it only happened this morning, that you just heard about it this afternoon, and that you never said anything about it being suspicious."

For some reason the conversation caused Toni's world to tip on its axis. When Buck told her about Dustin, she had been so shocked and grief stricken that she had not thought beyond the obvious. She shook her head in denial. "Buck would have said something if he suspected anything other than what it appeared to be."

"Would he?" Kara's question was soft.

Toni only had to think about it for a second. "No, he probably wouldn't. If he suspected anything wrong, he would only share that with his officers."

"Well, if there's anything out of whack, I'm sure he'll work on it. He's pretty savvy. He became police chief after I left here, but my parents have always said good things about him."

Kara finished her cider, put the mug down, and picked up her purse. "I need to go. My parents are expecting me."

After they parted at the door, Toni wrestled a wave of emotions. She was glad for the visit with her friend, and for Kara's improved state of mind. But now everything came back at her in a rush. She clamped down on her thoughts and went to check on the boys, relieved to find them getting ready for bed. She took a quick shower and crawled into her own bed.

Once under the covers, the horrible reality of Dustin's death began to replace the initial shock and denial. As it sank in, Toni let grief have its way. Deep, wrenching sobs wracked her body. The entire month had taken its toll. Marsha's death, followed by the attack on Garrett, and then the shooting attack on her, had left her stunned and uncertain. This latest death could not be borne. Her whole body churned with grief—and anger.

Dear God in heaven, how can such evil exist? Why are these things happening? Please stop them.

Gradually the tears lessened, and she lay staring up in the dark, struggling to breathe through stuffy sinuses. The tears had given her a small measure of relief, but now she was numb. She tossed and turned for what seemed like hours, unable to stop the horrible visions flashing through her mind. Finally she fell into an exhausted and troubled sleep.

A hand on her shoulder woke her sometime later. Toni forced her swollen eyes open to find Kyle sitting on the side of the bed. The small bedside light glowed behind him. He stared at her red puffy eyes.

"What's wrong?" His voice was deep with concern.

Toni reached for him, grateful when he pulled her into his arms. She buried her face in his shoulder and told him about Dustin.

He simply held her, while the front of his shirt grew wet from her fresh torrent of tears.

*

They had an excellent pastor, but in church the next morning Toni had a difficult time focusing on his sermon. Then suddenly the scripture he was reading from the book of Jeremiah penetrated her fuzzy brain.

"A voice was heard in Ramah, lamentation, and bitter weeping; Rahel weeping for her children refused to be comforted for her children, because they were not."

Toni had lost track of the context of the sermon, but she had an instant sense of empathy for women, and men, weeping for their children. She thought of the Guthries, and of her personal feelings regarding her own child being threatened, and she began to pray silently.

Lord, please be with the Guthries. And don't let anything happen to Garrett. Please don't let any more of these awful things happen.

After the benediction, she was solemn as she exited the church with Kyle and the boys. When they were in the minivan, she glanced over at Kyle, and then back at the boys. "I don't feel much like being around people. Would you mind if we just go home and make hamburgers?"

"Sounds fine to me," Kyle responded.

"Great idea, Mom," came from Gabe. Garrett just nodded.

By the time lunch was over, all Toni could think about was a nap. The amount of sleep she had gotten the night before had been broken and not restful. That, plus the emotional toll, had her exhausted. She started for the bedroom, but was waylaid by the ringing of the phone.

"There will be an assembly in the gymnasium first hour tomorrow morning," Ken Douglas said when she answered.

"I'll call Loretta," Toni said lethargically.

She made the call and then crawled onto the bed, thankful that Kyle had taken the boys to get milk shakes. She knew he had made the offer to give her some time alone, as well as giving him a chance to spend time with his sons. She appreciated it.

*

A somber crowd of ninth through twelfth graders assembled in the gymnasium Monday morning immediately after attendance and lunch counts were taken. The students filed in and took their seats without their usual boisterousness. They sat in sections by grade on one side of the gym, while teachers occupied chairs along the wall facing them.

A small portable amplifier, microphone, and lightweight podium were positioned on the floor. Having drawn another tough assignment in his short tenure as acting superintendent, Ryan Prewitt stepped to the podium and addressed the students and staff in a strained and somber voice. "As I'm sure you all know by now, we have suffered another tragic loss among us."

Faces stared straight ahead, listening silently, with eyes being dabbed around the room. Toni's pain paralleled the thick grief and pain of the students. The acid in her stomach slithered up into her throat, strangling her.

"Our sympathies go out to the Guthrie family," Ryan continued. "They have informed us that there will be visitation at the funeral home tomorrow evening from five until nine. The funeral will be Wednesday at two p.m. at the Woolison Funeral Chapel. School will be dismissed right after lunch to allow all those who wish to attend to do so."

He paused and motioned for the small group of adults sitting with Kelly Graham to come forward. "We have counselors from other schools in the area who have volunteered to make themselves available to any students or adults wishing to speak with one."

There were introductions of the counselors, along with directives as to where each would be located. When students began stepping forward to indicate their desire to talk to one of them, the meeting was dismissed with instructions to report to second hour classes. Those remaining were assigned to specific counselors.

As Toni exited through the gym doorway, Ryan caught up with her. "Chief Freeman brought Marsha's computer back this morning. Can you look at it during your free period?"

"I'll be there. Your office or the superintendent's?"

"Superintendent's. See you then." He took off up the hall.

At the end of second hour Toni took a blank flash drive from the supply cabinet in her room and slipped it into her purse. Then she hurried to the administrative offices.

"Come on in," Ryan said when she peered inside his doorway. He stood and rounded the desk. "It's all yours for now. There are some matters in my regular job that need my attention, so that's where I'll be if you need me."

Anxious to get started, Toni perched behind the desk and booted the computer that someone—she assumed Ryan—had taken the trouble to hook up for her. She wasn't interested in the kind of in-depth checking that the technicians would have already done. She located Marsha's word processing files, which were voluminous. There was no way she could scan them meaningfully in the forty-five minutes she had. She took the flash drive from her purse, put it in the drive, and copied all the files and folders onto it.

Next she accessed the e-mail account, discovering that it had been previously opened and the password saved. *Thank you*, she breathed silently to whoever had done it, not caring whether it had been Marsha, or if a technician had figured it out. She added copies of those folders to the flash drive and put it back in her purse.

The remainder of the time Toni spent browsing through everything she could think to check, and finding nothing of significance. She shut down the computer and returned to her classroom with only five minutes to spare before the bell would ring.

Classes were conducted in an abnormally quiet atmosphere with no pressure being exerted. Toni kept the students as busy as possible without any kind of stress, allowing them to work individually or in groups, and making no objection if they drifted into quiet conversations or even periods of despondent inactivity.

Seventh hour was the worst, because Dustin's absence was such a noticeable and harsh reminder of its permanence. Jodi Garrison was present. Sidney

Rayford was not.

When the bell rang at the end of class, Jodi approached Toni's desk. "Uh, do you have any work you would like help with?" she asked quietly.

Toni smiled. "I can always use an extra pair of hands. Why don't you make sure all supplies are put away and computers shut down and covered properly? I'll be back in a few moments."

She went next door to John's room. He looked up as she entered. "I'll get the boys," he said, reading her face before she could speak.

She thanked him briefly and returned to her own room.

"Everything's in order," Jodi said.

"How long do you need to stay?" Toni asked while scooping a jumble of work sheets from the last class into a stack for grading.

Jodi gave her a half smile, half grimace. "An hour or so."

"Fine. Why don't you get comfortable and do your homework. But before you start, would you run down to the vending machines and get us both a cold drink?" Toni took some money from her wallet.

"Oh, I don't want you buying anything for me." Jodi shook her head in refusal.

"I'd really like to," Toni insisted. "Please?"

After a hesitation, Jodi took the money and left.

Toni called Kyle and explained that she would be home a little later than expected. Without asking questions, he said he would start supper. She disconnected and started grading the papers. Minutes later Jodi returned and plunked a can of iced tea onto her desk. She laid some change beside it. "Thanks."

Gabe and Garrett charged into the room.

John waved from the doorway. "I need to run." He disappeared.

"Have a seat and eat those," Toni told the boys, indicating the Popsicles they carried. "Then you can get a game from the supply cabinet."

Jodi settled in with her homework, and Toni continued grading papers. Her eyes were getting bleary when the sound of Jodi's book closing made her look up.

Jodi got to her feet. "I can go now. Thanks."

*

Kyle was taking a ham and broccoli casserole from the oven when Toni and the boys arrived home. After they ate, he took the boys to McDonald's for Blizzards.

Even though Toni had wished for time alone with Kyle, right now all she wanted was some time totally alone. Grateful for it, she settled on the sofa with her laptop, plugged the flash drive into it, and began browsing through the files she had copied. It was quite a hodge-podge, everything from notes from Jack Rayford, to memos from state departments, to notices of e-Bay purchases. She started working through them alphabetically. *A+ School. Accelerated Schools. Accounting and Procurement. Accreditation and Classification. ACT. Building Codes.*

It was dry reading, test scores and percentages, comparisons of each to the one before it. Halfway through *Career Ladder,* the doorbell interrupted.

When Toni opened the door, she found a distraught teenager standing under the porch light. Sidney Rayford's face and eyes were red and blotchy, and tears glistened on her cheeks. She drew a ragged breath and burst into speech. "Mrs. Donovan, Dustin didn't commit suicide. He wouldn't have done that. I know he wouldn't."

Toni extended a hand. "Please come inside."

The next thing she knew, the sobbing girl was in her arms. She pulled Sidney close and rubbed a hand over her shoulders. "Let's get to where it's warm."

Toni closed the door and steered the girl to a seat on the sofa, carefully moving her laptop onto the coffee table and closing the lid. Then she just held Sidney while she wept, stroking her long blonde tresses that lacked their usual sheen from brushing. She cried with the teenager, her heart aching as their tears streamed.

When the storm eased, Sidney shuddered and drew from Toni's arms. She ran a hand over her tear-ravaged face. "You tell us in class to study the evidence," she challenged brokenly.

Toni lifted the box of tissues from the coffee table. "Here. Let's talk about it."

"He didn't commit suicide," Sidney repeated, pulling a tissue from the box. She wiped her eyes and blew her nose. "I know he didn't."

"Tell me how you know he didn't." Toni took the girl's hand in her own.

Sidney sat up straighter and struggled for composure. "Mrs. Donovan," she said when she could speak. "I know I haven't always been the best student for you."

"It's okay, Sidney." Toni fought the tightness in her throat.

"I knew you were the one person who would

listen to me," Sidney went on doggedly. "You respect the facts."

"What *are* the facts?" Toni asked. "Can you just relax and tell me about it?"

Sidney nodded. "Dustin could be a pain. I know that," she began, her mouth trembling. "But he wasn't suicidal. He had an ego, and he hadn't been depressed or withdrawn. He drank sometimes, but he didn't do drugs, and he was never bored. He was a guard on the basketball team, full of life and looking forward to winning the district championship. Does that sound like someone considering killing himself?" she demanded, her voice rising in pitch.

"It doesn't seem to fit the profile of a suicidal person," Toni agreed carefully.

"He loved life. He loved a lot of things," Sidney added, her speech trailing to a halt. After a moment she struggled on. "I thought he loved me, and I still think he did, but…"

"But what? Are you afraid he loved someone else as well?"

Sidney nodded. "He was seeing someone else, but I don't know who."

"How do you know?"

Sidney took a long shuddering breath. "I'm a teacher's aide for Coach Hopper during sixth hour. I help him get things set up in the gym before games, or when an assembly or community meeting is scheduled in there. I also help in the office, typing schedules and things like that."

Toni listened in silence, letting the girl tell her story her way.

"Lately Coach's PE supplies have been

disappearing, and some equipment has been vandalized. So I decided to investigate."

Now Toni smiled. "Putting your detective skills to work, huh?"

Sidney shrugged and gave her a weak smile in return. "Monday, while Coach Hopper was in the gym with his class and I was in the office typing schedules, I hid my digital camera on a shelf in the room. I set it to automatically take a picture every five minutes."

"I remember you being upset Tuesday."

"That's because I was mad at Dustin for breaking our Monday night date. Anyhow, during sixth hour that day Coach Hopper sent me to deliver some memos to teachers, so I didn't have time to retrieve my camera until after school while Coach and the team had basketball practice in the gym."

Toni began to grasp the significance. "You found the picture after school Tuesday."

Sidney nodded miserably. "As soon as I checked the camera, I found that picture of Dustin with…with some other girl." Her voice broke.

Toni knew what was coming next.

"I was so mad at him for lying and two-timing me that I couldn't sleep that night. So Wednesday morning I got up early and e-mailed the picture to all the kids on my address list. Now he's dead, and it's my fault," she wailed, dissolving into tears again.

"No, it's not your fault," Toni assured her. "You were hurt and striking out, but you didn't cause his death."

"I was mad and looking for revenge," Sidney insisted.

"You're growing up. We all make mistakes. Some of them are just worse than others. The important thing is to learn from them and not repeat them."

"Is there anything I can do?" Sidney pleaded.

"You can't erase anything, but you can answer a couple more questions for me."

Sidney hiccupped and rubbed the back of her hands over her eyes. "I will if I can."

"Are you sure you have no idea who Dustin was with in the picture?" She didn't mention that she had seen it.

Sidney shook her head. "No. I was so stupid. I thought I was the only one he was going out with, until Monday night when he cancelled our date. I was suspicious then, but I had no proof."

"Until your camera caught them in the coach's office. Did you and Dustin date much during the week, or mostly on weekends?"

"Our parents wouldn't let us go out more than once or twice a week, said we had to get our rest and keep our grades up. Not that Dustin worried about the grades," she added, her mouth twisted and trembling. "Monday night we were supposed to go to the ballgame together, but he caught me in the hall second hour and said he had to run some errands for his parents before the game and wouldn't get done in time to come get me. I thought it was pretty lame."

"Which ticked you off, and you were letting him know about it in class the next day."

Sidney nodded. "Sometimes he would tell his parents he was going hunting. Then I would make up an excuse to leave my house, and we would meet somewhere."

Toni's brain spun. "Like Saturday?"

She nodded. "He was found at one of the places we used to meet."

"So you think he met someone else there."

"Yes," she whispered, her eyes pinched shut.

"But if he was there for a meeting—and not hunting—why did he have the gun with him?"

Sidney only thought a moment before coming up with an explanation. "He always took his gun so his parents would believe he was really going hunting. When he got there he always kept it with him. He would never leave a gun in his truck where it could be seen and stolen."

Toni squeezed the girl's hand. "I am so sorry about all this. I wish I could fix it, but I can't. You've given me a lot to think about and discuss with the police, though."

Sidney had calmed down considerably. "Thank you for listening," she said, withdrawing her hand and reaching for her purse. "I need to get home. I told Mom I'd only be gone an hour."

As Sidney pulled out of the drive, Kyle and the boys returned. Toni sent the boys to take their showers and told Kyle about the girl's visit.

"I think you need to call Buck," Kyle said when she finished.

She did just that.

Chapter 14

Toni Donovan again," she said when Buck answered. Then she launched right into the story of Sidney's visit. "The girl is convinced Dustin didn't commit suicide, and I think she made some good arguments."

"The kid's gun was a twenty-two rifle, he was using long rifle twenty-two shells, and there was a small amount of gunshot residue on his hands," the chief enumerated thoughtfully.

"But did he pull the trigger on his own, or did he have help?"

The chief's heavy sigh whistled across the line. "Toni, are you just looking for trouble where there isn't any, or are you saying you think someone killed him?"

She didn't want to antagonize him, but she couldn't just drop it. "I had Dustin in class every day, and I never saw any indication that he was suicidal."

There was a long pause. When Buck finally spoke, his voice was tinged with irritation. "It looked like a suicide, and there was a suicide note."

Almost afraid to say more, but driven by an invisible force, she persisted. "What if it was just made to look like a suicide? And what about the note? It was printed, not cursive. He never printed his classroom assignments. Are you sure he wrote it?"

"Listen to me, Toni," Buck snapped. "There was nothing to indicate it was anything but a suicide. Besides, who would kill a kid like that? I understand your reluctance to accept that a student would do such a thing, but there's just nothing to suggest otherwise."

Toni decided she had no choice but to drop it. "Okay, I just wanted to let you know about Sidney's visit. I'll talk to you later."

After she disconnected, Toni sat staring at the phone in her hand.

"What's the matter?" Kyle, still holding the remote, had muted the television. "Don't you think it was suicide?"

"I think Sidney made some very valid points," she said slowly. "When Kara told her fiancé about the suicide, his first reaction was to point out how foul play is always suspected when there's a suicide in crime shows. It seemed like a joke at the time, but now I can't get away from the idea. I'd hate to see something get overlooked."

"And someone get away with murder."

She put the phone on the coffee table. "It doesn't feel right. There aren't many coincidences in this world. And I can't stop thinking about the two deaths and wondering if they're connected."

Creases formed between his brows. "You think the same person who killed Marsha may have killed a student?"

She shook her head slowly. "I don't know. I realize the causes of death were completely different. One was beaten, the other shot. The beating was a crime of passion, committed with the first weapon handy. The second, if it was murder, was premeditated. But the area where Dustin was found isn't unusual. His parents said he often went hunting there, so other people surely knew that as well."

"But what would have been the reason?"

"That's where I'm stuck. They seem so unrelated. Of course..." She became silent, pondering.

"What?" He put the remote on the table and leaned forward, his elbows on his thighs.

"What if whoever killed Marsha felt threatened by Dustin for some reason? What if the boy found out who did it and was making threats?"

His mouth pulled back in a tight frown. "That's pretty farfetched."

Everything Toni could remember bounced around in her mind, trying to connect. Marsha had made a lot of enemies. The teachers resented her, as did the support staff. She had offended people in the community. She had convinced a married man to leave his wife and kids for her.

Dustin, on the other hand, was too young to have left such a string of broken relationships. But he *had* caused trouble for a number of people. He had disrupted classes. He had been unfaithful to his steady girlfriend. Toni froze.

Marsha had been involved with Jack Rayford. Dustin had been involved with Sidney Rayford. In both cases a lot of people were hurt and angry, but the common denominator was Janet Rayford. Janet would have hated Marsha for taking her husband, and Dustin for hurting her daughter. Could Janet have killed Marsha? Toni could kick herself for not checking on the woman more thoroughly.

Another possibility floated through her brain.

Could Dustin truly have killed Marsha? Could Janet have recruited him to do it? He had been dating her daughter, which meant he was a familiar face at the Rayford home. If Janet had recruited him, could Dustin have become scared of getting caught? Or maybe he just saw a way to pull Janet's strings and threatened her. Or was there a completely different rationale? Maybe, if he became a threat, Janet changed her approach and seduced the boy, and then killed him.

Even if all these things were true, would anyone listen to her? Toni doubted it. Everyone accepted that it was a suicide. The case would be closed.

*

The first thing Toni did when she got to her classroom Tuesday morning was call the technology director and cancel her request for him to trace the e-mail.

As she finished the call, Ken Douglas entered her classroom, his countenance drawn and fatigued. His eyes swept over her forest green blazer and matching green shoes, but he didn't comment as he normally would have. "I wanted to catch you before classes start and apologize for forgetting to check that e-mail you sent me. Things were hectic, but I should have gotten to it."

"Don't worry about it. It wouldn't have made any difference."

His brow furrowed. "You know where it came from?"

"I rushed to get here early this morning so I

could tell Dillon to not waste any more time tracing it. I planned to talk to you if I could catch up with you." She gave him the condensed version of Sidney's visit.

He covered his face with his hands. "When is this nightmare going to end?" he groaned, his head rotating back and forth in misery. Then he glanced up at the clock and gave a startled jump. "I have to run. The first bell rings in about thirty seconds."

Toni went next door and peeked inside John's room. "Would you like to go with me to talk to Janet Rayford after school?"

He looked up from adjusting a microscope. "Sure. I know Jenny will be happy to look after the boys."

"I'll fill you in later," she promised as the bell rang.

*

As soon as Jenny left school with the boys, Toni and John headed for her red minivan. The sun was out, but the inside of the van still felt like an icebox.

"You're turning into a real detective," John commented while they waited for the heater to warm. "Did you ever think about going into police work?"

"It crossed my mind several times," she admitted. "Having a dad in law enforcement taught me to question acts and motives. I learned to love science from both my parents, but from different perspectives. My dad saw it as helpful in getting evidence. My mother saw it as important in saving lives. I respected both."

"Did either of them ever pressure you to follow in their footsteps?"

"Not really." She put the van into motion. "Dad was stern, but the boys and I knew he loved us. He always seemed to enjoy my interest in his work, but he never tried to make a cop of me. As for Mom, she was gone a lot and always too busy, but we understood the importance of her work. I know this sounds corny, but teaching is my way of making the world a better place. I like the challenge of managing a classroom and sharing knowledge that could benefit the lives of my students."

John grinned. "Your teaching has always been simply classroom science, but now you're using it to solve actual cases."

"Maybe." She steered out of the parking lot. "I don't seem to be very successful at this point."

"You're not giving up the effort," he pointed out. "Whatever the outcome, you'll have given it your best. It sounds like you had a good childhood."

His return to the earlier topic surprised her. "I did, but don't get the idea that everything was perfect. We had our good and bad times, our little conflicts and differences. But we always worked through things. What about you?"

"My mom was the stay-at-home kind. My dad was a workaholic and gone a lot, but overall we had a solid upbringing."

Toni pulled into the Rayford driveway. "Okay, here goes nothing."

They marched up the walk together, and Toni pushed the doorbell. "I wonder if Janet will be sober or drinking again."

Janet appeared in the doorway, dressed in a business suit, her long dark hair done up in a stylish arrangement. Her expression was pleasant enough—until she recognized them. Then the smile turned to a scowl.

"Hi," Toni greeted her cheerfully. "May we visit with you for a few minutes?"

"I'm pretty busy," Janet hedged, obviously not thrilled at their presence.

"We won't take much of your time," Toni promised.

"Oh, all right." The words and tone were ungracious, but she backed up to allow them entrance. "Come on inside."

John went to an occasional chair, while Toni sat on the sofa. Janet took the rocker across from them and tugged on her stylishly short skirt as it rode high on her legs. "What do you want now?"

John gave her a disarming smile. "We both have Sidney in class, and we know how much Dustin's death has upset her."

Janet seemed to relax a little at the mention of her daughter. "Yes, she's taking it really hard. Everyone is," she added stiffly.

"I assume you knew Dustin pretty well," Toni ventured.

Janet frowned, and her gaze became frosty. "What is it you really want to know?"

Toni steeled herself to say what she must. "We've had two tragic deaths in the past few weeks, and we're just looking for any information that might help us figure out exactly what happened."

"I can tell you what happened to Marsha Carter," Janet hissed bitterly. "Someone did the world a favor and killed her. The police have asked hundreds of questions and haven't figured out who to give a medal to for the deed, and now here you are still asking questions. What's going on?" Her voice had risen in shrillness.

"We're aware of your circumstances and how much that death affected you," Toni said, hoping to placate the woman. "We're aware that this latest death has also affected you through your daughter. We were wondering when the last time you spoke with Dustin was and what you can remember about his behavior."

Janet's eyes narrowed. "Exactly what are you asking?"

"We just want to learn more about his contacts and behavior over the past few days. Did he seem depressed or upset? Was there anything unusual about his behavior, anything that would indicate he was thinking of taking his own life?"

Janet's tone chilled. "No, I don't recall anything different."

"When was the last time you saw him?"

"Sometime last week, not that it's any of your business," she snapped. "And if the next question is where was I Saturday morning, that's none of your business either. But I'll tell you anyhow. I was here talking to my dear departed husband—not dead, just departed," she added with acrid sarcasm. Then she emitted a harsh laugh. "He wanted to know if we could patch things up and try again. And, no, I can't prove it. Considering that I told him to take a flying leap, and knowing that Jack isn't Mr. Straight-and-Narrow, we have to expect that he probably would take great delight in not providing me with an alibi—

if I need one."

"I'm sorry, we didn't mean to…"

"Yes, you meant to ask me for alibis for the times of both those deaths," she interrupted. "And now this conversation is over." She stalked to the door and jerked it open.

In the car a few seconds later, Toni looked over at John and winced. "Ouch!"

John grinned, then sobered. "Do you think this is a case of a lady protesting too much?"

"I'm not sure," Toni responded thoughtfully. "She sounds pretty believable, but she certainly managed to avoid providing alibis for when Marsha was killed, or for the times of the rundown in the parking lot and shooting at the lake."

"Did you have anything else in mind for today?"

"I wish we could talk to the Guthries, but they're distraught and facing the ordeal of their son's funeral. Even if that weren't the case, I'm not sure I'm tough enough for another eviction right now."

"The police chief probably wouldn't be too happy with us talking to them right now, either," John said with a philosophic shrug.

*

The next morning Toni wore a sensible blue pantsuit with navy shoes and blouse to school, determined to appear calm and keep her mind on academics. But by lunchtime more questions had risen to plague her. She went next door to see John. "I'd like to talk to the coaches after school."

He nodded and waved her on her way. "I'll get the offspring and wait for you here."

As soon as her last class dismissed, Toni headed

for the gym to find Jordan Hopper and Lisa Baker. She marched across the shiny floor to where the dressing rooms, showers, and offices of the coaches were located.

Jordan's door was ajar. When Toni stuck her head inside, she was happy to find him seated at his desk. It looked like he was going over game schedules.

He looked up. "Hi. What's on your mind?"

She stepped into the small room. "Got a minute?"

"Sure," he returned amicably. "Have a seat." He reached for the peanut butter and jelly sandwich that lay near the desk calendar he was studying. "Got to stay over tonight, run a few drills, and then get on the bus to go to an away game. Teachers eat so elegantly," he said dryly before taking a big bite.

Toni nodded agreement. "Twenty minute lunches and after school duties don't allow for much fine dining. No wonder we're such pigs."

"What can I do for you?" he asked between inelegant bites.

"I'd like to ask you and Lisa about Dustin's recent behavior."

"Lisa had a dental appointment right after school, so there's only me."

"That's okay. You should be able to help me. In addition to being teacher aides in the P.E. department, I believe Dustin and Sidney spent a lot of time in the gym after school."

Jordan frowned. "I suppose so. Dustin was on the basketball team, and Sidney is a cheerleader, so it was a natural hangout. Dustin had practice nearly every day, and Sid hung around a lot. She ran errands for us."

"What about Dustin's behavior? I mean, did he seem depressed or upset lately?"

Jordan gave her an intense look. "Are you implying that you don't think he committed suicide?"

Toni shrugged. "Sidney is convinced that he didn't."

"You've talked to her?"

Toni repeated the tale of Sidney's visit. "I think she made some valid points. Can you tell me anything that will confirm that he was suicidal?"

Jordan swigged from a can of Dr. Pepper, eyeing her over the top of it. "No, I can't really think of anything out of the ordinary," he said when he put it down.

Toni's gaze swept over his office. A picture of his wife and kids adorned the wall behind him, and an oversized calendar and pictures of the basketball team filled the wall to his left. The calendar was covered with notations of game times and locations, along with names of game officials. The wall to her right was lined with shelves loaded with sports equipment and scorebooks. She noticed a long handled, heavy-duty flashlight lying along the back of a shelf. She forced her attention back to what Jordan was saying.

"As a matter of fact, I was just talking with Lisa this afternoon before she left, and we were wondering what could possibly have been going through Dustin's mind."

"So you're saying you never noticed any kind of personality change or physical complaints, anything like that?"

"No," he repeated. "But I have to admit that it

doesn't sound like he was on a suicidal track. I remember one day last week he was kind of worked up over wanting to buy a jeep. I got the impression that his parents weren't in favor of the idea, thought since he already had a pickup that he didn't need to add to his collection of wheels. I think he also has a four-wheeler and a motorcycle. Had, I mean," he amended grimly.

Toni glanced at her watch. "I guess I'd better run. My boys are waiting for me."

Back in John's room, she found him wearing a serious expression. "I heard your phone ringing across the hall, so I went over and answered it. Chief Freeman wants you to stop by and chat with him."

"I'll swing by on my way home."

Gabe had his coat on, his trombone case clutched in his right hand. Garrett pulled the last chunk of Popsicle off its stick into his mouth, making him look like a chipmunk. He tossed the stick into the trash. "Um..um..um," he mumbled, motioning that he was ready to go and grabbing his coat.

"Do you have something to occupy yourselves with while I visit with the Chief?" she asked as they climbed into the van.

"I could practice my trombone," Gabe said with an impish grin.

Toni raised her brows and made a fake swipe at him.

"I have something to read," Garrett said. "Or the deputies might talk to us."

Buck Freeman was in the front office when Toni entered and parked the boys in their usual chairs near the door. "Glad you could make it. Come inside my office and have a seat."

She followed him and took the chair near his desk.

He met her curious look and got right to the point. "I've decided you might be helpful to me. Sometimes a person outside law enforcement can add a fresh perspective. Overall, you've been a pretty good sounding board, and your role at the school is especially helpful in this case. I'd like to hear a little more of your thoughts."

Toni gave him a wide-eyed look. "That's high praise. I'm flattered."

"First, let's talk about your bookkeeper and her alibi," Buck began in his gruff, no-nonsense manner. "We found an attendant at the gas station who knows her personally, and he remembers seeing her put gas in her car the evening Marsha was killed. He says he remembers the date because he's a student, and he had gotten out of school early that day for Christmas break. The other reason he says he remembers it is because Dana seemed so upset. He said she looked pretty chewed up—his words, not mine—like maybe she had been in a fight or something. Said her face was red and swollen on one side like she'd been hit, and she was crying."

Toni nodded. "I guess that means she didn't do it."

"I don't think she did," the chief agreed. "But she's still on the hook for embezzlement."

If Dana had been the killer, it would have been a relief to have the matter settled. But Toni had to admit that, deep down in her gut, she couldn't fathom poor Dana committing such a violent act. Not only was she physically small, but she didn't have an explosiveness about her.

Buck continued speaking. "I'm ready to admit that you might be onto something with the Guthrie boy. I did some refresher reading on the warning signs of teenage suicide, and then I started checking on the kid's activities prior to his death. The Guthries say he didn't seem upset to them. In fact, they say it was more like he had been on a high lately. I went through that list of suicide warning signs with them, and they denied every one. According to them, nothing really bad had happened, and they aren't aware of any major quarrels between Dustin and anyone."

"There was the spat with Sidney," Toni pointed out. "But she's truly broken up over his death and even blaming herself. I don't think she had anything to do with it."

"Dustin hadn't been giving away his favorite possessions," the chief said. "Dennis showed me his room and said that nothing was missing. His wife even showed me a stack of movies that he bought just recently. They both said Dustin wanted to buy a jeep."

Toni nodded. "That checks with what Coach Hopper told me today. We've already established that his Saturday morning hunting trip was not unusual. I think there's a killer out there."

The chief looked troubled. "You might be right."

"One or two killers?"

His expression clouded even more. "The big question is Dustin's whereabouts on the night Marsha was killed. If he didn't kill her, my guess is that there's only one killer. Whoever killed Marsha killed Dustin to shut him up, at the same time putting the blame for her death on him to get us to stop looking."

"There's something else you might check," Toni said uneasily.

Buck's eyes rolled upward. "What have you done now?"

"John Zachary and I went to see Janet Rayford, and she pretty much threw us out."

His eyes drilled her, unblinking.

"I was trying to make a connection between the two murders," Toni explained defensively. "It occurred to me that Marsha's involvement with Jack Rayford, and Dustin's with Sidney Rayford, might somehow be a connector. I hoped to find out where Janet was during the times of the murders and the attack on my son."

Buck's head bobbed in understanding. "I'll put someone on it."

"Janet said she was home talking to Jack Saturday morning. She said he wanted to try to patch things up and get back together, but that he probably won't give her an alibi because she turned him down."

"That would be a petty motive for lying. We'll have to find out."

"Good."

"Okay, I guess that's it," the chief said. "Unless there's something else on your mind. You have that look on your face."

"I've been putting some thought into how a murder could have been staged as a suicide."

Interest flashed across his face. "Have you come

up with a scenario?"

"I think so. I tried to imagine that I wanted to commit such an act and figured out how I would go about it."

He grinned at that.

"Dustin could have been shot, and then the killer could have put his hand on the trigger and fired a second shot," she theorized, envisioning it in her mind. "The gun would have been wiped off after the first shot, and only one of the shell casings left behind."

"An interesting theory," the chief allowed. "Almost makes sense."

"I know that rifles aren't as likely as small guns to test for residue on hands, and that collecting evidence as soon as possible is important, which are problems in this case," Toni continued. "But I'm hoping your tests were good."

He shrugged. "The results weren't great, but we took pictures of what we got. The one thing that's in our favor is that it didn't look like anything had been disturbed at the scene. The best pictures are of the clothing. Nothing out of order was noted."

"I'd like to know if Dustin's prints were on the forearm of the gun."

He stared at her, his expression thoughtful. "No prints there would mean that he could not have fired the gun?"

Toni nodded. "He would have had to touch more than just the trigger to anchor it in position and fire it."

He made a note. "I suppose it's worth checking."

"May I see the pictures and the actual report? I'd

also like to see the file on Marsha if I may."

Buck made another note, grinning this time. "As you may know, we have our autopsies done in Farmington. We haven't gotten Dustin's body and paperwork back yet, but they're supposed to be here in the morning. I'll visit with you again after I get them. Anything else?"

"No, but if I think of anything, I'll let you know," she said with an impertinent wrinkle of her nose. She picked up her purse to leave.

"One more thing," Buck said before she could get away. "I talked to all three of your administrators, and they agreed to schedule a special faculty meeting tomorrow after school. I want to lay out some facts to the staff and see if we can find any help there."

"Good idea."

As soon as she got home, Toni called her parents and arranged for them to pick up the boys from school the next day. John and Jenny would have to attend the faculty meeting.

Chapter 15

Toni, Jenny and John entered the cafeteria together and sat at a table in the second row for the faculty meeting. The three principals, the chief of police, and the resource officer stood facing them from behind a table at the front of the room.

Buck Freeman walked around the table to them and leaned down to speak softly to Toni. "The medical examiner rechecked that autopsy report. He says the evidence and pictures aren't the best. The index finger that pulled the trigger was completely clean on top, but it probably means nothing."

Her fists clenched. "It may not be good enough for proof, but it's significant to me."

"He also took another look at Marsha's autopsy report, but he didn't find anything new."

"We've got a second murder," Toni muttered in fury as the chief walked away, but low enough that only John and Jenny heard her.

Toni constrained the anger boiling inside her and studied the room. Members of the board, with Dennis Guthrie significantly absent, sat at a table to themselves. The secretary, counselor, and technology director sat at a table to the right of them.

Darren Brown, the industrial arts teacher, entered

the room with Lisa Baker and Jordan Hopper. Darren's jeans still showed traces of sawdust and splotches of varnish from the shop. Jordan and Lisa wore their customary gym shoes and sweats. Jordan's dark crew cut was a sharp contrast to Lisa's ash blonde ponytail and Darren's light brown hair.

Ryan Prewitt introduced Chief Freeman, and Buck took his place at the podium.

"What I want to do this afternoon is lay out some facts for you," the chief began.

Loretta Mullins came bustling through the door, late as usual, and took the only vacant seat near the front.

She's probably pleased that this meeting isn't being held in her precious inner sanctum, Toni thought uncharitably. A sudden vision of short, plump Loretta trying to kill someone caused Toni's mouth to twitch.

She banished that thought and studied her colleagues, wrestling with the grim thought that someone in their midst could be a killer, and that he or she could strike again if threatened. Her insides quivered.

"We know that people are far more likely to be killed by those closest and dearest to them than by strangers, colleagues, or mere acquaintances," Buck continued. "We're reasonably sure that the person who killed Mrs. Carter is right handed. That person is also strong enough—or highly motivated enough—to have moved the body from the primary crime scene to the site where it was found. The weapon was a large blunt object."

Around the room of grim faces, heads nodded.

And hands jotted notes.

"We think that person is intimately familiar with the school and its personnel, a belief that is reinforced by the fact that an attempted hit and run was made on someone after a school event."

"What attempt was that?" came from the rear of the room.

The chief outlined how a car had charged at Toni and Garrett Donovan. He didn't state a reason for the attack, allowing the impression that the intent had been to harm Toni. She breathed easier when he left it that way.

"Then there was the shooting attack on Mrs. Donovan," he continued. "We think that has to be related. In addition to those incidents, we're looking into the question of whether the death of Dustin Guthrie was a suicide or something more sinister."

That revelation elicited gasps of shock.

Buck made a few more remarks before turning the meeting back over to Ryan, who announced that there would be visitation with the Guthrie family at the funeral home Friday evening, and that the funeral would be at two o'clock Saturday afternoon.

After a brief question and answer session, Ryan concluded the meeting. "If anyone knows anything that you even suspect might be helpful, please give the police a call."

As the room began to empty, Jordan Hopper paused next to Toni. "Sorry I wasn't more helpful yesterday. Got boys running drills in the gym. Better get out there."

"Say, Lisa," Toni called as she and Darren started to follow Jordan. "I came by the gym to see you yesterday, but Jordan said you had left for a dental appointment. Would you have time to chat in the morning if I come in early?"

Lisa glanced around, impatience etched on her face. "I'll be in the gym by seven-thirty."

"How's your hand? Did that cut heal up all right?" Lisa had brought the student council a new jar of pickles the week after the broken jar incident.

Lisa gave a shrug that indicated it was of no importance. "I pulled it open a couple of times. That's what I get for playing ball with the kids."

"Did you get the stitches out?"

She flexed the hand that still sported a band-aid. "Last week. See you tomorrow."

On her way home, Toni experienced a sense of running in circles and getting nowhere. Panic was growing inside her. If the killer was not found, there might be more deaths. But the murderer's identity seemed more elusive than ever.

The next morning she found Lisa Baker in the gym watching a group of students shoot baskets. Toni kept to the perimeter of the floor. Street shoes were forbidden on it, and her peach pumps that matched her blouse and cinnamon colored suit slipped on the glossy surface.

Suddenly a basketball flew across the floor and hit her in the thigh, knocking her off balance. Toni flashed a hand up against the wall and struggled to stay upright.

"Sorry, Mrs. Donovan," a boy called across the gym.

Lisa rushed to Toni's side. "Are you all right?" she asked huskily, a basketball clutched in her hands.

Her ash blonde ponytail swung behind her.

"I'm fine." Toni steadied herself and looked up. The boy who had let the ball get away from him stood a few feet away, staring at her in concern.

Toni gave him a wave. "I'm fine, Mike. Don't worry about it. Accidents happen."

"Thanks for being a good sport," Lisa said softly. "Go on into my office and have a seat. I'll be there in a minute."

Lisa's office, next door to Jordan's, was a bit smaller, but furnished identically. Her shelves were fuller than his, and her desk was cluttered with a music player, a stack of CD's, an oversized desk calendar, and other assorted debris.

Toni had just gotten seated when Lisa came rushing through the door. She went behind her desk and plopped down. "Friday mornings are open gym before classes. Someone else is on duty today, but I like to keep an eye on things."

"I stopped by and talked to Jordan yesterday," Toni explained. "We discussed Dustin and his recent behavior. I had hoped to do the same with you."

Lisa's countenance became grave. "All this has been a terrible shock. The kids have been upset, especially those involved in the athletic programs."

"Dustin and Sidney were both athletes."

"Sure." She nodded and brushed her bangs away from her eyes. "Dustin played basketball, and Sidney cheered, so they spent a lot of time around the gym. They were both teacher aides, as well."

"What can you tell me about Dustin's behavior? Did you notice any personality changes or hear him making complaints recently?"

Lisa shook her head, a hand fisted over her pursed mouth. "Nothing unusual that I can think of. Of course, I didn't have him in class. He was Jordan's aide and in his Team Sports class, so Jordan spent more time with him than I did."

"So they were close."

Lisa shrugged. "I suppose so."

"Did Dustin seem depressed or upset recently? Had he had any serious arguments that you know about?"

Lisa stared at Toni, her brows knitting. "There were a couple of arguments, but nothing major."

"I know about his little upset with Sidney over a broken date, and the fact that he wanted to buy a jeep and his parents didn't approve. Is there anything else?"

"Well," she said slowly, as if judging whether to share something. But then she did. "One day last week in ball practice he and another boy got into some horseplay, and they ended up yelling and rolling around on the floor. Jordan stepped in and sent both boys to the showers."

Was Jordan hot tempered? Toni didn't remember him as anything but friendly and laid back—and competitive, a necessity for coaching.

"Do you have any idea where Dustin spent his time or what he did just prior to his death? We're trying to determine who was the last person to see him alive."

Lisa leaned forward on the desk and gave her ponytail a flip behind her. "I have no idea what the kid did or where he went after practice Friday afternoon. I remember seeing him leave when the other guys did. Sorry I can't be more help to you."

Her words seemed friendly enough, but Toni sensed an underlying reserve, or insincerity. "Sidney's convinced he didn't take his own life," she said evenly. "I don't know what happened, but my gut says she might be right."

"Is your gut what convinced Police Chief Freeman it wasn't a suicide?" Lisa asked, her eyes cool and assessing.

Toni got the feeling that Lisa didn't think much of her questions—or her personally. "I told him how Sidney feels. He reached his own conclusion. Maybe I'm paranoid, but it doesn't feel like a suicide."

Lisa tipped her head, frowning. "How does a suicide feel?"

Toni ignored the question that smacked of sarcasm. "Maybe it really was a suicide. Maybe it wasn't. If it was, there has to be a reason. I want to know why. If it wasn't, I want to see justice served. His family deserves to know the truth."

"I guess I see your point," Lisa conceded. Her mouth moved, as if to say more, but then stilled.

"Thanks for your time. I have to run."

Back in her room Toni laid out supplies for her first class. Then she dashed across the hall to John's room. "Why don't you and Jenny come to my house for supper? We can go to the funeral visitation together and drop the boys at my folks on the way."

"I'll call Jenny and get back to you."

When she peeked inside his door during third hour, John gave her a brief thumbs-up and went on with his lecture. She called Kyle and told him they would be having company.

Kyle was home and had steaks grilling and potatoes baking when Toni arrived. She made a salad and had everything ready when John and Jenny arrived. They ate promptly, and then everyone piled into Toni's van. They dropped the boys with her parents and arrived at the funeral home by seven o'clock. At the entrance they joined the line wending its way inside the chapel. The room was already overflowing, so they moved with the crowd that pressed forward to express their condolences.

After passing the closed casket and shaking hands with the hollow-eyed Guthrie family members, they spent an appropriate time in respectful memoriam. As their little foursome started out the door, they met Buck Freeman just arriving to pay his respects.

He pulled a couple of folders from under his arm and handed them to Toni. "I recognized your van in the parking lot and brought these in, hoping to catch you. Look them over tonight, and I'll pick them up in the morning."

On the way home Toni fought anger and frustration as she remembered the despairing, empty look in the eyes of those parents. Why did tragedies like this happen? Seventeen was too young to die.

Why, God? Why?

She slapped a hand on her thigh. "We have to stop this."

"Every time we think we have the answer, it falls apart," John said from the back seat.

Toni held up the folders. "When we get to the house let's start over, lay out everything we have or know, along with these reports. There has to be something in here. And we have to find it."

*

"First, let's establish a timeline," Toni said when she, John, and Jenny were gathered around the dining table with coffee and Cokes. She placed the autopsy folders and a notepad on the table before them. The television blared from the living room where Kyle had taken the boys to keep them out of the way.

"The Christmas party was December twenty-first," John began. "So that's the original crime date." He wrote it down and scooted the pad back to the center of the table.

"The gym was empty by about five o'clock, everyone except Marsha scattered for the Christmas break," Toni continued. "We know where some of them went, others we don't. But there was plenty of time for someone to leave and return well before the time of the murder, which is believed to have happened about ten-thirty." She jotted dates and times on the notepad.

"Jimmie Huff and Dana Smith have alibis for that time," John said. "We don't know where Dustin was then."

"Or Janet." Toni wrote her name under Dustin's.

"You two found the body on January third," Jenny interjected. "It was right after we returned to school from the holiday break." She took her turn making a note on the pad.

"The incident in the parking lot happened on January tenth, only seven days after finding the body," was Toni's next contribution.

"I still think that was because the killer thought Garrett could find him," John said. "I just can't figure out how the killer knew about Garrett's role."

A long silence fell. "I can't either," Toni admitted at last. "Someone must have seen the chief's notes. And because of that I don't dare let my children out of my sight. Someone shot at me on January fourteenth," she said, adding it to the list.

"Dustin's death wasn't until January twenty-eighth." John made another note.

Toni reviewed the timeline in her mind before speaking. "At this point Janet and Dustin are the only ones on our suspect list for Marsha's death. I talked to the coaches, Jordan on Wednesday and Lisa yesterday. They both basically said they saw nothing unusual in Dustin's recent behavior, other than Lisa mentioning some sort of scuffle in practice one day last week."

"You mean the kind of argument that kids get into all the time?" Jenny asked.

Toni nodded. "That's what it sounds like. But I did see something that may or may not be important. When I was talking to Jordan, I noticed a flashlight on a shelf in his office, one of those heavy duty ones like Buck Freeman thinks was used to kill Marsha." She jotted that on the list. "I know anyone can buy those anywhere, but just knowing that the athletic department keeps that kind around might be significant."

"Maybe you should mention that to the chief," John suggested.

"You're right. I'll do that next time I talk to him. Now let's look at these." She opened Marsha's autopsy folder.

After going over everything in it, they agreed that

nothing struck them as new or helpful. They put it away and removed everything from Dustin's folder.

All three of them reached for one of the photos in the small stack, and then made grimaces as they studied each one and passed them around. When they had each seen all of them, Toni reclaimed one in particular. She stared at the picture. "There's no doubt in my mind that the boy was killed. Look at the gun. It looks positioned to me. If Dustin pulled the trigger on his own, the impact would have thrown the gun away from him at an odd angle, not neat like that."

John and Jenny examined it closer. "I see what you mean," Jenny said. John nodded.

Toni stared at another photo. "There's another thing. Look at the gunshot residue on the clothing. The picture's fine, except for this spot here." She moved her finger to where she meant.

"What does it mean?" Jenny asked, frowning in perplexity. She was not steeped in science, but seemed as intrigued by the reports and pictures as Toni and John.

John's face brightened. "I know what you're thinking. It's out of place for the death shot. There were two shots."

"That's right. I think it's out of place. Let's see what else we have here." They each picked up a form and began to read.

When they all finished reading, Toni returned to the fingerprint report. "Dustin's prints were found on the trigger and stock of the gun, but the forearm was clean. There's no way he could have held that gun in place to fire it without leaving prints there."

John nodded agreement. "It was wiped. Do you

think the chief knows?"

Toni considered. "I'm betting he does, now that he's viewing it as a possible murder." She grinned. "I think he's testing us."

"I give you an A." Jenny used an index finger to draw one in the air.

John's brow furrowed. "If those mistakes were made, we have an amateur killer, or amateur hunter—someone who doesn't spend much time with guns."

"Good thought," Toni said. "But it would take someone strong to drag Marsha's body that far. And now we have a man included on our suspect list."

John tipped back in his chair and groaned. "So who did it?"

"Nobody!" Jenny chirped with a grin. Then she sobered. "Sorry. It's not funny. It's just that it's so frustrating."

Toni became serious. "Let's go back over our suspect list. Janet Rayford is at the top. She gave us an alibi for Saturday morning, but there's enough leeway in the time of death. And she doesn't strike me as very physically strong. The Medical Examiner says, based on partially undigested breakfast food in Dustin's stomach, he died between eight and ten a.m. I don't know if it's possible she could have done it."

"Dustin's off the list now, isn't he?" John asked.

"I think so." Toni nodded as she drew a line through his name. "Buck is checking on both Janet and Dustin's whereabouts. Since Sidney, Jordan and Lisa have all mentioned the amount of time Dustin spent in the gym, I think we should try to find out how important that is. I'll see if I can learn anything about Jordan and Lisa's activities during the critical hours. Although," she mused, pausing for a moment, "I don't see how either of them could have driven that car at Garrett. They were both coaching ballgames that evening."

"So we still have more questions than answers. Where do we go from here?" John asked.

Toni thought about it. "Since we're backtracking, I think I'd like to talk to Tom Keller again." She began putting things back in the folder. "I'm not sure that interview was valid. He had been drinking and was pretty fuzzy, but I still got the feeling he wasn't telling me as much as he could have. I'll try to catch him after the funeral tomorrow. Maybe that early in the day he won't be tanked yet."

When Buck Freeman stopped by the house the next morning to pick up his folders, he refused to come inside, but stood just inside the foyer and took them from Toni. It was early, and Toni was still in her robe as she told him about the session with John and Jenny and the points that came out in their discussion. When he admitted that he agreed with their conclusions, Toni mentioned the flashlight in Jordan's office. He just nodded.

"It seems that the gym is a center of activity," Toni added as he turned to leave.

"Yes, it does." But he didn't pursue it further.

Chapter 16

A surrealistic atmosphere at the funeral made Toni hug her arms and pinch them, as if that would wake her from this terrible dream, the second in such a short time. While soft music played in the background, she watched from the back pew where she and Kyle sat next to John and Jenny in a section of non-family members. She noted a large representation of school staff and students as the pews finished filling. An overflow of people lined the back walls and spilled out in the hallway and foyer.

By the time someone sang an appropriate solo and the minister delivered a poignant eulogy to a hushed crowd, punctuated by occasional bouts of stifled sobs, Toni felt utterly brittle and drained. When the crowd filed out and left Dennis Guthrie and his family alone for a final private moment at the front of the casket, she breathed gratefully of the cold clear air outside.

At the conclusion of a brief graveside service, John and Jenny went home, and Toni got into the van with Kyle. "Will you drive by the Railroad Bar so I can see if Tom Keller's car is there? If it is, you can drop me off and go get the boys while I talk to him."

The look her husband gave her said he didn't think much of the idea, but he didn't bother to argue. "I'll come right back for you."

Toni nodded, realizing he meant to keep guard over her. "That'll work. Thanks."

Kyle drove slowly away from the cemetery and back to town. When he turned onto Elm Street, sure enough, Tom's dark blue vehicle sat in its usual spot at the end of the street.

He pulled to the curb to let Toni out. "I'll be back in a few minutes. The boys and I will wait out here for you."

Toni entered the bar and did a quick scan of the room. It was fairly light, and it took only a moment to spot Tom at what must be his usual table near the west wall. Dressed in worn blue jeans and a plaid flannel shirt, he hadn't bothered to remove his heavy coat. It was unzipped, exposing a large belly.

As Toni walked toward the table, she spoke to the waitress cleaning the adjacent one. "I'll have a Coke when you have time."

"Gotcha." The older woman finished wiping the table and hustled away.

Toni took a seat across from her quarry. "Hi, Tom. May I speak to you for a moment?"

She was met with an unwelcoming silence that spoke volumes.

"What do you want?" he growled, his expression bordering on hostility.

"I need your help." She tried to sound suitably humble.

"I already talked to you," he huffed.

"I know, but I don't think you told me as much

as you could have." A Coke appeared on the table in front of her, and she thanked the waitress.

"I told you all I could remember," Tom snapped, his tone becoming a snarl.

"Listen, Tom, I'm not here to cause you any trouble. Someone took your car and tried to hurt my son with it. I'm here to plead for your help."

He peered at her closely, and his expression softened just a bit. He heaved a sigh of resignation. "What do you want to know?"

"I need to find out who took your car. I'm not implying that you know who it was, but I don't think you were entirely honest with me when we talked before."

Tom took his time pulling a pack of cigarettes from his pocket and extracting one.

"Will you tell me about it again, and not leave anything out this time?" she asked quietly.

Tom lit the cigarette before answering. "I really can't remember much. But I don't think I was driving it."

"I don't either. And I don't hold you responsible. No one else does either."

"Well," he said slowly, seeming relieved. "I always park in the same spot, get here ahead of the crowd so I can."

"On the corner, right?"

He nodded. "I know I put it there, because I always do. And I always put my keys in my pocket."

"What about that night? Did you let anyone have your keys?"

He shook his head. "No, but maybe somebody got 'em and I didn't know it."

Toni's heart leaped. "What happened?"

"Well," he began in a slow drawl. "When I was getting out of my car that day, a guy came barreling around the corner and ran into me. I tripped and fell. He stopped and helped me get up."

She leaned forward on her elbows. "What about your keys? Did you drop them?"

"I think so." Tom rubbed an arm over his face. "I don't remember pickin 'em up. I didn't think about 'em til later, you see. I put my hand in my pocket, and they weren't there. But I thought I musta left 'em in the switch and didn't go looking for 'em."

"Where did you find them?"

He hesitated, but then came clean. "When I went out that night to go home, they were in the car. In the switch."

"You think you had them in your hand and dropped them when someone ran into you," she repeated thoughtfully. "But you remember that they weren't in your pocket during the evening. Right?"

He nodded and shrugged. "Yeah, I guess so."

"What did the guy who ran into you look like?"

Tom's face twisted into a grimace. "I don't know. He was wearing one of those winter caps that covers the whole head, like a ski mask."

"Did the voice sound like a man or a woman?"

Tom shook his head. "A guy, I guess. The clothes were just a running outfit, some kind of sweat suit. I thought it was a guy. All he said was 'Oops, sorry,' or something like that.

"So it could have been a man or a woman," she said slowly.

Uncertainty crept across his face. "I guess."

"What time was it when this happened?"

He shrugged. "I guess about six o'clock. That's when I always come down here during the week. I come earlier on Saturday, like today."

Toni couldn't think of anything else he could tell her that would be helpful. "Why didn't you tell me this before?"

Tom dropped his head for a moment, and then looked back up at her. "I was afraid of losing my driver's license. I can't afford another DUI, and I was afraid they were gonna blame me for whatever happened to your boy."

"Well, they're not," Toni assured him. "I appreciate you leveling with me."

Toni finished her Coke in a quick gulp and paid for it. Then she joined Kyle and the boys, her mind whirling. It could have been either a man or a woman. The athletic clothing and the running led her right back to thoughts of Jordan and Lisa. But they had both been coaching ballgames in the gym that evening.

Sunday morning it was snowing, big fat flakes drifting leisurely to the ground. During church service, Toni sat on the edge of the pew as the pastor once again spoke of how people who say they love God, but hate their brother, are liars The sick feeling festering deep in her stomach made her bend forward in pain.

Growing up, her parents had dragged her and her brothers to church every time there was a service. Bill, the ever-obedient child, had always gone willingly. Quint had been resistant at times. Toni had been—well, neither. In a painful bout of self-examination, she realized that she had been like the people of Laodicea spoken of in the Bible. Not hot. Not cold. Just lukewarm. Despicable.

Not liking the sting of what she saw in herself, Toni ached for better. *Lord, my life seems to get more hectic every day. Please help me change that—and expose the killer in our midst. And please don't let me ever hate anyone again.*

Warmth stole through her, easing the raw ache and bringing moisture to her eyes.

By the time they exited the church, a couple inches of snow had accumulated, giving the ground a glistening cover. The boys wanted to play in it, but Toni was reluctant to let them be alone, even in their own yard.

"I'll go out with them after I hear a weather update," Kyle promised.

Satisfied, they ate the bowls of hot chili Toni served and escaped to their room. When Kyle settled in the rocker with the television remote, Toni returned to her laptop and the files from Marsha's computer.

The number of them was daunting. It would take hours to read everything thoroughly. Picking up where she had left off earlier, she started scanning through them, doing her best to ignore Gabe's beginning musical efforts emanating from the bedroom. All she could say about it was that it was loud.

She continued thumbing. *Curriculum. Guidance. Interface. Jobs for Missouri Educators. No Child Left Behind. Show-Me Standards. Staff Realignment.*

Toni halted at that last one, her heart rate quickening. She pulled it out and began to read more thoroughly. It was a study on how to reduce staff. Could it be related to the report Sam and the board had expected Marsha to present at their next meeting? It began with some lengthy introductory statements, but as Toni read further she discovered that it was a two-part document. The first part contained material from state reports and was general in nature. The second part was vastly different. In Marsha's own writing, it applied to the local district and included a list of all staff by departments. There were notes regarding the number of students served by each, along with other dry statistics.

The final paragraph indicated that an across the board ten percent cut of certified staff and eight percent of support staff was, in Marsha's opinion, necessary. Toni could only surmise that the woman had indeed intended to propose this plan to the board.

Reductions? Reassignments? Who had Marsha planned to terminate or move to another position? Had she acted on anything before her death? Toni reached for the phone.

"Sorry to bother you on the weekend," she apologized when Sam Brinkman answered. "I need to ask another nosy question."

"I wasn't busy. What would you like to know?"

"I've been reading reports from Marsha's computer, and I found one that indicates she planned to reassign and reduce staff. But it doesn't state specifically who. Had any of this been acted on by the board?"

"There was some discussion about ways to reduce expenses," Sam said in his slow, thoughtful way. "But no formal action had been taken. Which, in hindsight, is absolutely terrifying. The woman was skimming money and planning for others to lose their jobs to cover it."

"Do you think she might have already been putting some of those things in motion, figuring it was a simple matter to get the board to rubber stamp it?"

There was a long silence before he spoke again. "It sickens me to admit it, but we probably would have done whatever she proposed." Self-disgust laced the admission.

As much as Toni hated to admit it, he was right. Marsha would have gone right ahead with whatever she intended to do, confident of their approval. "I have a pile of stuff here yet to read, so I'd better get busy."

As she put the phone beside her, the weatherman appeared on the television screen. Kyle turned on the sound, and they listened to a forecast for light snow to continue throughout the night and stop by mid morning, with no hazardous accumulation. However, sleet was predicted to move in sometime in the afternoon.

"It looks like you can count on going to school in the morning," he commented.

"But what happens after that is questionable," Toni added.

Kyle took the boys outdoors, and Toni curled up to continue reading, content in the knowledge that he would be home every other night the next week. She read until she finished the last report about eleven o'clock.

*

On the way to her classroom the next morning, Toni tracked down Ken Douglas in the cafeteria where he was having a donut and coffee at the table reserved for staff. Two teachers at the other end of the table were absorbed in conversation. Toni slid onto the bench next to him. "I found out some interesting information about the car that tried to hit Garrett." She gave him a quick summary of Tom Keller's revelation.

Ken's reaction was a look of silent puzzlement.

"I don't know how relevant any of that is," she said quietly. "But there's something else I wanted to discuss with you. I copied a lot of stuff from Marsha's computer, and yesterday I read a report that indicates she was planning to cut and realign staff. Sam Brinkman says there was some discussion, but no final plans had been approved."

"That's right." He picked up his coffee cup, drained it, and set it back down.

Toni considered how to phrase her request. "I'm wondering if Marsha went ahead with anything in that respect, taking board approval for granted. Could you check with department heads and see if they can confirm any orders for reassignment or termination?"

He pushed to his feet. "I'll get on it as soon as the bell rings and the halls clear."

"Thanks." They left in opposite directions.

Third hour Toni didn't waste any time getting to the office to see Ken. "He's expecting me," she said to Pam as she entered.

Pam jerked her head in the direction of the door behind her. "That's what he said."

When Toni peeked inside his doorway, Ken was

on the phone, but he saw her and motioned to a seat. She sat and waited for him to conclude his conversation.

"I've been calling department heads," he said when he finished. "They all say that Marsha contacted them the week before Christmas and told them to anticipate cuts. They were to let her know by the end of the first week after break who in their particular department they thought they could survive without."

Toni shook her head in a weary rotation. "She had total confidence that the board would approve whatever she proposed, didn't she?"

Ken scowled. "She was a very confident person, and it sounds like the January board meeting was meant to be a downsizing one."

"I wonder who all escaped the axe," Toni mused.

He stared hard at her. "We'll never know exactly, because the departmental recommendations would have been a mere formality. Marsha would have already known just who and where she intended to cut, and you can bet that my name was at the top of the list."

"I don't really see how this information can help, but thanks for checking."

"You went to bat for me," he reminded her needlessly. "I haven't shared anything privileged with you. All this stuff is common knowledge."

Toni got to her feet. "I'd better run."

Back in her room, she went to the window and stood watching the snow. It was a light, gentle downfall, and the temperature was still forty degrees, so an early dismissal was not likely. When the bell rang, she turned to meet her fourth hour class.

When Jodi arrived seventh hour sporting another black eye, Toni's heart sank. She watched until the girl sat at her desk, and then walked over and leaned down next to her. "Can you stay after school and talk?" she whispered.

Jodi didn't answer. She just stared at the white board, as if she hadn't heard.

Toni returned to the front of the room and began her lecture.

Jodi seemed to listen to instructions, and she participated in lab. During cleanup at the end of class, Toni watched to see what the girl would do. She held her breath as the bell rang and students filed out, then exhaled a long sigh of relief when Jodi remained in her seat.

Toni stepped out into the hallway and spotted John. "My boys?" she mouthed over the chatter of departing students and nodded back at her room, hoping he understood.

"I'll get them," he called, giving her his usual thumbs up and heading down the hall.

Toni returned to her room and took a seat facing her abused student. "Jodi, I'm sorry this has happened again. I want to help you, but I need you to be honest with the authorities about what's happening to you."

After several moments of silence Jodi spoke in an unsteady whisper. "You mean the police?"

"You could talk to the principal or counselor. I know they're both concerned and have already spoken with Protective Services." Toni hoped she could reach the girl.

Tears glistened in Jodi's eyes and leaked in a trail

down her cheeks. Self-consciously she reached up and wiped her face. "I wish I'd never met him," she choked in a rush.

"Let's not waste time being sorry for things we can't change," Toni said gently. "Let's get tough and do something about it."

"I'm afraid to complain to the police," Jodi said. "They probably wouldn't lock him up, and then he would just get real mad and find me and take it out on me."

Toni thought fast. "How about if we approach it a little differently?" She heard John and the boys arrive and go into his room across the hall.

"How?" Jodi's voice was low, but there was a tiny spark of interest.

"Well, what if Donnie were arrested for something besides abusing you? Do you know anything he's involved in that the police could catch him in the act of and arrest him if they had a tip? They could keep your name out of it, make sure he thought they got their information from another source."

There was another long silence. "They might not be able to do that," she said at last.

Toni sighed. She was tired, and she needed to go home, but she couldn't walk away from a student in need. "Jodi, you have to get out of this relationship. It's dangerous."

"I know," the girl admitted, nodding and choking back sobs.

"Sometimes we don't have a choice about things," Toni pressed gently. "Sometimes things get so bad that we just have to square our shoulders and do what's necessary."

Suddenly Jodi did just that. She took a deep breath and sat up straighter. Then she looked Toni in the eye. "There is something. I don't know the details, but I heard Donnie talking on the phone. He told someone, a customer I think, that what he needed would be in by Wednesday morning. After he hung up, he told me that he had some night work coming up tomorrow night."

"Do you think he's planning a robbery for tomorrow night?"

Jodi bit her lip and nodded. "I played dumb and didn't say anything then, but later I asked him if he was going to go to Bennie's party tomorrow night, like I forgot the phone call. He laughed and said no, he had to pay a visit to the tire shop."

Toni's eyes widened with comprehension. "You think he's planning to steal tires from a shop, instead of taking parts from cars like he's been doing?"

Jodi nodded. "That's my guess. The only tire shop I know of is Palmer Tire."

"Will you repeat this to the police if I call them?"

"I guess so." The look on Jodi's face was a mixture of determination and fear.

Toni rang Buck Freeman quickly, before Jodi could change her mind. "I have a student here with some information you should hear," she said as soon as she had him on the line.

By the time Toni and the boys left the police station about five, the snow had turned to rain and was washing away the snow that had fallen earlier. But she felt somewhat better. Jodi had driven behind them to the station and repeated her story to Buck.

After she finished and left, Toni had explained to Buck that Donnie was responsible for the condition of the girl's face.

"We'll get him," Buck had promised.

Chapter 17

The next morning Toni shivered as she and the boys climbed into the van. The rain that had fallen during the night was lighter, but it was turning to drizzle, with the temperature hovering just above the freezing point.

As she walked up the hall to her room, her gut knotted. A picture was beginning to form in her mind, one that she dared not share with anyone yet, not without proof.

Her first and second hour classes didn't go as smoothly as normal. Thoughts of the murder investigation, and the robbery planned for that night, kept her on edge. And the students were restless, watching the weather through the windows. Twice Toni lost her train of thought in the middle of an explanation and had to pause and refer to her notes. It was a relief when third hour arrived. She removed her lab coat and put her cell phone in the pocket of her black wool blazer. Then she locked her door and headed for the gym.

When she entered the big room, neither coach was in sight. A class of students was being led through warm-up exercises by a substitute, which meant that at least one coach was absent. Toni waited until there was a break in the exercise routine and approached the sub. "Who are you filling in for?" she asked politely.

"Coach Baker," the young woman said. "Do you need something? Can I help you?"

"No, I just needed to speak to Coach Baker. Thanks."

Toni swallowed frustration and returned to her room. It was like having an itch she couldn't scratch. She felt drawn to the gym for answers, but Lisa was elusive. She wasn't sure how everything fit together, but she was convinced that the coaches held the key.

By sixth hour keeping the attention of her students was a challenge. They kept staring out the windows at the light rainfall that was turning to sleet and pinging against the glass panes. Whispered murmurings circulated about the chances of an early dismissal. Toni doubted that would happen, since it was so near the end of the day and the precipitation was melting almost as fast as it fell. But a slight drop in temperature could make all the difference.

During last hour, while keeping an eye on the developing weather outside, Toni moved among the students, checking bookwork and facilitating labs. She stopped beside Jodi, who was adjusting a microscope over a slide. "How are you?" she asked softly while keeping an eye on the activity around them.

"Okay." Jodi didn't look up.

"You're welcome to go home with me if you'd like," Toni whispered.

Where you'll be safer.

Jodi looked up then, her eyes large and troubled. "Thanks for your concern, Mrs. Donovan," she whispered, "but my dad didn't go to work today. He's home sick with the flu."

With a parent present Donnie would not be likely to bother her. It wasn't a guarantee, but it was encouraging. With a small, reassuring touch to the girl's hand, Toni smiled and moved on.

By dismissal time, that drop in temperature was happening. Everyone rushed to get the buses loaded and the buildings cleared. Toni picked up her boys and went straight home.

She had just taken a chocolate pie from the oven when Ken called to say that school had already been cancelled for the next day. Toni immediately called Loretta and relayed the message.

As she disconnected, she heard Kyle's truck pull into the drive. It was a relief to have him off the roads. They weren't hazardous yet, but it definitely wasn't a good time to be out.

He sniffed as he entered the kitchen. "It sure smells good in here." Then he spotted the pies. "Chocolate?" His face took on a little boy expression.

Toni grinned. "Of course. Is there any other kind?"

He tossed his bag and grabbed her in a bear hug. "Now I know why I married you."

During supper Toni told Kyle about Jodi, and then about her boyfriend's plan to break into the tire shop that night. "Do you think even Donnie would try anything on a night like this?"

He placed his fork beside his plate. "A guy like Donnie might see it as an excellent opportunity. He wouldn't expect the police to be as vigilant in this bad weather."

"Are you worried, Mom?" Garrett studied her

face across the table.

"Yes, I am, but everything will be all right," Toni assured him.

They let the boys stay up later than usual, since they could sleep in the next morning. Once they were in bed, Toni took a shower. When she emerged, pulling her robe over her nightgown, she found Kyle sitting on the side of the bed. He patted a spot beside him. "Let's talk."

She tied the belt and sat, not sure she was ready for whatever he had to say.

Kyle turned her to face him and put his fingers under her chin to force her face up. "I've missed you."

His forthright statement took her off guard. Toni swallowed and placed her head on his shoulder. The scent of soap on his skin was so familiar—and comforting. "I've missed you, too. I've never meant to neglect you."

"I know that. I'm sorry we've let ourselves get so busy that we don't have time for one another. You're a good mother and a dedicated teacher."

She raised her head. "But not so good at the wife part, huh?"

He grinned. "You're good at that, too—when we can squeeze it into our schedules."

Toni pulled back enough to meet his gaze. "I know I've let things steal time from us, and I feel bad about that. But I'm not sure how to fix it."

He stroked her hair. "I feel bad about it, too. But recognizing our problem has to be the first step toward fixing it. We've both gotten caught up in our jobs and other activities."

Something in his tone put Toni on alert. She drew back and placed her hands on his shoulders. "Don't give up your job. I'm selfish. I would love to have you home with me more. But I know how much you love what you do."

He inhaled sharply. "You know I was thinking of doing that?"

"I sensed it." *I know you.*

"But we don't have time to spend together, just the two of us the way we used to do."

His words touched her, reminded her how much she loved him. Toni took a deep breath and looked directly into his eyes. "I miss you, too. But don't give up your job. Instead, let's concentrate on finding ways to slow down and enjoy what time we can together."

His eyes bored into her. "You mean that?"

She nodded. "I mean it."

He kissed her and pulled her tight. "I understand that you have to keep Garrett safe, and that finding out who is behind all this tragedy is not something you can ignore. But please be careful and stay safe."

She nodded and snuggled up to him. "I will. As soon as all this is over, why don't we take some time off and get away from everything for a few days?"

His arms tightened around her. "I'll schedule some vacation time for right after school is out for the summer."

She unwrapped herself from his arms. "I'd like that."

He smiled. "I still love you. And I'll be here for you, no matter what."

*

They had only been asleep a short time when the phone rang. Kyle reached over and snagged it. "Yeah, she's here," he mumbled and handed it to Toni. The digital clock read eleven-thirty.

"Yes," she mumbled sleepily.

"We have a casualty." Buck's voice sounded gravelly and grim.

She came instantly awake, her stomach wrenching. "What do you mean, a casualty?"

A cough came across the line, followed by a clearing of the throat. "Donnie showed up at the tire shop about ten o'clock. He jimmied the back door and was filling the bed of his pickup with tires when we drove up. He jumped in the truck and tore around the building and out onto the highway. The roads weren't safe, but he put the pedal to the floor."

Dread curdled her stomach. "What happened?"

"He lost control on Scenic View Hill, went off the road, and rolled his truck."

"He's alive, isn't he?" She held her breath.

"He's in the emergency room here at the hospital. I don't know just how bad he's hurt, but it's serious."

"Thanks for letting me know. I'll call Jodi in the morning."

Toni relayed to Kyle what had happened. Then she tried to go back to sleep, but it was a long time in coming.

*

The next morning Toni started to fix breakfast, and paused to gaze out the kitchen window. Ice glistened on the trees, but the sky looked like the sun might come out. She put the coffee pot on and dug out the phone book.

"I'm sorry he's hurt," Jodi said in an uneven voice when Toni related what had happened to Donnie. But she didn't indicate she would go see him. "Thanks for calling me."

Instead of getting busy, Toni just stood there, staring at the icy trees and letting loose thoughts and memories ooze around in her brain. She felt better about her marriage, but she couldn't relax while a killer still ran loose. She knew all the pieces were there, but they weren't clear enough to present to anyone. She had to connect the dots, establish a link between the crimes.

Newspaper articles had reported Marsha's death as a community travesty and left the impression that a monster had killed her. But a monster hadn't done it. It was another human being, just like herself and many others who lived and worked in the community.

In her silent introspection, a cog suddenly clicked into place. With her heartbeat quickening in her chest, Toni went to the desk in the den to check the calendar where she kept notes. There had been three basketball games the night of the attack on Garrett. Each of them ran a little over an hour, with a ten to fifteen minute break between, a total of about an hour and a half apart. She looked at the game times she had jotted on the calendar when working on student council concession plans. The first game had started at five. Either coach could have lifted Tom's keys before that.

Lisa would have been coaching the first game, during which Jordan could have gone out the back door of the gym to where coaches and officials parked their vehicles. He could have driven to the

Railroad Bar, parked, and driven Tom's car back to the school parking lot in readiness for the attack later.

On the other hand, Jordan coached the second and third games, making it possible for Lisa to leave. But Lisa had been to the concession stand during one of those games and conspicuously noticed by everyone in that hallway. Toni was sure the pickle jar incident had happened during the last game. That left the middle game time slot for it to have been possible for Lisa to leave and return.

It would have been a simple matter for either coach to park somewhere near the bar and take Tom's car. All he or she would have had to do was drive Tom's car to the school and use it, return it to the bar, and drive away in his or her own vehicle.

Toni shook her head. If all she suspected were true, could she handle it? What if she, or anyone in her family, got hurt? Then there was still the nagging question of Dustin's involvement and death. She had too much on her plate—and not enough on the breakfast plates—to dwell on this right now.

Right after breakfast Kyle and the boys went outside, leaving Toni alone again. At eight-thirty she decided it was late enough to call Buck at the station.

"Hi, Toni," he answered tiredly. "I assume you want an update on Donnie."

"That's right. How serious are his injuries?"

"He'll live, but his back was broken, a spinal injury that will keep him in a wheelchair the rest of his life." His voice relayed weariness, not just from the long night, but that it was all so unnecessary.

"While I have you, may I ask if you've been able to verify the alibis for Janet Rayford, Jordan Hopper and Lisa Baker?"

"I guess you just did," he responded gruffly. "We've checked their stories. Jack confirmed that he was at Janet's house with her the morning Dustin was killed. Maybe he thinks it's time for a little honesty, or he could be hoping Janet will change her mind and take him back if he gives her an alibi. Or maybe he just feels too guilty to do anything else. Whatever the case, Janet seems to be in the clear."

"What about Jordan?"

"He was with his family the evening of December twenty-first, but he admits that he went out to gas up their van sometime during the evening. They planned to leave to visit family the next morning. The timing is pretty close to Marsha's time of death, but he wasn't gone very long, probably not long enough to have killed her, dragged her to the body farm and driven her car to the airport."

"What about the morning of January twenty-seventh?"

"We're still working on that. Jordan says he went out for donuts that morning. Once again, he was away from home about the right time, but probably not long enough. I plan to talk to him again, see if he can get the time frame more precise and verified."

"Okay. What about Lisa?"

"That one's even harder. She says that, at the time Marsha was killed, she was at home packing to leave for Kansas City the next morning. She's single and lives alone, so there's no family to vouch for her."

"What about when Dustin was killed?"

"Same problem," he said with a heavy sigh. "She

claims she was in Poplar Bluff shopping that morning, that she left early. We're trying to locate a sales clerk who saw her, or a surveillance camera that caught her, anything to prove she was there."

Toni rubbed her brow. "I'm worried. I can't prove anything, but I'm getting the feeling that one of them was involved."

A long silence met that assertion. "I hope you're wrong. I'll work more on those alibis, see if we can clear them."

Toni spent the rest of the morning at the computer, doing paperwork for her classes and an upcoming student council project. Having a day off was nice, but this one had her feeling trapped. She wanted to be able to go about her business, take action and see people in person, to read their faces as they responded.

During lunch Kyle received a call saying that runways were clear and flights moving again. As soon as he finished eating, he packed his flight bag and left. His promise to call that evening made Toni feel better—but only a little.

She caught up on some housework while Gabe practiced his trombone. Toni didn't consider herself a great cook, and she disliked housekeeping, but she liked to eat and hated clutter, and she prided herself on being organized. She knew just where the dust bunnies hid. It felt good to her ears when Gabe's trombone quieted and he joined Garrett in a video game.

By mid-afternoon Toni couldn't bring herself to do any more housework. She stared out the kitchen window again and noted that the ice was nearly gone.

There would surely be school the next day.

She heard Gabe and Garrett relocate to the living room, apparently tired of the video game. She peeked around the doorway and saw them setting up the carom board on the coffee table. As she mixed jello at the counter, the clinking of caroms rang through the house.

"I wish we could go out and ride our bikes." It was Gabe speaking.

"Me, too," Garrett said. Clink. One carom hit another. "But Mom would worry if we went outside without her or Dad."

Toni went still, forgetting to stir the jello as she listened.

"Yeah, I wish whoever killed Mrs. Carter and Dustin would be caught."

A pause was followed by a couple more clinks. Then Gabe spoke again, his voice more thoughtful. "Mom's scared for us, and I'm scared for her. I don't want anyone to hurt her."

"Do you really think someone would try to hurt us?" Garrett asked. "We're just kids."

"Dustin wasn't much older than us, and he's dead," Gabe pointed out in his blunt, logical way. "And somebody tried to hurt you."

Toni's heart constricted, and tears welled in her eyes. She hadn't realized the true depth to which they were affected, or how they looked at things. She picked up the bowl and took it to the refrigerator, glad they couldn't see her crying. Placing it on a rack, she returned to the counter and began to wipe it, hardly able to see through the film in her eyes.

Her emotions were on overload, fear for her

children and herself a churning conflict. Any reasonable person would surely back off in the name of safety. But she couldn't just quit. The mother part of her had to reconcile with her professional part—and her sense of justice. The only way she could be sure of their safety was to find the killer. Kyle understood that.

Lord, please keep my boys safe. Show me what to do.

"Oh, no!" Garrett's moan rang loudly.

"Ha, ha," Gabe chortled. "You put one of mine in. You lose your turn."

Garrett didn't answer, and Toni assumed that play was continuing without argument. That assumption was confirmed when Gabe shouted, "I got the queen."

"But you have to get one of your own to keep her," Garrett challenged.

There was silence, and then a click. Then a moan.

"You missed. Put the queen back," Garrett demanded in smug satisfaction.

Toni began to assemble the ingredients for goulash.

"My bike's getting too small for me." Gabe had reverted to their former topic with lightning speed.

"You mean you're getting too big for it," Garrett retorted, delighted to find an opportunity to correct his older brother.

"Okay, you know what I mean," Gabe responded impatiently. "I need a bigger one."

Another click.

"Can I have your old one when you get the new

one?" Garrett asked, not doubting that there would be a new one.

Toni stifled the urge to correct his grammar.

"Sure," Gabe said magnanimously. "I want a mountain bike this time."

"What kind is that?"

"It's an ATB. That means All Terrain Bicycle," Gabe explained.

Count on Gabe to have done his research.

"It's for riding on dirt trails or other unpaved areas," he expounded to his younger brother.

"What do they look like?"

Gabe laughed. "Like a bike, silly. They have thick, knobby tires for extra traction and to absorb shock." He quoted facts in a manner that indicated he had been reading up on his subject. "It's the kind of bike Coach Baker rides. Sometimes it's parked behind the gym."

"Yeah, I remember now," Garrett replied.

More clicks.

"Do you know what a bicycle calls its dad?" Garrett asked.

Gabe moaned. "Don't you ever get tired of reading all those dumb jokes?"

"Ha, ha, you're just mad because you don't know the answer," Garrett taunted.

"No, I don't know the answer," Gabe admitted in disgust.

"It calls him Pop-cycle!" Garret said loudly, and then paused. "Hey, let's have a Popsicle. I want an orange one."

Toni hid her grin as both boys came rushing into the kitchen and headed for the refrigerator.

Chapter 18

After a restless night, Toni crawled out of bed and dressed in dark green khaki slacks and an avocado colored blazer with matching wedge-heeled shoes. She tried to curb her edginess as she served breakfast to the boys and took them to school. When she entered the high school, her body prickled with apprehension, but she forced herself to relax and headed directly for the gym.

Lisa Baker's office door was open. Inside, Toni saw the red athletic warm-up jacket clad woman at her computer, her back to the door. Toni tapped on the doorframe.

Lisa spun her chair around, and the smile on her face vanished. "What do you want now?" Her husky voice was barely civil.

"I have one more question I want to ask you," Toni said with more outward confidence than she felt. She eased on into the room and perched on the edge of the chair in front of the desk. "I hear from other students and staff that Marsha used to spend a good deal of time around here."

She was bluffing, but if her suspicions were correct, it was worth a try. "I'm trying to learn more about her behavior toward other staff members."

A flash of irritation—more like malice—crossed

Lisa's face.

Toni pressed on, determined to not be intimidated. "What I specifically want to know about is Marsha's behavior toward you. How close were you?"

Lisa stared at her, as if trying to decide how to rid herself of a pesky gnat. Then she issued an impatient huff and leaned forward on her elbows. "Oh, all right. Marsha started coming around the gym several months ago, complaining of an aching back and shoulders. She wanted to know if we could help her."

"By *we*, do you mean Jordan and yourself?" Toni wanted it spelled out clearly.

"She talked to Jordan at first. He told her that massage therapy was a good idea and that she should come back when I was here, since I have experience with that."

"You've had training in physical therapy?"

Lisa hesitated before speaking, obviously weighing her words. "When I was in college I worked for a sports medicine clinic and learned to do massage therapy," she said at last. "In fact, I married one of the physical therapists, which was a colossal mistake. It only lasted a year. I was in the process of divorcing him when I came to work here."

Toni just nodded, not quite sure what to say to that. Thinking fast, she decided to bluff some more. "I heard that Marsha made overtures toward Jordan. Do you know if there's any truth to that?"

A fleeting look of surprise crossed Lisa's face, but she recovered quickly. "That doesn't shock me," she said in what seemed a false show of unconcern.

"If he didn't respond, which I assume he didn't, she just moved on. She liked men. Look how quickly she moved on to Jack Rayford."

"How did she act toward you? Was she friendly? Did she come on to you?"

"That's none of your business," Lisa snapped, smacking a hand down on her desk so hard that a pen bounced off onto the floor. "Why don't you stay in your lab where you belong and leave me alone?"

"Because I can't," Toni returned heatedly. "I admit that I was driven by curiosity at first, but when someone tried to hurt my son, and then me, it got personal. Deadly personal. All I did was find Marsha's body and answer some questions about it to the Chief of Police. Then someone, for some reason, decided that my child had become a threat and set out to get rid of him. Then that person tried to shoot me. So, no, I can't leave it alone. Or you, so long as you know more than you're telling."

Lisa visibly struggled for control, and then seemed to get a grip on herself. "Okay," she relented grudgingly. She hauled a big breath and came upright in the chair. "I treated her with massage therapy, and she started coming around regularly."

Toni found this picture unsettling. She had never found Lisa an easy person to get to know, but she had never questioned the woman's abilities or professionalism.

Lisa shrugged. "Anyhow, she started paying a lot of attention to me and my programs. One thing led to another."

I'll just bet they did. "You became lovers."

"I'll admit she had me mesmerized for a while,"

Lisa confessed in a manner meant to portray nonchalance. "She came on so smooth and fast that I didn't realize what was happening, until one day she was all over me."

"You didn't know she liked women as well as men?"

Lisa shook her head. "Not until that afternoon." She still maintained a façade of matter-of-factness.

"What was the outcome?" Toni watched every mannerism and muscle movement.

Lisa made a dismissive shrug. "That scene wasn't for me, and I told her so." She swiped a hand in the air, as if brushing away something offensive. "She stopped coming for massage therapy, and we both moved on."

The warning bell rang, startling both of them. In five minutes students would be pouring into classrooms. Toni bounced to her feet. "Thanks for your time."

Her head buzzed as she hurried to her classroom. Something else had been nagging at her for days, a vision in the back of her mind. Inside the room, she pulled her grade book and papers from her satchel, almost frantic with the need to do more things than she could manage at once.

The final bell rang and Toni's day rolled forward. Once she had the lecture portion of the first class covered and the students working on their pig dissections, she was able to relax a bit. As she moved about the room, observing, making suggestions and answering questions, a small part of her brain raked through her memory, going back over every conversation with each staff member with whom she had talked.

A kaleidoscope of pictures flicked in her head. Classes. Encounters with individuals. Funerals. Faculty meetings. Her mental camera stopped on the faculty meeting right after Dustin's death. One image stood out—Lisa Baker and Darren Brown together. Like electricity running along a wire, the connection clicked. Darren's brother, Dale, was a deputy—with access to police reports.

"Mrs. Donovan, is this the pancreas?"

The question reclaimed her attention. Toni put other thoughts on hold for the rest of that class period. And the next. As soon as third hour arrived, she called Buck Freeman.

"I think I've got Marsha's killer pegged," she said without preliminaries. "But I can't prove it. Will you check one more thing for me?"

There was a pause before he answered. "Toni, I don't want you putting yourself in danger." His voice was gruff, but concerned.

"I'll be careful," she promised. "All I have at this point is a strong theory, but I've remembered something that might back it up."

"Tell me what you're looking for."

"I remember seeing Lisa Baker and Darren Brown sitting together in a faculty meeting. They seem to be much better friends than I realized. Darren is Dale's brother."

"You're wondering if either of them asked Dale about why you went looking for a body." He spoke slowly, following her train of thought.

"Yes, that's exactly what I'm wondering."

"Dale's out on patrol. I'll contact him and get

back to you. Can I ring straight through to your classroom?"

"Yes, it's extension two hundred."

As soon as she disconnected, Toni headed straight back to the gym, determined to pump more information from Jordan. She found him sitting at the scorekeeper's table in the second row of bleachers, operating the clock while two teams of students ran up and down the floor. Two more groups occupied the bottom bleachers, apparently waiting a turn in a class tournament. She climbed the steps to the table and scooted onto the bench next to him.

Jordan's head whipped around, and his expression wasn't exactly welcoming when he recognized her.

"I need to talk to you."

"Can't it wait?" He looked back at the action on the floor.

"No, it can't," she said urgently, her hands clenched so tight the knuckles whitened. "I have to have some answers *now*."

Jordan seemed startled. "Just a minute." He entered a score on the clock and scanned the students at the bottom of the bleachers. "Hey, Bryan, come here."

A lanky blond boy stood and came to the score table. "Whatcha need, Coach?"

"Take over here for a few minutes. I'll be right back."

When he headed toward his office, Toni followed. He stopped just inside the open door, where they could have a semblance of privacy, and Jordan could still keep an eye on his class.

"Look, Toni, aren't you pushing this thing a little too hard?" he asked, his famous grin nowhere in sight.

"No, I'm not," she shot back angrily. "Someone killed two people and tried to hurt or kill my son and me. I have to make sure that person is stopped."

He exhaled heavily in exasperation. "I just don't see how I can help you. What kind of questions do you have that you haven't already asked?"

"I need to know if Marsha ever made a habit of hanging around the gym." She wanted to hear his version of things.

"No," he said quickly, and then paused. "Not recently anyhow."

"Does that mean she did earlier?"

He went silent for several moments before muttering, "Yeah, I guess it does."

"How much earlier?" Toni struggled to keep from shouting.

"I don't know." He glanced out at the action on the floor. "It was several months ago, not long after she signed on as superintendent. She came in complaining of aching shoulders and neck. She had heard that Lisa was good at massage therapy. She is, you know. She's our own in-house first aid and physical therapist person. She's the one the students go to if they have minor injuries, sprained ankles, things like that."

"I know Lisa worked for a sports clinic and married a physical therapist. How did Marsha act toward you? Did she ever make any kind of personal advances?"

Jordan winced. "She made subtle overtures," he

admitted. "Which I ignored until she finally directed her attentions elsewhere."

"Do you know where that elsewhere was?"

"It could have been anywhere," he said flatly. "She was a predator. I was so relieved to be off her radar that I didn't care who she went after."

"Did Lisa take care of her shoulder and neck problems?"

He shrugged. "She must have. Marsha started coming for sessions, and she continued for several months. I think she and Lisa became pretty close during that time. Then she quit coming. I don't remember when. I just realized one day that I hadn't seen her around the gym in a while."

"Thanks for leveling with me." Toni moved to leave.

"One more thing," Jordan said, looking her straight in the eye. "I told Ken when he called this morning that Marsha informed me just before Christmas that we might have to take a budget cut in our department, maybe reassign some classes. She didn't get specific. I haven't discussed it with Lisa yet."

*

Buck Freeman didn't call back until the middle of fifth hour while Toni was at the white board illustrating a point to her biology students. She put the marker down and made her way to the phone in a normal pace, resisting the urge to run.

"Hello." She spoke softly, keeping her peripheral vision on the class.

"You nailed it. I know you're in class right now, so just listen and answer as simply as you can. I drove out and talked to Dale. He had read the file, including my notes about Garrett. He says he thought nothing of it a couple of days later when he and his brother were chatting and Darren asked him how come you and John happened to be up at your farm at that particular time. Do you think Darren's involved in any way?"

"No, I don't think so," Toni said carefully in a low undertone, turning her back on the class for just a moment. "I don't think Dale is either. I think Darren was asking Dale what someone had asked him, and Dale was just having a friendly conversation with his brother."

"I think I need to come by the school and talk to Darren. I'll try to get there before classes dismiss and he leaves." The phone went silent.

Toni continued with class, but inside she was a jumble of nerves and fear. The clock seemed to stand still, the hands refusing to move any faster as she kept a steady watch on it. A glance out the windows confirmed that it was beginning to sleet again.

During sixth hour Toni forced herself to remain calm enough to present her lecture and lab instructions. But when the students broke into groups and began to work independently, her mind reverted to the massage therapy and how good that might feel on her tight muscles right now. From there her imagination traveled along a path of possibilities. If Marsha found the massages helpful, and stimulating, Toni could see how a patient could become drawn to the masseuse.

From there her thoughts drifted to Lisa's first aid services, to the students, and at the amount of physical contact that might develop. Sprained ankles and pulled muscles could benefit from massage, and massage entailed physical contact. Could that have developed into more? Her heartbeat quickened.

Toni went to the computer between classes and looked once again at the picture in Sidney's e-mail. She peered at it closely, but couldn't see anything definitive.

When seventh hour finally ended, Toni stepped across the foyer to John's doorway. With the sleet picking up, the halls were emptying faster than usual. "Please get the boys for me," she said, her voice strained. "And don't let them out of your sight."

John read the tension in her. "Will do." He loped off up the hall.

Toni grabbed her purse, tucked her cell phone into her blazer pocket, and locked her door. Then she speed walked down the hall to the office of the technology director. Dillon was walking out his door. "Will you please do something for me before you leave?" she asked, her voice so strained she could hardly speak.

After a puzzled glance, Dillon stepped back inside his office. "What do you need?"

Toni followed him into the room. "Remember the e-mail I forwarded to you? I'd like you to enlarge and enhance that picture for me."

Something of her thinking must have communicated to him, because he didn't ask questions. He simply booted his main work computer and plunked down in front of it. "What am I looking for?" he asked when the machine was fully booted.

"I'm not exactly sure," Toni admitted. "Something—anything—that will identify the boy's partner."

"Got it." He opened the picture in a photo editing software program. "Drag a chair over here if you want." He pointed at a workstation across the room.

Toni got the chair, settled next to him, and watched as he worked with the resolution of the picture. She edged up nearer the screen and peered at it intensely. "Can you crop that section and sharpen it?" She touched the screen with a finger to indicate where she meant.

"I can try."

When he had it as clear as he could get it, Toni studied it again. Suddenly she drew in a sharp breath of discovery, feeling faint. "Can you print a copy of that for me?"

"Good as done. I'll even put it on photo paper for you." He reached into a drawer and took out a sheet, put it in the printer, and clicked the print button.

He handed her the picture moments later. "Is that all I can do for you?"

"Yes, this will do it. Thanks for the help." As Toni moved toward the door, she struggled to keep her hands from trembling. All doubt had been erased.

"Glad I could help." Dillon shut down the computer and followed her out of the room. "Have a good evening." He locked the door and marched ahead of her down the hall and out of sight.

The empty rooms and halls seemed eerie so soon at the end of a school day. The light sleet that was falling outside had caused all after-school activities to be cancelled and everyone sent home. There would probably be another snow day tomorrow.

Toni started up the hall, but when she rounded

the corner to return to her room and call Buck Freeman, she found herself face to face with Lisa Baker.

Lisa wore a heavy jacket and sweats—and carried a baseball bat.

Chapter 19

To a casual observer, there was nothing menacing about Lisa's appearance, but Toni knew better. Sure, it was normal for a physical education instructor to be carrying a baseball bat. But not in February. Some people might not consider a baseball bat a lethal weapon, but Toni was sharply aware that a mere flashlight had killed Marsha Carter. The look on Lisa's face told Toni that this meeting was no accident. The woman had been lurking around the corner, waiting.

Help me, God. Please.

"Why, hello, Lisa." Toni tried to inject a lilt into her voice while paralyzed by fear. She glanced up and down the hallway and realized how eerily alone they were. The place resonated with silence.

Lisa didn't answer. She just stood there, her eyes raking Toni from head to foot.

Fighting panic, Toni forced herself to make conversation. "The weather's nasty out there, and getting worse. I should get home before it's too bad to drive. It looks like everyone else has already gone." The words rattled from her to echo off the walls and up the hall.

"You're not going anywhere." Lisa's husky voice

was amazingly calm, the tenor of the words deadly.

"Aren't you anxious to get home before it gets any worse?" Toni asked, playing dumb.

Is she fully aware of how much I know? Should I attempt to walk away? Or try to brazen it out and look for an opportunity to get away?

"I'm not worried about it," Lisa returned, her voice as icy as the precipitation falling outside. A murderous glare pierced Toni.

At that point Toni realized she was in deadly trouble. Lisa knew she was found out—and that Toni had fingered her. Fear slithered up her spine. She inhaled a quick breath of panic.

"I know all about it, Lisa." Toni uttered the calculated lie in a spurt of fear induced courage. She knew a lot, but not all the details. She had to bluff her way along.

"You meddling busybody," Lisa snarled. "You just couldn't leave it alone, could you?"

"I don't know exactly what happened between you and Marsha, but I know you killed her." *Are you there, God? Please let someone see or hear us.*

"She couldn't accept rejection. She came onto me like a…a…"

"A predator is what Jordan called her," Toni supplied, desperate to keep her talking. Buck Freeman had said he would be here by the time classes dismissed, but that had been nearly a half hour ago. She had no way of knowing if he had arrived on the premises, or where he might be if he had. Her cell phone was in her pocket, but she couldn't get to it without Lisa seeing her do it.

"She was an expert manipulator and liar," Lisa

snapped bitterly. "She thought she was irresistible to everyone, and when I told her I didn't want that kind of relationship with her, she said it was my decision. But she was the boss."

"She found ways to make life miserable for you," Toni said, guessing. "You resented her power over you."

"In spades." Lisa's face twisted in an expression of hatred.

"So the situation deteriorated," Toni continued, glancing around frantically for a possible escape route. They were at a point where two hallways intersected. Classroom doors on each side of the hall were locked, and they were too far from the bathrooms and offices for her to get to them. "Did you know about the cuts she was planning?"

"I knew," Lisa snapped harshly. "That was what I came back to talk to her about that night. Now, let's take a little walk." She raised the bat in a menacing gesture.

Toni froze, desperation dulling her thought processes.

"I said walk." Lisa shoved her toward the north exit.

"You went home and rode back here on your bicycle," Toni said over her shoulder, as if she were certain.

"Well, give the lab nerd an A," Lisa snarled, her voice dripping with sarcasm. "Yes, I came back to reason with her. But she had it all laid out. The PE department was going to have one staff person cut, and I'm low seniority. Since I'm tenured, she couldn't just fire me. So she had to offer me another position in the district." She prodded Toni with the bat. "Get moving."

"She offered you something menial and insulting," Toni guessed with sudden insight, stalling for time and watching every movement, hoping for an opportunity to get to her cell phone.

Lisa laughed bitterly. "Theoretically she had to offer me something lateral, not a demotion or pay cut. She was assigning me to full-time ISS monitor." She gave Toni another shove that knocked her off balance.

Toni stumbled forward and landed against the wall with one foot beneath her. Her purse landed on the floor beside her. She took her time getting straightened out. Looking up at her enraged colleague, she fought to hide her terror. "I can see how furious that would have made you."

"Then she found out about…about something personal," Lisa continued, shoving Toni forward. "She threatened me. She said we could start over, be special to one another, or she would keep me in that ISS room until she found a way to fire me. That's when I lost it." Lisa's trembling voice and body indicated she was near the point of losing it again. Toni had to keep her inside the building as long as possible so someone could find them.

"She threatened to reveal your relationship with Dustin." No longer bluffing, Toni reached inside her purse and pulled out the picture Dillon had enlarged for her minutes earlier. Maybe using it now would provide distraction.

Lisa snatched it and stared at the cropped enlargement of her hand. Her eyes dropped to her palm. "So you know that, too," she snarled.

"Just a small section of the band aid on your hand is visible in the picture, but that told me it was you," Toni confirmed. "I also know you tried to run over my son with Tom's car, and that you tried to shoot me."

"Your kid knew too much, and you wouldn't stop meddling," Lisa roared. Then she reached down and grabbed Toni's hand. She yanked her to her feet with so much force that the twist to her shoulder nearly made Toni scream from pain. "Get going." Lisa shoved her toward the exit.

"What I don't understand," Toni stuttered, stumbling and nearly losing her balance, "is why you killed the boy. Once Marsha was dead, why hurt him? Did he find out that you killed her?"

Lisa pushed her again, harder this time. "Yes. He made a joke of us, took that secret picture and sent it around to scare me."

"No, he didn't," Toni shouted over her shoulder, whirling and stopping so abruptly that Lisa was startled into stopping as well. But only for a moment.

"What do you know about it?" Lisa demanded, raising the bat in warning.

Toni leaned backward, her eyes following the motion of the bat. "Sidney took it. She told me that she hid a camera, trying to catch whoever was pilfering PE supplies and vandalizing equipment."

Lisa's face showed genuine shock, but she quickly regained control. "So what. He knew too much, and he would have eventually told."

"He was just a kid," Toni said through clenched teeth.

"This is all your fault. You should have stayed out of it," Lisa hissed.

"I might have, if you hadn't tried to hurt Garrett," Toni shot back, her voice harsh.

"Everyone's happier with the witch gone," Lisa said, ignoring the comment about Garrett.

"I doubt her children would agree."

"Shut up!" Lisa swung the bat, striking Toni in the right shoulder that already had her in agony. "Get moving."

"The police are coming." Toni struggled for balance and glanced back over her shoulder. "In fact, they're probably already here."

"You're lying. Move. Faster." She prodded Toni repeatedly with the bat.

"Two people are already dead. Killing me will only make everything worse," Toni gasped, forced to move forward. "The police have you on their radar. Turn yourself in."

"Not on your life." Lisa hit her again.

Toni lurched forward. "Think about the families of your victims," she pleaded, hoping to reason with her, at the same time realizing the woman was beyond reason. "Think about the effect this is having on the school."

This time the prod of the bat shoved her into the exit door. A hand reached over her shoulder and pushed it open. Then the bat prodded again.

Stumbling out into the bone-chilling cold was shocking, but maybe an opportunity, Toni realized in a frantic flash. She shivered and shoved her hands into the pockets of her blazer, pulling them around her and hunching against the cold. "I hate February," she complained loudly, wrapping her hand around the cell phone in her right pocket. "I *hate* February," she repeated, speaking a little louder while working the phone around in her hand and managing to locate the notch that identified the top. It slipped from her hand.

"Quit stalling." Lisa gave her a furious shove off the step onto the parking lot.

"I gripe about February a lot," Toni chattered, grasping the phone again and tracing her index finger over the sides of the phone, searching for the spot to put it on vibrate. She pushed it and moved her finger to one end of the device, looking for where the charger connected to determine whether it was right side up or upside down. When she felt it, she turned the phone upright.

"I have a philosophy," she continued, clutching the phone tightly and hoping her chatter would create enough distraction to camouflage her hidden actions. "I figure everyone is entitled to a certain number of gripes." She moved her finger to the bottom of the phone screen. Visualizing the phone icon, and then the one for recent calls, she traced the finger to the right over where she estimated them to be, and paused at what felt like the middle of the screen where the contacts icon would be. She held her breath and pressed it.

"Shut your mouth," Lisa rasped.

"I use up all my gripes in February, so when summer comes and it gets hot, I don't have any gripes left," Toni prattled on loudly, praying that her panic affected brain would get her through this. Knowing the stored numbers were alphabetical, she moved her finger back to the bottom of the screen, traced to the right of the center, and pressed what she hoped was the keyboard icon. Then she traced to where she thought the Z should be, thankful that John's cell number was the first and only 'Z' number stored in her list, and pressed again as she stumbled across the parking lot. She couldn't be certain, but she thought her call had connected.

"I said shut up!" The bat struck her in the shoulder again. "Get going."

Toni released the phone and pulled her hands from her pockets while praying that John's phone was ringing. She hugged her arms around her and glanced back at her tormentor's distorted face.

"Lisa, I'm freezing," she yelled over her shoulder. "You're wearing a coat, but I'm not." She hoped John could hear and interpret from her words that they were outside the building—and who was with her.

Seeing the bat raise again, Toni changed her tactics and did the only thing she could think to do. She broke into a run.

God, please don't let her kill me. She's already killed twice. She couldn't finish the thought.

Then, with a flash of insight, Toni knew exactly where Lisa meant to take her. And it was exactly where she wanted to go. She visualized the box of tools at the body farm. If she could get there first, maybe she could grab something and defend herself. She was amazed at how much clearer her thinking was getting.

Toni ran across the road and darted into the trees, the sound of Lisa's running footsteps right behind her.

"John, I hope you can hear me," she gasped, nearly tripping as she kicked a loose rock. "Lisa's trying to kill me, and we're headed for the body farm. Get Buck."

She couldn't say any more, needing all her breath for running. Her wedge-heeled shoes were awkward, but shedding them would be treacherous and freezing. The terrain was rough, but more familiar to her than to Lisa. The sleet made visibility poor.

"Dear God," she prayed under her breath, zigzagging around a big tree. "Please give me strength. Don't let her kill me. My babies need me." A sob burbled from her.

With a final burst of energy, Toni reached the body farm gate and grabbed the latch. Fumbling in the cold, she shoved it up and pushed the gate open just as Lisa scrambled up behind her. She plunged inside the little cemetery and resumed running, slipping and sliding over the sleet covered leaves and woody debris. It was slicker here in the clearing than back under the trees. Behind her she could hear Lisa having the same problem and faced one horrifying, deadly fact. Lisa had every intention of killing her. This race was for her life.

Taking a deep breath of air that was so frigid it hurt her lungs, Toni propelled her body toward the toolbox and landed on her knees beside it. She shoved the lid up, reached inside, and grabbed a shovel. She turned just as Lisa ran up behind her. Seeing the raised bat coming at her, Toni ducked sideways, still on her knees, at the same time swinging the shovel with every bit of strength she had. It connected with Lisa's left leg.

Lisa grunted in pain and fell to her knees. She raised her head and glared straight at Toni, her eyes wild and venomous.

Toni scrambled to her feet, her instinct for survival kicking in with renewed strength.

God, please don't let her kill me. I don't want to die this way. You're the only one who can help me now.

Lisa got to her feet at the same time and edged nearer, the bat gripped firmly in her hands. Intent on destruction, she was closing in for the kill.

Toni faced her, the shovel drawn back, and watched every movement. When Lisa's arm drew back in a pre-swing motion, Toni did the same. When the bat started its deadly forward motion, Toni swung to block it.

Hard wood connected with the thin metal of the shovel, and the jarring impact forced the shovel from Toni's hands. It went flying through the air and tumbled across the ground.

Lisa's foot slipped from the force of the blow, and she fell to her knees. In the seconds it took her to right herself, Toni took off for the gate. She shoved it hard as she went out, and had the satisfaction of hearing Lisa slam into it and grunt in rage.

Thinking desperately, Toni had a burst of inspiration. Just over the ridge was a big shelf of rock that Lisa probably didn't know about. If she could just get there, it might give her an advantage. She dug in and ran for all she was worth. Back under the trees, the ground was not as sleet covered, but loose rocks and debris made her fight for traction and balance as she scrambled up the incline.

Muscles straining, her face dripping from the sleet, and gasping for breath, it was only the adrenalin of desperation that propelled Toni to the top of the ridge. At that moment she heard two things. One was Lisa's feet right behind her. The other was a siren.

With a heave of her chest, Toni crested the hilltop and flung her body into a sideways dive. She landed ungracefully on her belly, the breath knocked out of her. Winded but still thinking, she rolled to one side just as Lisa came running over the top of the ridge after her.

Toni looked around, still not breathing, as Lisa spotted her and tried to stop. Taken by surprise, she couldn't stop quickly enough and ran onto the edge of the icy shelf of rock. Her feet flew out from under her, and her body flailed backward. She emitted a husky yelp and landed with a thud. Her head bounced off a boulder.

Toni lay where she was, unable to move and fighting for breath.

"Toni, where are you?" John's yell came from down the hill. "Toni, answer me."

"Up here," she croaked, pulling in a huge gulp of air. She hurt, having landed on the shoulder already battered by Lisa. She made a hysterical little giggle as the term *bat*-tered flitted through her mind.

"Toni, tell us where you are." John's shout sounded a little closer.

"I'm up here," she called, a little stronger this time.

Suddenly he and Buck Freeman topped the ridge and took in the scene before them. Buck went to Lisa while John rushed to Toni and dropped to his knees beside her, gasping for breath. "Toni, are you okay?"

"I'm so c-c-c-cold," she whimpered, shivering and hugging her arms around her.

Buck joined them, speaking into the radio on his shoulder. "Get an ambulance out here. She's unconscious, and I'm afraid to move her."

Finished with the radio, he assessed Toni and how she was shivering. Shrugging out of his coat, Buck squatted on the ground beside her. He reached over and carefully pulled her upright, and then wrapped the coat around her.

"Keep her warm while I look after that one," Buck ordered with a jerk of his head toward where Lisa lay. His eyes took in the fact that John, like Toni, was not wearing a coat.

Sitting there huddled in the chief's coat and unable to move her right arm, Toni looked up anxiously at John. "Where are the boys?"

A sheepish look came over his face. "Uh, I locked them up," he said, and paused briefly. "In my room."

"You locked them up," she choked, hysterical laughter mixing with sobs.

Awkwardly John placed a hand on her arms. "When my cell phone rang and I realized you were in trouble, it was the only thing I could think to do. I locked my door and took off. I met Buck in the hallway near the gym and told him where I was going."

Phil Norton came over the hill in a run. Right behind him was Russell Nash.

"Gabe called and said you were in trouble," her dad said, dropping to the ground and claiming her from John.

Suddenly a pair of cops arrived. "Are you all right?" Dale Brown asked, glancing from Toni to Lisa.

"I'm alive," Toni told him. "That's enough for now." *Thank You, God.*

"Sounds like Gabe did all right in captivity," John said, regaining his equilibrium. "I wonder who else he called."

"His dad," Toni said with certainty, glad she had given in and gotten him a phone.

Buck approached them again. "Do we need an ambulance for you?" he asked Toni. "Or should we just call Faye and have her meet us at the clinic?"

"Mom," Toni said without hesitation.

"Good choice," her dad said, scooping her into his arms. "You go get the boys, and your coat," he instructed John as he started down the hill with Toni. Obviously freezing, John loped on ahead of them.

Minutes later they met John, now wearing his coat, and the boys at the parking lot. Russell put Toni into the back seat of her van and drove her to the clinic, with John and the boys following them in John's car.

Faye Nash met them at the rear entrance, wearing her nurse practitioner persona until she knew that Toni, although battered, was okay. Once she had her checked out and her arm strapped into place to protect the injured shoulder, she segued over into mother mode.

"I'm going to give you something to help you sleep and take you home with me," she informed Toni when she was done cuddling her.

Epilogue

The distant sound of a ringing phone pulled Toni from a sedative-induced sleep. She instinctively reached for the alarm, but the pain in her shoulder and ribs made her fall back onto the pillow. She must have moaned, because there was a sudden movement beside her. She opened her eyes to find Kyle sitting on the side of the bed, staring at her in concern. His hair was rumpled, and dark smudges rimmed his eyes.

"How do you feel?" he asked gently.

"Like I've been trampled by a bull," she muttered grumpily. "What time is it?"

He grinned. "Nine-thirty."

Toni looked around her parents' sky-blue carpeted guest room and dimly remembered Faye helping her put on a nightgown and crawl into bed. "I assume school was cancelled. It is Friday, isn't it?"

"It was, and it is," Kyle answered with a grin. Then his smile faded. "How are you really?"

She winced. "My shoulder hurts like the blazes, and my ribs throb when I move. I guess I jolted them pretty hard when I made that dive."

He reached over and tapped her lightly on the nose. "As much as I want to grab you and hold you, I'm afraid to touch you. So I guess I'll just sit here and look at you."

Toni swatted him on the arm, and then winced from pain caused by the movement. "Gabe called you, huh?"

"Of course. He takes his responsibilities seriously. In fact, he called twice. The first time was about three-thirty when John went to find you. The second was after your parents brought you home."

"What time did you get here?"

"About three a.m. I guess you know you're scaring years off my life."

"That was never my intent." She shifted so she could see his face more clearly, her sore body protesting. "Believe me, I have a new appreciation for all I have—you, the rest of my family, everything."

"We love you, and we're proud of you." Kyle leaned over and placed a soft kiss on her mouth, being careful not to touch anywhere near her shoulder or ribs.

A tap sounded on the bedroom door.

"Come in," Kyle called.

The door opened, and Russell Nash stuck his head through the opening. "I don't want to disturb you, but I heard voices and knew you were awake. I thought you'd want to know that Buck Freeman just called. He said Lisa Baker died about an hour ago."

Grief washed over Toni, but it was mixed with relief that the nightmare was over. She breathed a prayer of thanks for God's protection through all of it. And His forgiveness. Never again would she let hate disrupt her life.

"Faye says if you want to get up, we'll have brunch." Russell's head disappeared.

"Tell her we'll be right there," Toni called after

him.

When Kyle escorted her into the living room, they found Gabe and Garrett sitting on the sofa, their eyes round and troubled. "Are you okay, Mom?" Gabe asked, his serious gaze raking over her battered appearance.

"I'm fine." She attempted to sound perkier than she felt. "Come here." She held out her left arm.

Both boys got up and walked over to where she could hug them.

"We were scared," Garrett said quietly, snuggling his face against her good arm.

"So was I," Toni told them. "But it's over now, and I want both of you to try to forget it."

"Can't you remember where you put it?" Faye's voice carried from the kitchen.

"No, I can't," Russell snapped.

"Okay, we'll look for it after we eat." Faye emerged from the kitchen carrying a large baking dish. "We have egg casserole and pancakes. Everyone be seated."

Toni eased onto the chair Kyle pulled out for her.

"I want you to take a couple of pain pills with your juice." Faye placed them next to Toni's plate and ran a critical eye over her. "I've seen you looking better." She placed a kiss on one cheek and took her seat.

"John Zachary called last night to check on you," Russell said. "He also said he had just gotten his school cancellation call."

"Your dad has already lost one of his new hearing aids," Faye said as she poured herself a glass of juice. "He finally broke down and bought some good quality ones."

"Paid five thousand dollars for'em," Russell muttered.

"And he's lost one of them," Faye repeated in vexation.

Toni understood her mother's frustration, but she also sympathized with her dad's increasing difficulties. She refrained from comment.

As they were leaving the table after the meal, the doorbell rang. Russell went to answer it and admitted John and Jenny Zachary. John carried a bundle of roses.

"We came to call on the sick and maimed," he said, handing the flowers to Toni. He and Jenny sat on the sofa. "We're glad to see you up and about."

Toni and Kyle took chairs facing them. "Believe me, I'm glad to be up and about," Toni declared with fervor. "I know it's trite, but I never expected anything like this to happen around here."

John nodded. "I hear you."

"It's all so sad," Jenny said. "I can't sleep for thinking about it."

"The only good thing I can think of right now," Toni said, "is that Marsha's family and the Guthries won't have to endure the ordeal of a trial."

John grinned. "I think you showed real guts. I'm pleased to be working with you."

"Now don't get sentimental on me," Toni scolded.

"Actually, I have an agenda," he admitted. "When Ken called last night to tell me school was cancelled for today, he asked if you and I will be coming back next year to help him hold things together. I told him that I never really wanted to leave in the first place, so I probably will, but that I couldn't speak for you."

"I never wanted to leave either," Toni said with a sigh. "Now that Marsha's gone, it changes things. I guess I'll stick around."

"That's what I told him I expected you to say. He says he plans to give it another year, but he wanted to know if we would be there to support him."

"I guess the first thing the administration will have to deal with is the financial mess Marsha created."

"I talked to Ryan Prewitt yesterday," Jenny spoke up. "He told me that the board has already met with some people in the state education office, and they want to work with us. It may take a while to determine just how much money was received fraudulently, but they said they'll work out a payment plan for reimbursement if it's needed."

"Good." Toni nodded in satisfaction.

"I hope you guys never experience anything like this again," Kyle said.

Toni nodded. "Me, too." But if they did, she would be less trusting, and a little smarter. Life was going to change. She couldn't control all the circumstances of her life, but she could curtail some commitments. She would no longer say yes to everything asked of her—committees, social functions, any distractions that kept her from the people who meant the most to her. With God's help she would make her family her top priority.

"There are so many heavy hearts," Jenny said sadly. "One death affects a lot of people, and we've had three."

"I can kind of understand a crime of passion," Toni said thoughtfully. "In that respect I understand what happened to Lisa when she killed Marsha, how it got out of control. But she was in total control and fully responsible for Dustin's death, and then her attempts to harm Garrett and me."

After the Zachary's left, a motion across the room registered in Toni's peripheral vision. She turned to see Garrett beckoning to her from the hallway. When she struggled to her feet and walked stiffly across the room to him, he opened his clenched hand and revealed the hearing aid her dad had lost.

"You know, Son, I'm not sure I'm up to having you find things right now," she said softly, steering him into the kitchen where they wouldn't be heard. "Where did you find it?"

Garrett led her to the little telephone table in the dining room. "It was in the phone book." He pointed at the large directory.

Toni visualized what must have happened. The hearing aid had been bothering Russell, probably touching the phone and causing interference while he used it. He would have taken it out and laid it on the open phone book. After hanging up the phone, he must have forgotten about it and closed the phone book over it. She gave Garrett a conspiratorial look. "Why don't we put it back like you found it?"

He stared at her as if she had lost her mind.

"I think it might be better this way. Why don't you stand in the next room and listen."

His eyes slowly lit with comprehension. "Gotcha."

Toni returned to the living room. "Dad, Garrett tells me our heating system at home is making funny noises. Could you get me the number of that repairman you were telling me about a few weeks ago?"

"Sure. Give me just a minute." He got up and went to the dining room.

There was silence for several moments, then, "Hey, Faye, guess what I just found."

THE END

What will Toni do when members
of her forensics class stumble
across a human skull during an
educational field day scavenger hunt?
Find out in
PREYED IN MURDER,
Book 2 in the Toni Donovan mystery series.

BOOKS by Helen

Ozark Sweetheart
Ozark Reunion
Ozark Wedding

Bandit Bride
Prairie Bride

Bootheel Bride
Bootheel Bachelor
Bootheel Betrothal

Show Me Love
Heartland Illusions
Mozark Vision
Missouri Catch

Paige's Proposal
Brooke's Bargain
Haley's Hero
Kelsey's Keeper

NOVELLAS by Helen

Hawthorn Hope
Tree of Hope
River Town Romance
(Hawthorn Hope &
Tree of Hope 2 in 1)

Pasque Plight
Black-Eyed Susan's
Secret
Love Blooms (Pasque
Plight & Black-Eyed
Susan's Secret 2 in 1)

Shamrock Ruby
Dream Team
Mother Road Matches
(Shamrock Ruby &
Dream Team 2 in 1)

Secrets in the park

Made in the USA
Middletown, DE
08 November 2019